We all have tragic backstories in today's world...

I wake up chained to the wall of a dark cell aware of two things: I failed my sister, and I smell my enemy.

When I'm taken to meet Dare, the alpha of the Silver Tip pack, I'm sure I'm about to lose my throat. The last thing I expect is for the Alpha to recognize me as his fated mate. No way is he going to let me go now, and I still have to find a way to rescue my sister.

As I plot my escape to save her, I find that if I leave, Dare could be killed by power-hungry members of his pack. And now he's more to me than my fated mate—my heart is involved. With time ticking by on my sister's life, I have to make a choice I never thought I'd face—my sister's life or my mate's? That's *if* I can survive the undead shifters intent on killing me first...

Dedication

To Scott Speedman, who made a damn fine werewolf in Underworld.

And to Jon Bernthal, who was the best zombie killer on The Walking Dead.
They did you dirty, Shane!

Table of Contents

Author's Note

There is a glossary at the end of the book for terms used relating to geography and shifter life.

Thank you for reading!

CHAPTER ONE

Reese

FOR ONE BLISSFUL MOMENT, AS my body came awake, I felt nothing. Then my brain clicked online, synapses firing, and with that came the hot, branding sear of pain.

The motherfucking pain.

I didn't move from where I lay on my back. The floor beneath me was hard, so even breathing was sending bolts of agony up my spine and through my ribs. I hoped I had no permanent damage. I was too weak to shift, and even if I had been strong enough—I blinked out of my non-swollen eye at the silver cuff on my ankle—that right there would prevent me.

Jude.

My brother's name was a bright light through the fog of pain. I tried to say the word, but only managed a puff of air. My throat was sandpaper, and when I licked my dry tongue across my lips, I tasted the iron tang of crusted blood.

This was my worst nightmare. If they found Jude too…

I'd been in Xan's isolation pits before—pure fucking torture for a species that needed companionship like air—but this wasn't a hole dug in the ground, covered with a crude locked grate.

The room was dark and small—maybe twelve square feet. My depth perception was fucked up, because only one eye was functional. A large metal door seemed to be the only entrance in or out. One single beam of sunlight snuck into the cell and lit a foot-long patch on the ground. Maybe this was a special place for wolves he planned to kill in slow, torturous ways? Probably.

I scraped my fingernails on the dirty concrete floor, then my gaze followed the length of the chain to where it was attached to a bolt in the corner. I lifted myself onto my elbows, gritting my teeth as that simple motion stole what little energy I had left.

I inhaled, expecting the ever-present scent of wolves, fear, and starvation.

Instead, I sniffed dirt, blood, and Were.

Were.

My entire body went tight, my canines punching down as my body sought to protect itself from an enemy. I was a werewolf, which meant I had two forms—human and four-legged wolf. Weres had three forms—human, four-legged wolf, and Were. Their Were form was like a giant wolf/human hybrid. They stood upright about eight to nine feet tall, with clawed hands and feet, wiry hair coating their bodies, and massive jaws the size of my torso. Werewolves and Weres were separate species with no real love between them, which was why the smell of Were was enough to send me into a frenzy.

My heart raced as I took stock of my injuries. It was

always good to know which limbs were in working order, especially when I had to defend myself.

My ribs were fucked, and one knee was not bending like it was supposed to. Oh, and I was pretty sure my left arm was broken. So...two out of four functioning appendages. Wonderful. Great. Grand.

I'd wanted to get my siblings away from Xan's rule and the tyrannical way he ran the werewolf Bluefoot pack. Well, I'd gotten past step one. Step two? I rattled the chain. Apparently step two was surviving Weres.

Piece of fucking cake.

Something moved in the corner of the cell, and the hair on the back of my neck rose as I bared my teeth—instinct even though I wasn't able to shift.

A hand, its fingernails caked in dirt, entered a beam of light. Then a dark head and a face with familiar blue eyes peered at me with trepidation. "You're awake."

Ignoring the pain and the dread, I scrambled toward Jude as he came toward me, and we met in a clash of limbs under the beam of light. I inhaled him, snuffling my nose into his neck as he did the same to me. My brother was alive and for right now, I'd celebrate that victory. He clung to me, his slender body shaking as I ran my hands over his skin. "Are you hurt?"

He shook his head. "Not hurt." He wasn't chained like I was, probably because he was a novus and couldn't shift yet. His fingers grazed my swollen face as his eyes hardened. He was so close to his muto, and although he was a wisp of a thing now at seventeen, he'd be formidable once his first change hit. "I saw it all." His teeth were clenched. "If you hadn't made me promise to stay hidden, I would have tried to stop them." His lip trembled. "I thought they killed you."

My memory was fuzzy, but I knew the members of our old pack hadn't even given me a proper cast-out as a shifter. They'd prevented me from shifting and then took turns beating the shit out of me. "Well, they didn't," I mumbled, my tongue thick, my throat swollen.

He was trying not to cry, my brave brother. "Selene's still there."

As if I weren't already in enough pain, the guilt over failing to save my sister threatened to suffocate me. We'd planned this escape for months. I got Jude out first, stowed him away in a small cave outside the walls of the compound, and had been on my way back inside to get Selene. Except Xan's men, for once, didn't do exactly what they were supposed to be doing. I got caught and nearly killed.

Despite the pain now, I'd do it all over again. Selene was still there, and in a month, Xan planned to mate her. I'd seen what he did to mates, and there was no way I'd allow that to happen to my sister while I was still fucking breathing. I'd be back to get her, as soon as we figured out how to get out of here.

"I know, man." I glanced around. "So where the fuck are we now?"

He curled in on himself. "Shit, Reese. I'm sorry."

The dread intensified. "Sorry for what?"

"When you were unconscious, they carried you outside the city and left you for the Noweres. You had no protection.

I couldn't… I didn't know what to do."

Noweres. Even now the name sent an arrow of poison-tipped fear through me. A century ago, a virus eradicated the human population and killed two-thirds of all Weres. But those dead Weres? They became…undead. Stuck in their Were form, they roamed the earth in packs, feeding from or infecting any living thing they could. As a werewolf, I couldn't be infected like Weres, but I sure as hell could be very, very dead. If a Nowere had found me last night, it would have ripped me apart and scraped the meat from my bones with its rotting teeth. I gripped Jude's chin. "What're you sorry for?"

"I asked for help."

My stomach dropped. "From who?"

He swallowed. "Weres."

"Ju—"

"The Silver Tip."

My muscles gave out. I collapsed onto my back and stared up at the ceiling, unsure whether I should cry, laugh, or just kill us now before the Silver Tip did. It was promising they hadn't killed Jude and me on sight. But then, I was chained to the wall in a cell, so it wasn't like they'd given us some excellent hospitality.

The Silver Tip and the Bluefoot pack had a truce that went back decades. The only rule? We left each other alone. And we certainly didn't step foot in each other's territories.

"I'm so sorry," he said, full-on crying now, and I closed my eyes, trying to summon the willpower to comfort him when I didn't even have enough energy to comfort myself.

"They were the only ones I knew who would enter Nowere territory. They shut me in here while they went to get you. You were still unconscious when they tossed you in with me and chained you."

He sniffled, and I didn't move. I'd never actually met a Were. Rumors about the Silver Tip pack and their ruthless Alpha were all the rage in the Bluefoot pack. I had absolutely no idea what they'd do with us. Starving under Xan's rule might have been preferable. What had I gotten us into? Out from under the dictator's thumb and right into the path of the killer's giant jaws.

I raised my hand to my throat. I kinda liked my throat. Not sure how much longer I'd have it, to be honest. "I'm surprised they didn't kill you on sight."

"I know everything we've been told about them, but I couldn't do nothing. And they haven't killed us yet."

A key rattled in the door's lock, and despite my seriously broken body, I stumbled to my feet, shoving Jude behind me with my one good arm. I pushed us into the corner as far as the chain would allow. "Reese," he hissed. "You don't have to protect me."

I ignored him. Despite my injuries, I wasn't a novus, and at six-five in my human form, I had a good couple of inches on my brother, as well as about fifty pounds.

When the door opened, I sucked in a breath as a massive Were in his human form filled the doorway. His scent was overwhelming, like dirt and pine. His head was square and sat on a neck as thick as my waist. His skin was dark and his scalp bald. He could have tossed me around like a rag doll, and he could have eaten Jude in two giant bites.

His black eyes shifted from me to Jude, then back to me. I swallowed.

The giant Were stalked toward me, and I braced, because even though I'd lose this fight, and lose badly, I'd fucking go down fighting, especially with Jude still alive to protect. The Were stopped in front of me, then reached down, and with one yank tore the silver chain out of the bolt in the wall.

Jude whimpered behind me. And yeah, I had the same reaction, but fortunately kept my noises to myself.

The Were straightened and pierced me with those black eyes, the end of the chain in one of his massive fists.

"Come with me." His craggy voice dropped the words like boulders between us.

The Were started walking, and I had no choice but to follow or else I was damn sure he'd drag me by my leg. I limped along behind him, concerned about all my body parts but having no other choice. He was moving way faster than I could walk, his tree-trunk thighs eating up the distance as he took us down a dark hallway. When I stumbled, he stopped and turned, watching as Jude tried his best to help me along with his arm around my waist.

When he began to walk again, his pace was slower this time.

Did Weres...have empathy?

That was brand new information.

We reached the end of the hallway, where our guide pushed open a door. At that point, I lost all sense of direction as he guided us up some stairs and through a couple more hallways. The plaster walls were peeling, and the sun shining through large, cracked windows lit our way.

Finally, we entered a large room, and my bare feet made a hollow sound on the warped wooden floor. We seemed to be on the bottom level of a warehouse-type building. The ceiling was probably four to five stories high, with balconies on every level lined with Weres peering down at us.

Deep voices followed our movements as we made our way to a large platform on one end of the room. Beside me, Jude spun as he walked, taking in our new surroundings. I glanced up but wasn't in the mood to dwell. I followed our guide doggedly, refusing to get behind and end up tripping in front of this room of predators.

We reached a small group of Weres in human form, who stood with their arms crossed, waiting for us. They weren't as big as the one holding my chain, but they were still all giants.

Fuck my life.

"Whatcha got, G?" one asked.

The Were holding my chain dropped it onto the floor with a loud clank, probably assuming I wouldn't bolt with an entire warehouse of Weres surrounding me. He was right. "Dare asked to meet the Bluefoot wolves."

The sound of footsteps had me taking a step back, and Jude crowded against my back. With every thump of a footfall, my anxiety ratcheted up a notch, because whoever was making that sound walked with purpose. With authority.

With ruthlessness.

The footsteps stopped, and I held my breath until a

movement caught my eye. In one moment, the space in front of me was empty, and in the next, a Were was there, landing with a shuddering thud from out of nowhere, the dust swirling up around his black boots and legs clad in leather pants. My gaze rose. And rose. And rose. Up past thighs the size of my torso, a bare stomach rippling with muscle beneath tanned skin, twitching pecs glistening with sweat, over shoulders that could bench press three of me, and finally up to meet the green-eyed gaze of Dare.

Alpha of the Silver Tip.

I knew with every beat of my heart that he was alpha. If I had any hydration left in my body, I would have pissed myself.

He was by far the largest Were in the room. When he opened his mouth and bared elongated canines—even in his human form—Jude clutched my shoulders and muffled a small scream into my back.

"Hey Dare, we can put 'em to work," one of the Weres said. "Or you could give the little one to me. Wolf novus? Yes, please."

I'd kill myself and Jude before that fucking Were touched him.

Dare opened his mouth, his throat working like he was about to speak when he paused and sniffed the air.

My nose was half-clogged with blood, and I could barely breathe. But a whiff of a scent caught my attention. I inhaled as much as I could, and as soon as the sweet aroma hit my nostrils, my knees buckled.

That scent was nothing I'd ever experienced before...like

the pine of the Were mixed with honeysuckle…

This couldn't be happening. Not here. Not now. But that scent was overwhelming me, setting my blood on fire. My skin tingled, and my heart pounded like a drumbeat in my chest. When Dare locked eyes on me, I knew it.

He was my True Mate.

I'd finally escaped my former prison, and now I was stuck in another one. My life as I knew it was fucking over.

Dare

THE MOMENT THE WOLF SMELLED it, his expression morphed into terror. Pure terror. He scrambled backward, the chain slithering across the floor like a retreating snake. He tripped and continued to crawl backward on his hands and feet, gaze on me the whole time.

I flicked my fingers at G to take care of the novus as I stalked after my mate, who was hell-bent on getting away from me. Which was hilarious because he wasn't going to get any-fucking-where. This entire place was filled with Weres loyal to me. The solid stone walls of my territory were thirty feet high and three feet thick.

I'd never expected to find my True Mate. The odds of finding one were incredibly slim in this day and age where we all locked ourselves away behind fortified walls. True Mates were mostly an urban myth nowadays, but the deep recesses of my shifter brain knew the scent on instinct. And now that I smelled him—a minty, sweet smell—I understood why the True Mate bond was so coveted. I craved him, and my blood rushed through my veins like fucking fire. Of course, I'd have to wait to take him until he healed a little. The wolf was beat to shit, squinting at me through one good eye. His lips were split and he was holding his body in a way that made me suspect some rib damage.

G had told me the wolf's pack had beaten him and left him for dead. I typically wouldn't give a shit about one dead wolf left as Nowere bait, but his brother had begged for help. We didn't mess with the Bluefoot pack, but the novus had said they had been thrown out. My brother said I was going soft, but the thought of a pack leaving a member to be eaten by the Noweres didn't sit well with me—even if he was just a werewolf.

Well, now he was my True Mate.

Mine.

A possessive fire roared to life in my chest, and I knew within another minute or two in his presence, there'd be no going back.

The wolf was my mate.

Too bad he needed some convincing. I was sure it was a shock to his system to realize he was going to be tied to a Were all his life. An Alpha Were.

He somehow made it to his feet, stumbling away from me with a hand out. "Stop."

I kept walking. The pack was watching, and it was important for me to show I could control my mate, and that he *could be* controlled. He was a werewolf, naturally submissive and inferior, so he needed a firm hand.

"Please," he cried.

I only stopped because in another two steps, he was going to crash into the back wall. And with a thud, he did, then collapsed onto the ground once more before curling into a ball. Behind me, I heard anguished cries, probably from the novus, but I knew G would handle him.

My wolf was crying now, and I gritted my teeth at the sound, wondering what this odd ache in my chest was about, why I wanted to cradle him to my chest and protect him.

I shook away the sentimental instinct and gave him a moment before crouching down and fisting my hand in his black hair. I pulled his head back, and he pierced me with a glare, his face covered in dried blood and snot and tears.

He still smelled fucking delicious.

I held his gaze until resignation began to set in his features. If he knew anything about Weres, he'd know that once we found our mates, we'd never let them go. Already my blood was pumping, my instincts screaming at me to hold him down, make him mine, imprint my scent on him and in him. He needed to shift and heal fast.

He jerked his head to rip his hair from my grasp, but I held firm, surprised he'd even tried. My pack was watching this, and they had to see I could control him. Once he stopped squirming, I released him. He shied away, pressing his back against the wall. Finally, he spoke. "What're you gonna do to me?"

His voice was low and smooth, melting over my skin like butter.

"Mate you."

"Then what?" The demand in his tone had my cock hardening. I thought passive always did it for me, but this wolf with his demands was challenging that.

I didn't understand the question, so I cocked my head. "What do you mean?"

"After we mate, what're you going to do to me?"

"I'm going to take care of you."

His jaw clacked shut, and his brows drew in, as if that wasn't at all what he thought I'd say. I glanced down at the silver around his ankle and ripped apart the metal band with a tug of my hands. I couldn't tell if the red around his ankle was from the silver or from whatever had been used to beat him bloody. "Stand. You need to shift."

"Can't," he croaked. He swallowed, and his throat clicked.

I turned my head. "Water!" I barked at whoever was closest. There was a scuffling and then a glass of water was shoved in my hand. I held it to his mouth. He hesitated.

"Drink like this or drink nothing," I said.

He parted his lips and began to drink, although his eyes told me it was under duress. He drank the entire glass, and I ordered Rua—one of my guards—to get me another. She returned quickly, and I told her to get one for the novus too, who'd calmed down somewhat in G's arms.

At the sound of my command, my mate scrambled to his feet and ran in a halting, painful gait to the novus. When he reached G's side, he tore his brother from my guard's arms. Shoving the novus's smaller body behind his, he glanced around as they took a few steps backward. I was again unsure where he thought he'd go, but his instinct to protect was strong.

I admired that.

"What's going to happen to my brother?" he demanded, his uninjured eye flashing at me.

I didn't fucking care what happened to the brother, but since my wolf did, I'd have to compromise. I glanced at G, who stood stone-faced, his attention on the novus. "He'll stay with G."

My wolf's eye went wide. "What?" I ground my teeth, because did I have to fucking repeat myself? But my wolf wasn't done. "No fucking way. Jude stays with me, where I can watch him. I'm not just abandoning him because you have a hard-on for me—"

That was enough. I grabbed him around the throat and squeezed. Not enough to hurt, but enough to warn, and to the pack it would look worse than it was. His nostrils flared, and he halfheartedly clawed at my forearm.

I spoke through bared teeth. "You might be my mate, but you do *not* make the decisions in this pack." I shook him a little until he bobbed his head in a faint nod. I released him, and, although he stayed put and remained silent, his blue eyes flashed daggers at me. If looks could kill...

"G is the best guard in this pack," I explained. "If I tell him to watch over Jude and protect him with his life, he'll do it."

He sucked in air before whispering, "Can I ask one favor, please?"

His eyes told me he resented having to ask me for something. "Yes."

He reached back, brushing his knuckles along Jude's. "Please don't let anyone touch him against his will."

One of my guards, Vaughn, heard that. He joked in low tones that he was disappointed that he wouldn't be able to sample the fresh meat.

I turned to G. "Jude will stay with you in your room, and you'll guard him. No one is to harm him or touch him in any way, and that includes you. Got it?"

G nodded. "Done."

"Great. Get gone then. Kid looks like he's going to pass out."

Jude hugged his brother and said through tears, "I'll be okay, Reese. I promise." He glanced at me before focusing back on his brother. "Will you be okay?"

So, my mate's name was Reese. He murmured, "I'll be fine," as the brothers parted. Reese wobbled on his feet, and as the murmurs of my pack grew louder, I knew it was time to get him alone.

"Come on." I wrapped an arm around his waist. "Take a deep breath."

"Wha—?"

I leaped five stories. When we landed on the uppermost balcony, I checked on my mate, who had paled. *Oh shit.* I gripped his face, taking care to stay away from the worst of the swelling. "You all right?"

He shook himself and growled softly. "You coulda warned a guy. Damn."

"I said take a deep breath."

That glare was back. "That's a seriously inadequate warning for what you just did."

Even beat to shit he had an attitude. "Can we debate my warning system when you're not dead on your feet?"

He pressed his lips into a thin line.

I gripped his forearm and hauled him up the stairs in front of us. "This building houses the entire Silver Tip pack. We're about three hundred strong." Reese stumbled on the stairs, but seemed determined to climb them himself. "What we were just in is the main meeting room, and then the balconies on every floor lead to apartments where pack members live. As alpha, I have the entire sixth floor." At the top of the stairs, I spun the lock to the correct combination and the door opened. "That's the only way to get to the sixth floor."

"So...you jump to the fifth, then take the stairs to the sixth like a civilized person."

I wasn't sure if he was testing his boundaries to see how hard he could push me, or if he had a death wish. Of course, if he knew anything about Were mates, he'd know I'd never kill him. "You have a smart mouth with everyone, or am I special?"

He shrugged as he glanced around.

Eury—the land that was home to the Silver Tip, the Bluefoot, and a couple of other werewolf packs—had pitiful resources, but my pack was willing to venture into Nowere territory, so we built furniture from the trees we chopped down. We'd had a couple of casualties from Noweres over the years, but it was worth it to be able to sustain ourselves. I knew we were the only pack with our own greenhouse to grow produce and a large farm area where we tended crops and raised livestock. If other packs found out, we'd have a war on our hands. Good thing we weren't big on socializing.

Reese limped a couple of steps, taking in his surroundings, but his color didn't look good, and he clutched his side.

I scanned his body. "What do you mean, you can't shift?"

His back was to me as his head dropped forward. He mumbled, "Too weak."

I frowned. I'd been around very few wolves. As for Weres, it could take a couple of shift changes to fully heal, but we could always shift. "That seems like a genetic fuckup. Shifting is how we heal."

He turned around with a look. "Well, that's the way it is for us. I need some water and some sleep, and then I can shift and heal my most-likely-cracked ribs and various other broken bones, okay?"

When Jude had requested help, he'd told us that his brother had been beaten by his own Bluefoot pack and left for the Noweres. I wanted to know more, but now wasn't the time to grill him. He was barely conscious, swaying slightly like he could barely keep upright.

I scooped him up despite his grumble of protest and carried him to the far side of the room. I set him down on my mattress. It wasn't thick or luxurious—it was basically fabric stuffed with pine needles—but it was comfortable.

I kept a pitcher of water and cups on a table along the wall. I poured him some and brought it to him. "Here." He drank the entire thing in a couple of gulps and then collapsed onto his back.

His one working eyelid immediately began to droop. He flung it back open one last time. "I'll be safe here?"

I sat down in a chair and rested my elbows on my knees. "You'll be safe here."

He smiled faintly, then closed his eyes. Within thirty seconds, he was asleep.

I relaxed, breathing in the delicious scent of my mate, content that he was now safe.

CHAPTER TWO

Reese

THIS TIME WHEN I WOKE, the pain still hit me after a few seconds. But I also registered that I was laying on something much softer than a concrete floor. Oh, and something smelled fucking delicious.

Both my eyes opened now, although one only halfway. And when I blinked to focus, I met the steady gaze of a green-eyed Were. The Silver Tip pack—as the only Were pack in Eury—had a truce with all the wolf packs, including Xan's. We left each other alone. No interfering with each other's compounds or packs. That was how it'd been for decades. The Weres were dominant and would likely obliterate a wolf pack. But not without suffering casualties of their own. And if all the wolf packs combined forces? The Were pack could be defeated. The truce benefited all sides. There was no overriding authority in Eury, or anywhere that I knew of. Communication between packs was rare and based on the reliability of a messenger's memory.

I'd heard of Dare, Alpha of the Silver Tip pack—bits and pieces of whatever information Xan let trickle down through the ranks of the pack. So even though I knew never to believe what I heard, I had a hard time reconciling this Were with the ruthless, violent, bloodthirsty beast he was rumored to be.

And now, he was my mate. Why the fuck did my True Mate have to be a goddamn Were? An alpha at that? True Mates were legit as hell. My parents had been True Mates, so I knew how strong the bond was. I just never expected to have that for myself. Most wolves mated for love and pleasure or procreation, not because they were compelled to do so by instinct. It was unheard of to ignore the True Mating call, no matter how inconvenient it might be.

We stared at each other silently, and I inhaled his scent. The minty, sweet fragrance was fogging my brain with arousal. Dare's eyes flashed, and I knew he felt the pull too. I wasn't sure what to say. I'd run my mouth a little when we'd first met, and I'd gotten a hand wrapped around my throat, so I figured it was best to play it cool until I knew what my place was here.

Someone knocked on the door. I started, and he raised a hand to calm me. And fuck if it didn't actually work. This mate shit was weird, and we hadn't even formally mated.

I wasn't going to think about that yet.

As Dare opened the door, I closed my eyes. The moment my lids closed, I saw Selene back in the Bluefoot compound, still under Xan's thumb. The image made my lip curl.

Rescuing Selene was a real, live pull inside of me. It was the main reason I was fighting so hard to stay alive. But now there was another pull inside of me. And it was tugging me towards a seven-foot, fierce-as-hell Alpha Were. I wanted to know more, to feel out this mating and the hold that Dare had over me. Was instinct the only reason I felt drawn to him? Maybe I could use this mating to my advantage. Just maybe, Dare could help me rescue Selene. He seemed to have listened when I'd asked him to protect Jude.

As Dare murmured some words to whoever was at the door, I got a better look at his room. It was large, probably fifty square feet, with a sitting area in the far corner near a bookcase, the toilet surrounded by a curtain on the other side. A large wardrobe along the wall was half open, revealing Dare's clothes inside.

A memory crept into my mind, a rumor about how Dare kept a Nowere as a pet in his room and fed it wolves who wandered up to his gates.

There was clearly not a Nowere here.

My mate finished talking with whoever was at the door. He shut it and strode toward me with a plate. The fucker was sexy, there was no doubt about that. Even with my body aching like it was, the sight of him in his leather pants and nothing else was enough to make me hard. It was those eyes, the vivid green irises, that pinned me in place. I wondered what they'd look like when he came.

Fuck, get it together, Reese.

Dare helped me sit up with a lumpy pillow at my back, then set the plate on my lap. It was steak and vegetables.

Steak. And. Vegetables.

He pointed at the plate. "Eat."

Right, he didn't have to tell me twice. I picked up a carrot, twisting it in my fingers, squeezing it, then licking it to test if it was actually real. I took a nibble. "Holy shit, this is an actual carrot. I haven't seen one in…years."

Dare seemed proud. Thank fuck I hadn't managed to insult him yet. "We have our own greenhouse."

I stared at him. If Xan knew… "Wow."

"Eat," he said. "Then you might have the strength to heal."

I made love to my plate with my eyes. "I think I'll be able to do just about anything after I eat this." Xan's rations had been so stingy lately, I'd been living off watery potato and cabbage soup.

Dare grunted, and I dug in. There were no utensils, but I was able to tear the steak with my teeth. I crunched into the raw veggies with relish, savoring the flavor. Already my body was feeling renewed.

Dare sat down on a chair beside the bed. "Tell me about the Bluefoot pack."

I was glad I'd already eaten most of my food, because the reminder of my sister sucked away my appetite. She was still under Xan's rule, eating shitty rations. The food I'd just devoured was now a ball of guilt in my stomach. I had to focus on Dare right now, though, until I knew what my role here was. "Uh, okay, what do you want to know?

Dare's brows were drawn in, probably because the tension was swelling around me. "Were you born there?"

I shook my head. "My parents were from down south in Astria. Do you know about Astria?"

"Home of four packs. Overtaken by the largest Nowere pack ever documented."

"Right." I'd been ten at the time of the Nowere takeover, and the alarms from the breach, the screams, the sounds of ripping flesh, haunted me every night. "I was a member of the Whitethroat pack. My parents got us out while the Noweres ravaged everyone within the walls. My folks risked all our lives to travel to Eury. We walked for miles and miles, starved and half-dead by the time we arrived at Xan's gates. We thought he'd be our salvation." I shook my head. "Xan killed my parents on sight. Enslaved us because we weren't Bluefoot—we were outsiders, and he's not so accepting of outsiders. That was ten years ago. I've worked ten-hour days repairing Xan's walls, digging holes, whatever labor he could think of."

Now the tension was coming from Dare. His fists were clasped in his lap, knuckles white. "Were you a prisoner?"

"At first, we were kept under guard and locked away when we weren't working. As time wore on, we were given more freedom, but any outsiders who ventured to his front gates were his labor force. We didn't benefit from that labor other than being protected from Noweres. I didn't feel like I could do anything to get us out of that hell hole until I went through my first shift."

Omitting the information that I had a sister—okay so it was lying—felt so fucking wrong, but I couldn't tell him. His lack of knowledge about her existence was all I had going for me in my attempt to get her back. If he knew I wanted to escape, who knew how I'd be treated? Maybe thrown back in that cell, and only brought out when he wanted to fuck me? Hell no.

"Xan is a dictator," I continued. "The Bluefoot pack is going to waste away because it can't sustain itself."

Dare listened to me intently as I talked. He wasn't treating me like some dumb inferior werewolf. It was probably unwise to hope that I could be somewhat of an equal partner, but his questions and attentiveness to my answers were promising.

"What did you eat?" he asked.

"He has some crops, but he's done a shit job taking care of the land, so they grow poorly."

"So you escaped with your brother."

I nodded. "They didn't see Jude. They saw me."

"And their punishment was to beat you and leave you to the Noweres?"

"Guess so. Xan never liked me much."

Dare studied me for another minute. "Where'd you plan to escape to?"

"We were going to try to go back home. To Astria." I didn't know what awaited us there, but I'd never lost hope that we could return. Since we'd left, I'd lived with a constant ache in my gut, a pull that was drawing me back home. I'd never had relief, not for one day. I had to trust that fate was telling me where to go, where to be happy again.

Dare leaned forward, his fist closing around my knee and squeezing. Possessively. "Well, doesn't matter anymore. You're a Silver Tip now."

He released me, and I bent my head to stare at my plate so he couldn't read my expression. I was a Whitethroat. I'd always be a Whitethroat, no matter how much Xan beat it into me that it was bad. "Right." My sister's face flashed in front of my eyes. Long black hair, porcelain skin. Blue eyes clear as water.

Abandoning her wasn't an option. For now, I had no choice but to mate Dare and hope I'd be given more freedom to somehow escape.

At least so far, I'd been treated fairly. I wasn't sure how questions would go over, but I was curious. "So," I asked him. "Are you worried about the truce?"

Dare didn't seem to find my question intrusive. "The truce is important to this pack, because I have built my rule on peace," he said. "As long as you and your brother are telling the truth, and I am trusting that you are, then no."

"We are." I made sure to meet his gaze.

He nodded.

"I…do appreciate you taking Jude and I in."

"Of course. We give sanctuary and a place to rest to any Were or wolf that knocks on our gates."

That was so different from Xan's philosophy that I didn't know how to process it. Xan was unpredictable. Some wolves that showed up at his gate were killed instantly. Others were put to work like I was. A few were allowed inside and then never seen again.

By the time my plate was clean, the pain in my body had dulled to tolerable levels. I imagined I still looked like road kill.

"So, uh." I glanced around. "Where can I take a piss?"

He pointed to a curtained-off area in the corner of the

room. "There. We have basic plumbing."

That was something Xan did have. I hopped to my feet and drained my full bladder, then came back feeling like I might actually be able to shift. I stripped off my clothes, Dare's eyes on me the whole time. With a crack of my neck, I called for the shift.

And, thank fuck, my body responded.

Bones popped and skin stretched. Fur grew. When I dropped to all fours, I was blissfully without pain for the first time since I took a punch from Xan's soldiers.

I bounced around, testing out my limbs a little, when I felt something brush my side. I leapt back and turned my head to see the black, furry chest of another wolf. I looked up higher to see green eyes staring down at me. In his wolf form, Dare was commanding and huge. With one howl, I imagined he could make his pack do just about anything.

Even now the urge for me to roll over and show my belly was all-consuming. I fought against it, wanting to play first. It'd only be a matter of time, though, before Dare had me on my back.

I leapt away from him, then dipped my head, tail high and wagging. He stood tall, peering down at me as if to say, *go ahead and get your energy out.*

He was a gorgeous wolf, solid and broad, with a glossy, black coat and a silver stripe running down his back to the tip of his tail. His ears were also tipped with silver, which was actually kinda cute. But I didn't think Dare would want to be called cute. I wondered what he looked like in his Were form.

For now, my body didn't hurt, so I bounded around Dare's living space with renewed vigor, knowing that every minute that passed was healing me. In my human form, my only discerning characteristic to other wolves was my scent, but as soon as I shifted, my pack roots were right there in my fur. I was a gray wolf with a white throat.

I sniffed Dare, then rooted around his bed, wanting to know if anyone else had been fucking my mate.

I smelled no one else. Interesting…

I wagged my tail, trotting back over to Dare, who still hadn't moved his body other than his head to track me as I studied his room.

When I nuzzled his chest, he shifted, and, even in my wolf form, I had to stare dumbfounded at the sight of a naked Dare. He was chiseled, molded to perfection. His thick dick was hard, the heavy weight pulling it down between his legs in front of large, low-hanging balls.

I licked my wolf lips.

Dare's eyes flashed. His fingernails were still curved into claws, his canines descended, and a dusting of fur still covered his shoulders. He looked wild and a little feral. "Shift." His voice was garbled, and I backed up a step, dipping my head as I whined.

He took a heaving breath and the fur on his shoulders disappeared. His eyes closed and when they opened, they were nearly black. "Shift," he ordered again.

My body obeyed.

Never in my life had anyone been able to command me to shift, but Dare could. His command was a swell of power that I couldn't deny. My bones cracked as I shifted back to human form, then I collapsed onto my stomach and panted as I tested my limbs. My ribs weren't even tender.

Fuck yeah, shifter power.

I rose to my feet, shaking out my arms as I lifted my head to meet Dare's gaze.

His teeth were bared, eyes cycling between green and black like a two-toned tornado.

He moved so fast, I didn't even see his arm, didn't realize he was in motion until a hand wrapped around my neck and claws dug into my throat. He hauled me against him, and with my feet not touching the floor, the only thing I could do was clutch his shoulders and wrap my legs around his waist.

"Mine," he growled against my lips.

Not gonna lie, I was fucking terrified. Dare was only half there, his Were pulsing inside his skin. I didn't know his Were, and I hoped to hell Dare had enough power to stay human.

I shifted my hands to grip his face, my fingers digging into his scalp as I rutted against him. The mating instinct overtook all my other thoughts. So, despite my terror, I was hard as hell. "Yours," I muttered back.

That seemed to appease the Were, because Dare's eyes stopped flickering, finally resting on green.

His chest rumbled, and he pressed our lips together— hard, punishing, furious—before delving his tongue inside.

The kiss was possessive and all-consuming. While I'd fucked around plenty, I'd never been kissed in my life, so I didn't know how to deal with it. My head was spinning, my body on fire, ass clenching in anticipation for being taken. I wanted it. God help me, but I wanted him to pin me down and fuck me until I broke.

I wanted to be owned.

So, I kissed him back, pushing against his tongue with mine, gnashing his lips with my teeth, which only seemed to spur him on harder.

The room tilted, and then Dare was looming over me, my back against the mattress as he gripped our cocks in one hand and began to pump. My cock was leaking pre-come, coating my stomach and mixing with Dare's pre-release.

His shoulders bunched as he held himself above me, his attention on stroking us. His gaze lifted to mine, and when our eyes met, I was thankful they were green. He peeled his lips back, revealing his sharp teeth. "I love the smell of you, but it's wrong. It's all wrong."

Great. I prepared to have my throat ripped out for mistaken mate identity. "What?"

"You don't smell like me yet." He ran his nose up the column of my neck and then nipped my ear. "I can't be around you anymore without imprinting my smell on you."

"Make me smell like you, then." I reached down to grip his balls. "I'm all healed now. Take me."

In the far recesses of my brain, I knew this meant the life I had planned for my brother and sister would change. But I couldn't help it, not while Dare's scent was in my nostrils, while his power was surrounding me, and as his hand left my cock to swirl through the wetness on my stomach.

I was going to be mated. To a Were. And there was no going back.

***

Dare

I'D WANTED HIM THE MOMENT I laid eyes on him, but once I saw him healed, with both blue eyes blinking at me, I lost control.

I never lost control. Sex before this was for pleasure or procreation. Strings not attached.

But now, my Were was rioting inside my brain. I beat him back, because he'd have to wait his turn to meet Reese. Right now, Reese was mine.

He lay beneath me on my mattress, black hair in disarray, eyes glazed with lust. He was coated in a mixture of our pre-come, his stomach glistening. I swiped my fingers through it and raised it to his full lips, swollen from our aggressive kisses. He parted them, gaze locked on mine as I slipped my fingers inside. He sucked immediately, hollowing his cheeks. I growled in my chest, imagining what those lips would look like wrapped around my dick.

Later. There'd be plenty of time for that.

I pulled my fingers out, and he let them go with a reluctant whimper. Gripping his face, I lapped at his lips, enjoying the taste of us together. Beneath me, his body shuddered.

I flipped him onto his stomach and ran my hand down his broad back. My mate was strong and well-muscled, although a little thin. We'd work on that. His ass was perfection. High and round. I slapped a cheek, enjoying the redness blooming on the pale skin.

He spread his legs on a moan, and I rubbed around his hole, happy to see werewolf males provided their own slick like Weres did.

I tapped the head of my cock at his entrance, and he squirmed. "God, please, I need this."

Yeah, well so did I. When I thrust inside, he cried out. I sucked in a breath as my blood sang, knowing I'd found my home. The feel of him clenched around my dick, the smell of him in the throes of arousal—all of it was fucking perfect. When I began to move, pumping in and out of him—that was when my body went a little wonky.

My vision blurred, and my skin prickled as my Were, wolf, and human forms battled. My brain went offline several times as each form fought to take our mate. But Reese wasn't some Were I could fuck and forget, so I tried to pull out, to abort, to do anything I could to preserve him. Except the control I held on to so tightly at all times was nonexistent. I dug my claws into the mattress on either side of him to anchor us and gritted my teeth, my hips slamming into his smaller body as he jolted higher on the bed with each thrust.

He was saying words. My name. Some other things that weren't registering. All my forms knew he was our mate, that he was home, that nothing felt as good as being inside of him.

Beneath me, his mouth dropped open, and he screamed, his fists clenching around my wrists. When the smell of his release hit my nostrils, my Were went berserk. I heard myself howl, and then everything went black.

WHEN I CAME TO, I smelled blood.

Blood and...something else that was *right*.

My head was foggy, my body like lead. I was laying on my side, arm thrown over something hot. I blinked open my eyes, knowing I needed to get my bearings. I had something to protect now. *My mate. Protect. Reese.*

So, when the first thing I saw was his neck dripping with blood, I bolted upright and hauled him into my arms.

"Reese!" I yelled, licking at his wound so my saliva could heal it. "What happened? Are you okay? Wha—?"

"Stop yelling!" He batted me away and blinked sleepy blue eyes at me. "Why are you yelling?"

"You're bleeding." I frowned at him, anger seeping into my voice. But I wasn't angry at him. I was angry at myself for losing control, for hurting him. Because those puncture marks in his neck were bite wounds. From me. I'd lost control and *bitten him*. I'd never bitten a partner during sex. But with Reese, I'd been compelled to do it. I needed to dig up a book on True Mates or talk to an elder. I didn't want to hurt Reese again.

He patted his neck, then shrugged. "Yeah, you bit me."

I stared at him as he yawned. "I bit you," I said again.

It was his turn to frown at me. "Yeah, Captain Obvious. Can we move on now?"

I glared at him.

His eyes widened. "Wait, did you think you hurt me?"

I gripped his chin. "Yes." His mouth formed an O. I caressed his jaw with my thumb. "I lost control. That's never happened to me before. I couldn't stop, and then I blacked out."

He placed a hand on my chest. "Yeah, you howled, then you bit me when you came. And, uh, it made me come again. I guess your teeth and my neck equals Reese g-spot. Cool, huh?"

I pushed him so he fell back onto the bed with a bounce. "Hey!" he protested.

"I was worried I killed you."

He lifted onto his elbows. "You didn't kill me. Not gonna lie, I saw my life flash before my eyes about three times. But apparently, I get off on that."

I wanted him again. Right now. After all of that, after the fear I'd hurt him, I wanted him again. He must have seen it in my eyes, because he licked his lips, and his eyes dropped down to my cock.

I could have buried myself in his throat, but as he moved toward me, his ribs shifted under his skin. My mate was too thin. Also, I wanted some time to clear my head. I didn't understand this True Mate pull well enough yet, and my instincts regarding Reese were messing with my head. I still had a pack and responsibilities to think about. Even if lying in bed with a naked Reese was the only thing I wanted to do.

I stepped off the bed and pulled my pants on with my back to him.

"Where are we going?" he asked.

"I'm going to get us food."

He started to speak then paused. "As in, just you?"

I didn't want to deal with his questions right now, not while I felt vulnerable toward him. "Yes. You're staying here."

"Why can't I go with you?"

I didn't like being questioned. My pack didn't do it. Why should my mate? Maybe I'd been too soft, too accepting of his smart mouth. But even now, I only wanted to kiss said smart mouth. I clenched my jaw. "I'm going, you're staying here, and that's all you need to know."

"When am I going to be able to leave this room?"

"I'm not sure yet."

His face was flushed, his hands balled at his sides. "I thought I was your mate, not your prisoner. Are you just going to keep me locked in here? What about Jude?"

I thought I'd made it clear that this wasn't Q&A time. As I walked toward the door, he scrambled after me. "Hey, wait—"

With a hand on the knob, I whirled around. "I'm not sure what you think this is, but my commands are not up for debate. My reasons do not need to be explained to you. You will stay here, and I'll bring you food, and that's the end of it, do you hear me?"

Reese's eyes were wide, and he didn't move. Then he slowly gathered himself together, his face hardening, his spine straightening. He took a measured step back and, with a jerky nod of his head, he said in a dead voice, "Yes, Alpha."

Fuck, why did his tone send a chill down to my bones? I walked out the door, slamming it behind me, then leapt down the stairs. I paced along the landing, listening for sounds from behind my door, but there was nothing. Those words had felt like a punch to the chest, and I had no idea why. What was wrong with me that I regretted snapping at him? I hadn't treated him badly. I'd fed him, I'd let him sleep and shift. And I'd fucked him so well, he begged for it and came twice.

This was ridiculous. He had to learn how to be an alpha's mate, was all. That didn't stop the uneasy feeling in my stomach.

CHAPTER THREE

Dare

GETTING REESE FOOD WAS A priority, but so was my pack. I swung by my brother's apartment on my way to the kitchens. It was late now, and the only natural light was from the moon filtering in through the windows at the top of the Hive.

Bay lived on the fifth floor in an apartment that was supposed to be nice, but he kept it a mess because he had no proper home training.

I knocked on the door and waited as muffled voices reached my ears. "Who is it?" Bay's voice called.

"Me," I answered.

More muffled voices, until eventually the door opened, and a female Were emerged, yawning. "Hey, Alpha," she said.

I greeted her with a nod, then stepped inside, closing the door behind me. Bay was on his bed, shoveling a banana in his mouth. My brother was smaller than me, but seventy-five percent more charming and attractive. His green eyes sparkled as they tracked me across the room, and he grinned around his mouthful of food. "Hey, brother."

"She looked like she was barely a novus."

He ran his hand over his short hair. "What? Nah, her muto was like three years ago."

I raised an eyebrow. "That's Pullo's granddaughter. Three years, my ass."

He pursed his lips. "Okay, a year and a half." I laughed and he threw up his hands. "Hey, she came knocking! Not the other way around."

"She's cute."

"Damn right. So, what's up?"

"Wanted to see how things were."

Bay smirked. "You took a break from being balls deep in your mate to see your brother? I'm touched."

"Bay." I growled.

Again with the grin. "When do I get to meet this wolf? I'm so pissed I wasn't here when he got dragged out of his cell."

I regretted chaining up Reese, but he and his brother were refugees from a pack we had a truce with. I hadn't wanted them free inside the Hive until I could question them. Of course, as soon as I scented him as my mate, all bets were off. "Soon. I still feel protective of him. And I'm not ready for him to be judged by the pack yet."

Bay threw his banana peel in the trash. "Look, I get you're anxious over this, but the pack will respect him because they respect you. Unless he's a total asshole."

"He's not," I said. "He smart and curious." I heard Reese's voice in my head calling me Captain Obvious. "He's funny too."

Bay's eyes widened. "Funny? Did you just say he's *funny*? Well, fuck, you barely laugh at my jokes and I'm hilarious as shit."

"You're dumb."

"*I am funny*." He drew out the words. "So tell me his story."

"It's pretty shitty."

He snorted. "We all have tragic backstories in today's world, Dare. Just tell me about him."

Point taken. "He's a Whitethroat from Astria."

Bay squinted. "Astria." Then his mouth dropped open in an O. "Shit. They got attacked about fifteen years ago, yeah?"

I nodded. "Reese was ten. His parents got him and Jude out and took them to the Bluefoot pack hoping for sanctuary. Instead Xan killed his parents and put Jude and Reese to work."

"Damn."

"Then he tried to escape, and you know the rest."

"I thought Xan was doing okay over there, but he's killing and forcing wolves to do labor?"

"According to Reese. Why else would he risk escape?"

Bay sighed heavily. "I heard he was in bad shape. He's healed now?"

I nodded. "Yeah. He's really thin. I'm on my way to get him some food."

Bay was quiet for a moment. "And…you think he's legit?"

"What do you mean?"

"I mean, do you think he's telling the truth? He's not some sort of mole or spy or whatever?"

I bristled, my immediate reaction to defend my mate. "You think Xan would beat up his own pack member and send him here to spy on me?" Bay and I looked at each other, and then I sighed. "Okay, yeah he probably would. But he wouldn't have been able to anticipate that Reese was my mate."

"Fair enough," Bay said. "I thought I'd be a voice of reason while your brain is clouded with hormones."

"Since when are you the voice of reason in this family?"

Bay laughed. "Yeah, it's not a good fit."

"You're right, though, about the hormones. I don't—" I shook my head. "I don't know how to handle this. I don't know enough about True Mates to understand what's normal."

"What do you mean?"

"I bit him." I blurted out.

Bay didn't react. "You bit him?"

"Yeah, the first time I fucked him, I lost control. I half-shifted then I bit him and passed out."

Bay blinked at me. "Uh, that's intense."

"You think?" We didn't have any True Mates in the pack for me to look to for an example. In fact, I'd never met any in my life.

Bay held up a finger and hopped out of bed. He rummaged under some clothes on a table in the corner of his room, and I peered around him to see a stack of books. "Are all those books signed out?"

He turned around with a roll of his eyes. "Probably not."

"Bay! How many times—?"

He shoved a book in my face so fast that the cover smacked my nose. I grabbed it out of his hand with a snarl and read the cover. *Real Accounts of True Mates.* "Oh. Thank you. Still, sign the books out like everyone else, okay?"

He waved a hand at me. "Sure. I grabbed that a while ago because I was curious. There are all kinds of stories about alphas being able to control entire packs. Their mates gaining alpha powers. Stuff like that. True Mates are the real deal."

"I don't feel any different so far other than wanting to fuck him a lot."

Bay barked out laugh. "Well, I'm not sure how much that book will help because it doesn't have any mentions of True Mates between species. Only accounts of Weres with Weres and werewolves with werewolves."

I ran my fingers over the embossed lettering. "I wonder if, before the humans went extinct, there were any Were/human True Mate pairings."

Bay sat down on the edge of his bed. "Yeah, I don't know. It's rare enough to find it *in* species."

I smacked the book on my thigh. "So how's the pack?"

"They're fine. It's normal to spend a week with a new mate. Now that you found your True Mate? They'll get it. Take your time to get to know him, it'll be fine."

I blew out a breath. "It feels like a fine line. I want to make sure we're adequately bonded before introducing him to the pack, but too long and they'll think something's wrong."

"Well, you're still well within the line." He leaned back against the wall, folding his hands behind his head and crossing his feet at the ankles. "Except with Gage, but he hates everything you do."

Gage was our older cousin and an ever-present thorn in my side. My history with him was…nasty. Most of the pack knew about it, but we'd grown so much since then that the last thing I wanted to do was take the pack back to that violent, uncertain time. "Anything new?"

Bay shrugged "He's been asking about your mate."

"Oh?" I crossed my arms over my chest and worked to keep a hold on the lick of anger surging in my gut. "What kind of questions does Gage have about my mate?"

"He wants to know how it can be a True Mate pairing when Reese is a wolf. And…" Bay paused.

"And what?"

He sighed heavily. "And he's questioning if this is actually what's best for the Alpha of the Silver Tip pack—to be mated to a wolf."

I wanted to explode, punch a hole in the wall, shift and roar. Gage would find anything to undermine my authority. And using my mate to do it was low as fuck. Of course, that was how Gage operated.

My lips curled into a sneer, and a growl rumbled in my chest. Bay winced, and I willed myself to calm down. I breathed out slowly, even though I felt anything but calm. "His speculation is just that. Keep an ear to the ground for me."

"Of course, brother. I have been. What do you think you should do?"

It was a question I'd been asking myself a lot lately over the last few months. My father, may he rest in hell, was quick to challenge any enemies if they so much as looked at him wrong. It bred hostility and fear, which led to a lot of pack infighting. I refused to let the pack fall back into that under my rule. "He hasn't challenged me, and I'm not comfortable with being the type of alpha who'll initiate a challenge with someone who dislikes me."

"I get it. Although, this goes past dislike."

He had a point. "I know it does."

"I think you're right, though. Eventually, he'll either challenge or leave. And you can deal with him appropriately when that happens."

I respected the advice from my brother and the trusted members of my guard. I squinted at Bay. "Do you think I'm making the wrong decision?"

He shook his head. "No. I think you're making the best decision you can right now, based on the information you have. Plus, you've just found your True Mate. You need time to make room for that in your life."

"Yes, I do."

"You're a good alpha, Dare. And the overwhelming majority of the pack agrees."

"I want to make her proud," I said. He knew who I meant.

Bay's voice was raspy when he answered. "You are."

I rolled my shoulders, feeling the ache in my bones from

my separation from Reese. That was one side effect of the True Mate bond that I knew only affected Weres. The Mate Pain. The ache was bone-deep. Each time I left Reese's presence, it would ease somewhat, but it was Fate's reminder I was tied to Reese for the rest of my life. Literally. Because if Reese died, then so did I. "I need to get back to Reese."

"Sure, of course."

"Sorry I interrupted."

"Nah, she was heading out anyway."

"I'll bring him out soon, okay?"

"Of course, and I'm holding everything down while you're busy. No worries, Alpha."

I still worried. I had pack members, family, and friends who relied on me. "Check in with Mav and Cati for me?"

Bay grinned. "You got it."

I walked over to the side of the bed, gripped the back of Bay's head, and brought his forehead to my lips. "Don't know what I'd do without you."

"You'd make bad decisions and laugh a lot less," he answered, patting my cheek as I pulled away.

I did laugh at that. I couldn't help it. "You speak the truth."

"Always."

I pointed at him. "Be good, and I'll bring Reese around for you to tease soon." I smiled. "He'll like you."

"Of course he will. Everyone likes me."

I rolled my eyes and walked out the door to Bay's laughter.

As I walked back to the kitchen, I gnawed my lip, thinking about Bay's words of caution. Reese was telling me the truth about escaping the Bluefoot pack, of that I was certain. No way would they leave him as Nowere bait and hope we'd save him. It grated on me to learn how Xan was running his pack. Our truce stated that we would never intervene in other packs' politics, but how could I stick to that promise knowing Xan starved his pack and enslaved others?

I wasn't sure I could live with that. Gage would, of course, tell me to mind my own business, or better yet, raid Xan's compound, but that wasn't my style. I could be ruthless when I wanted to, and I had been in the past, but I had to justify it.

Could I justify breaking the truce to save wolves I'd never met?

Eh, I'd follow Bay's advice for now. I'd get to know Reese and watch him fatten up. I made my way to the kitchens, intent on spoiling my mate. The last look he'd levied at me had not been a happy one, which I probably deserved. I re-gripped the True Mate book in my hands. Maybe we could both stand to learn something from it.

Reese

I DIDN'T KNOW HOW LONG I stood there staring at the door after Dare closed it.

My mind was a jumbled mess. In addition to worrying about Jude and Selene, I was worried about my damn self. What the hell was my role as Dare's mate? Was I just a body he kept locked in his quarters to fuck when he wanted?

My parents were True Mates, but their bond was so much more than fate. They'd loved each other with an all-consuming passion. I'd always dreamed of having that with someone else. I'd expected that was the way True Mates were supposed to be, that right away we'd be in love. I hadn't considered that there would be a learning curve. Dare and I were strangers, forced together because of instinct, but we knew nothing about each other. I had no idea what this pack was like, what kind of alpha he was. All I knew was that I was alive and unharmed. For now.

I wouldn't do my sister or my brother any damn good if I didn't start thinking smart. This wasn't about me or my pride. This was about surviving long enough to be able to get out of here, rescue Selene, and be free.

I had to abandon this dumb hope for love and the idea I'd be a respected partner to Dare. He was a Were for fuck's sake. In his mind, I was an inferior species.

As a True Mate pair, my parents had been able to communicate silently, a gift of their bond. Apparently, each Mated pairing was special and any gifts that might occur as a result were different, depending on the bond. Well, so far, I didn't feel different except for a sore ass. Why couldn't this True Mate bond make me fly or give me super Nowere-killing powers? Super sister-saving powers would be stellar too.

Even though I was healed, in that moment, my heart felt battered. With heavy steps, I retreated to the bed, and crawled into it, covering myself with a knitted blanket. I lay on my stomach, hands under my head, and closed my eyes.

When Dare returned, he brought the smell of food with him. Delicious food. I wanted to stay turned away from him in a silent protest, but my growling stomach overrode my desire to pout.

I sat up as he set several plates in front of me. Chicken drumsticks. An omelet oozing with cheese. A big glass of milk.

He grabbed a drumstick and sat down on a chair beside the bed, crossing his feet at the ankles and propping them on the mattress. He bit into it and chewed without a word, green eyes on me. When I didn't move, he pointed to the food. "Eat."

I dug in, knowing I needed my strength. I hadn't eaten this well in years. So at least I wasn't the mate to some alpha with a rationed compound like Xan's. *Could be worse, Reese. Could always be worse.*

Hell, I could be in a Nowere's belly right now.

The chicken was juicy, the omelet fluffy as hell, and the milk cold. "How do you keep this cool?" I asked, licking the milk from my lips. "Am I allowed to ask that question?" I cringed immediately. Did I always have to run my mouth?

Dare looked unimpressed by my second inquiry. "We have underground bunkers where we store food that needs to be kept cool."

"Oh. That's great." I poked at my omelet. Now that I'd eaten, my energy was coming back, which was the only reason I decided to blurt out dumb shit. "Hey, do you keep Noweres as pets?"

Dare's face remained frozen. "Noweres as pets."

"Yeah."

"Why are you asking me this?"

"Never mind."

"Please explain. I'm curious why you're asking me."

Now I felt stupid. "Just a rumor over at the Bluefoot pack. That you kept a Nowere in your bedroom and fed him wolves who wandered into your compound."

Again with that impassive expression. "Ah, well, that's obviously incorrect."

I nodded. "Yeah, obviously—"

"I keep him in the kitchen."

I stared.

Dare's lips twitched.

I sat up. "I—are you making a joke?"

"I guess we'll cover that on the tour." His lips twitched again. Fuck, he was mocking me. I sneered at him, which only seemed to amuse him more. The damn Were's eyes were sparkling. With a small smirk at me, he placed his empty plates by the door, then rummaged around his bookshelf.

I made faces at his back.

"I keep him in the kitchen," I mimicked softly. "Jerk."

After a moment, he sat back down on his chair and resumed his favorite activity, which seemed to be watching me eat.

"Can I ask you one more question?" I took his silence as an affirmation. "Can I see Jude?"

He crossed his hands in his lap. "I'll check on him soon."

That didn't answer my question. I took another bite of food for courage. "Okay, thank you. But *when* can *I* see him?"

"Soon. When I'm ready for you to be out among my pack." I opened my mouth, but he cut me off. "G is a trusted member of my guard. I promise you that your brother is in safe hands."

I was about to remark that I didn't trust fucking anyone, but I kept my mouth shut. He'd given me an answer. Not one I wanted, but I could work with that. I smiled at him faintly and resuming eating.

When I couldn't stuff myself anymore, I placed the plates on a table beside the door, then walked back toward the bed. I sat in the middle of it, watching Dare down a large glass of water, his Adam's apple working as he swallowed.

I hated that I found him so sexy, that while he was kind of a cold bastard, I wanted him so badly, I ached for it. I knew that was the True Mate bond talking, but it didn't matter because I couldn't deny it.

He stood up, shucked his pants, and sat back down. His cock was half hard, and he stroked it a couple of times to full hardness before saying in a low voice, "Come 'ere."

Yes, okay, I was down for that. If I was stuck in this room with him, then I should go ahead and get laid as much as possible. Refusing would get me nowhere, and I didn't *want* to refuse.

I crawled toward him and when I was close, he gripped my hair tightly, leading me off the bed to kneel on the floor between his spread thighs. Fuck, being this close to his dick, the heat of his skin and the smell of his pre-come was making me dizzy with lust.

With a fist, he gripped his cock and held it up against his stomach, then guided my mouth to his balls. Sure, yes, I was totally into those too. I licked the soft skin, then sucked one into my mouth, relishing the salty, musky taste of Dare.

The color of his eyes swirled as I worked him. I tongued everything I could reach—all around his balls, the base of his dick, and even delving my face into his groin to take a heady whiff.

"You like the smell of your alpha." His grip tightened in my hair.

"Yes," I mumbled as I nuzzled closer, proud of myself that I actually formed a word.

"You like the taste of me too." His voice was thick as he guided my lips to the tip of his cock. "Go on, taste me."

I licked the head, and one taste had me moaning, eager for more. The slick around my hole was dripping down my thighs, and I was tempted to hump his leg.

He slowly entered my mouth, and I kept my eyes on him the entire time until he touched the back of my throat, making me gag.

If anything, that turned him on more. He pulled my head away, then began to fuck my mouth at a steady pace. I gagged the first couple of times, until I got the rhythm down, then I relaxed my throat and breathed in time to his thrusts.

Finally, he released his grip on my hair and leaned back in his chair. It was my show now, and while I'd blown a couple of guys before, I'd never enjoyed it as much as I did now. I never craved it like this, my body telling me I had to bring him to release. I kept one hand at the base of his cock and pumped him in time with the bobbing of my head.

He was silent above me, but his nostrils flared, his chest heaved, and he panted from between parted lips.

I knew he was close when his hand dropped heavily on my head, and his legs shook. "My mate," he moaned before shooting his load down my throat.

I got one last lick in before he tossed me back onto the bed and crawled over me. A large hand closed around my aching dick. "Please," I murmured.

"What do you need?" he rasped in my ear as he loomed over me.

"Need you to make me come."

He squeezed again, to the point of pain, and I cried out.

"Fuck my hand." He circled the rim of my ear with his tongue. "I want to watch you."

His grip was tight, but not too tight. I began to thrust my hips into his fist, and he watched me the whole time. Finally, with a slap to my hip to get me to stop thrusting, he began to stroke me off like a fucking expert, twisting his wrist at the top, whispering in my ear that I was his, that I smelled like him, that he couldn't wait to fuck me again.

With a silent moan, I came all over his hand and my groin until my body went slack.

My brain narrowed to one focus and that was to scent my mate. I managed to turn myself in his arms and nuzzle into his chest, rooting around his nipple and armpit, all the areas where his scent was concentrated.

A hand in my hair wrenched my head back, and my vision swam as Dare stared into my eyes. I don't know what he saw, but his brow furrowed. "Did this happen last time?"

I tried to talk, but the words wouldn't come, only a dry click in my throat. Last time, I'd passed out almost immediately, so this drugging need for him was new. I pulled against his grip, needing his scent. He muttered something and let my head go. I went right back to nuzzling against him. I tried to tell him what I was doing, what I needed, but his scent was all around, infecting me, and the last thing I remembered before I passed out was his hand resting gently yet possessively on the back of my neck.

CHAPTER FOUR

Dare

REESE SLEPT SO DEEPLY THAT even when an empty plate slipped out of my hand and clattered to the floor, he didn't stir. Not even a flinch.

After nuzzling into my chest and my pits with his lips parted and eyes glazed, he'd finally passed out, but I could still feel the phantom moist exhales of his breath, the brushes of his lips, the rhythmic way he inhaled me, like he couldn't get enough.

I sat beside the bed watching my mate sleep, *Real Accounts of True Mates* clutched in my hand. I'd spent the last three hours while Reese slept reading all I could, but I wasn't much closer to learning about the True Mate bond. I already knew about the Mate Pain, which only affected Weres. Related to the Mate Pain was the fact that if Reese died, so would I. Probably within hours. The physical separation from him while he was still alive was painful, but if he died, then the pain would kill me.

Reese would be unaffected by this. Of course, if I was challenged by another alpha and killed, Reese would be killed too as my mate. I shuddered thinking about it. I'd do everything in my power to make sure that never happened.

There were some documented reports of Alphas growing physically strong, as well as their True Mates. And many were able to link their minds so they could communicate silently. But every True Mate partnership was unique. And all the benefits of the bond often took weeks to months to fully develop.

As interested as I was in learning how bonding with a True Mate would benefit me, I found my concentration drifting during reading. Mostly to watch Reese. And to think about how it'd only been two days since we met and already I was consumed by him.

I'd had limited interactions with werewolves over the years. A few came by and sought shelter for a little while before moving on, usually to other werewolf packs in the area—often Xan's. I'd never thought sending them there would most likely lead them to a life of servitude. They were never comfortable here, and wolves made Weres restless. I'd always thought them to be weaker, less intelligent, and naturally submissive, but Reese didn't fall into those categories. Well, he was weaker physically just based on size, but I was impressed with the strength he did have.

He wasn't dumb. He seemed to have a natural curiosity and a craving for answers and understanding. And, while in bed, it felt as though he enjoyed his role, but it was obvious he didn't enjoy being bossed around elsewhere. While his body listened to me, his eyes told me he was not pleased.

Sometimes reading Reese was easy. He showed his emotions all over his face. Other times, he threw up a guard, the one I suspected he'd hid behind when under Xan's rule.

I ran my hand over my face with a grunt. When I'd first smelled that this werewolf was my True Mate, I had expected to fuck him, absorb the benefits that came with the True Mate bond, and that would've been it. I hadn't expected to be invested in his feelings, wonder what he was thinking or if he was content, or for fuck's sake, want him to *like* me.

Who gave a fuck if Reese liked me?

I did, apparently, because the idea of him hating his life, of hating me, was intolerable.

Shit, I had to get out of here, away from his scent, before I woke him and fucked him unconscious again.

With one last look at him, I left my room, locking the door behind me. I jogged down the stairs, to the fifth level of the Hive, our main building which housed everything from pack member apartments to meeting rooms. I made my way to G's room. I knocked on the door, and he opened it a crack.

"I want a meet," I said.

He nodded, and left the door open as he retreated to stuff his feet into his boots. Jude sat on the bed with a pad of paper and a pencil. He was too thin like Reese, and he had the same pale skin, dark hair, and vibrant blue eyes. He glanced up, and when he saw I was at the door, his eyes widened as he clambered off the bed and ran toward me. "Is Reese with you?"

The hope in his voice tightened my chest. I shook my head.

Jude came to a halt in front of me, and his face fell.

"Oh." He nibbled his lip and glanced at G, who was watching him silently. "Is my brother okay?"

"He's fine." My answer was curt, but I didn't like being questioned about my mate by anyone. Jude's expression darkened, and he opened his mouth.

"Jude." G's voice was a sharp crack of warning.

Jude immediately bent his head, and his bony shoulders heaved. Without a word, he shuffled back to the bed and picked up his pad of paper, avoiding eye contact with either of us.

Shit.

G met me at the door. "I'll be back soon," he said to the boy.

Jude ignored him.

"Jude," I said.

He ignored me too.

"The Alpha is speaking to you," G said, his voice softer this time.

Jude pressed his lips together, his fingers curling into his palms. Finally, his gaze met mine.

"I'll bring Reese by to see you soon."

Jude swallowed, and despite his eyes telling me he wanted to claw my face, his voice was even. "Okay."

Right, that was more than I owed anyone. I led G out of the room, and waited as he locked the door behind him. We made our way to the end of the hallway, into a spare apartment I often used for meetings. When the door was locked behind me, I turned to G. "How is he?"

My guard captain pulled an apple out of his pocket and

bit into it. "He listens to me."

"I see that."

"He's hungry a lot, and sleeps." A muscle in his jaw jumped. "And he has scars on his back, like he was beaten with something."

I blinked. As far as I knew, wolves didn't scar. Reese's back was smooth. The only way to scar would be if they cut him with something silver. "For fuck's sake."

G didn't respond as he polished off his apple. He tossed it in the trash can in the far corner. "Bay's been handling everything fine."

I smiled. My brother was not an alpha, but everyone loved him. "Yeah I visited him yesterday." Was it yesterday? Time was running together.

"You want to round up the guard and meet?"

I shook my head. "I gotta get back to my mate. I'm not ready to make an appearance to the pack yet. And Reese definitely isn't ready."

G didn't have to ask. I knew by his one raised eyebrow what he wanted to know. Not that I had to tell him, but I told G everything. "He's fine, but this is an adjustment for us both." I huffed out a breath. "Who told us wolves were the submissive, weaker species?"

G barked out a laugh. "I was going to ask you the same thing."

"Are these wolves defective?" I grinned.

"I don't know, but Jude is the same. He's smart. I have to watch him closely and, even now, I don't want to be gone long."

"You think he'll escape?"

"I don't think he'll leave the compound, but he wants to see his brother."

"Yeah, okay." I shook my head. My joints were starting to ache, as the separation from my mate stretched on. "I should get back to Reese. When I left, he was sleeping." With a jerk of my chin, I was out the door, intent on getting food for my mate, then back to him as soon as possible.

Reese

I CAME AWAKE SLOWLY, MY head still a little foggy from sex. Would it be like this every time? Because fuck, I was useless.

I rubbed my eyes and rolled onto my back, sniffing the air. I didn't smell my mate and with a groan, I raised my upper body to look for him.

Nope, no Dare.

I rolled out of bed, took a piss, and then checked the door. Locked. Figured.

I tested the bars on the windows, but even if I could squeeze between them, I'd never survive the six-floor jump to the ground. And where would I go even if I managed to get out of this room?

I needed more time to feel Dare out, more time to get to know the way his pack operated. There was a possibility I could trust him enough to tell him about Selene. But as an alpha, his own pack would be his first priority, and the likelihood I'd have to escape and go it alone was high.

I walked laps around the room restlessly. A couple of times, I swore I saw the doorknob turn, and the excitement that bloomed in my chest each time worried me.

Why was I so eager to see him?

This was routine apparently—fuck, sleep, eat. Repeat. Any other time, I would have been cool with this. Who wouldn't want a mate who could use his dick as well as Dare? But my sister's life was on a knife edge. *Fuck my life.*

I shifted, dropping down to four paws and shaking out my fur. I found an old chicken bone under the bed and lay with it pressed between my paws so I could gnaw on it. I was so into the bone, that I almost missed Dare's return.

I smelled him a split second before he entered the room. He held a couple of plates in his hands, and stared down at me with what looked to be amusement. "You're awake."

I shifted back to human quickly, then grabbed a plate he handed me. "What did you bring me?"

"Chicken sandwiches."

I sat down on the end of the bed and poked at the bread. "Oh damn, it's still warm." When I bit into it, my eyes rolled back in my head. Fuck, I could get used to this. I was halfway through my sandwich when I glanced up to see him still staring at me. "You going to eat?"

"Already ate."

"Oh." I polished off the rest of the sandwich, then started in on the carrots. "So how is everything…out there?"

"Fine." He answered so quickly that I wasn't sure all was fine. "And I saw your brother."

I stood up. "Yeah? Is he okay?"

"He's eating well, and he and G seem to be getting along."

"What do you mean by getting along?"

"Jude listens to G, and does what G asks."

I raised my eyebrows. "My brother is following orders?"

"Apparently."

My brother listened to me, and that was about it. He only listened to people he respected or...that he was scared of. Him obeying G didn't sit well. "You sure G is treating him well?"

"I'm positive." His tone was final.

Fucker. I slumped back down on the bed and ran my fingers over the crumbs on my plate, then stuck my fingers in my mouth. He was keeping me from my brother, locking me in this room so he could fuck me whenever he wanted, and the worst part was that I'd offered zero resistance and even now kinda wanted to get on all fours for him. Stupid fated instincts.

"Do you need another sandwich?"

I refused to look at him. "No."

"Reese, look at me."

I gave him my back by crawling onto the bed and lying on my stomach. I pillowed my arms on my hands, my gaze on the wall. I was anything but relaxed, my body tense as I waited to see what he'd do now that I'd blatantly disobeyed him.

There was no sound, not even a sigh. My heart pounded in my ears, and I curled my hands into fists.

Of course, he could just take out my punishment on

Jude. That's what Xan had done.

That thought shot a jolt of pure terror through me and had me bolting upright. "I'm sorry!" I held a hand out. Dare hadn't moved from his spot, and he stared at me with widened eyes. "Don't punish Jude. I'm sorry. I'll listen and obey." I crawled off the bed, every movement against my nature as I knelt at his feet. I hadn't ever prostrated myself before Xan, and he'd taken it out on Jude. These were Weres we were dealing with, and who knew what they'd do to him. Fuck pride. I raised my head and did exactly what he'd asked of me—I looked at him.

His chest rose and fell, and his lips were pressed into a thin line. "Stand up."

I did that, quickly, but kept my head bowed. Hands gripped my chin roughly and jerked my face up, his gaze meeting mine. His irises were swirling, and I swallowed, hoping he didn't sense my trembling too much. Five sharp points dug into my skin as his claws unsheathed. I was panting in terror. "I'll be good," I whispered.

His eyes fell closed, and he heaved a deep breath. He shook his head and let go of me with a shove. I fell back onto the bed as he turned around, picked up his chair beside the bed, and hurled it at the far wall.

As the chair shattered and pieces of wood rained down onto the floor, I scooted backward on the bed until I reached the wall, curling into myself, trying to be as small as possible. My heart was racing, my palms sweaty. I hadn't been smart. Blinded by the sex and the True Mate scent, I'd let my mouth run and my pride show, and now Dare was pissed. I heaved in a breath, prepared to do anything, *anything* to get back onto his good side.

He stood with his back to me for a long moment. When he turned to face me, his eyes were back to green, and he didn't look angry anymore. Instead he looked...disappointed.

I still held my breath, unsure what the hell he was thinking. He paced back and forth a couple of times before stopping. "Are you scared of me?"

"Yes," I answered quickly. "I'd be a fucking moron not to be scared of you."

He braced his hands on his hips. "Tell me why you thought I'd punish Jude."

Be smart, Reese. "Because you told me to look at you, and I didn't look at you."

"But why would I punish Jude for something you did?"

"Because that's what Xan did," I said. "One time I refused to work, he beat Jude with a silver-spiked cane."

"For fuck's sake," Dare gritted out.

I remained silent.

He ran his tongue over his top teeth. "And you thought I'd do that?"

I shrugged.

"What have I done to make you think I'd do that?"

He had a point. *But.* "What have you done to make me think you wouldn't? I'm locked up here, and I'm not even sure how many days it's been. While I don't deny I love what you do to me with your cock, I have no idea what my role is in this pack. I don't know how disposable I am. *I don't know you, Dare."*

His nostrils flared, and he glanced at the shattered remains of his chair. He walked toward me, and, although I was still wary, his expression didn't terrify me. He sat on the edge of the bed and pulled me into his lap. I came willingly, because, despite my brain shouting out words of warning, my body felt safe in the arms of my mate.

He smoothed his hand down my back, then with his thumb at my chin, lifted my gaze to meet his.

"You're right, you don't know me. So maybe my promise won't mean much to you. But I'll say it anyway. I promise to protect Jude as I would my own brother. I would never hurt him to punish you." He nudged my nose with his, in a gesture of affection I hadn't thought he was capable of.

Whether I knew him or not, an alpha promise was golden, and Dare's voice dripped with sincerity. He meant what he said, and my heart beat double-time. I kissed him, a soft press of my lips to his, a display of gratitude that I couldn't put into words. What started as a simple, hesitant kiss from me quickly morphed into Dare ravaging my mouth.

Kissing him was better than air, than any plate of food he could deliver to me. Kissing Dare was life.

The thought settled in my stomach like a cocktail of elation and dread. My heart was being tugged in too many directions. I pulled out of the kiss and ducked my head, hoping to hide the swirl of emotions.

Dare's hand sifted through my hair, then he tucked my face under his chin. I breathed him in, feeling his hardness rub against mine, but neither of us was in a hurry to deal with it.

I gripped his arms, squeezing the hard flesh. "Thank you for that promise."

He was quiet for a moment. "I thought I knew what your role was, and now I'm not so sure."

"What do you mean?"

"You're not what I expected. From a wolf and from a mate. If you're patient with me while we figure this out, then I'll be patient with you."

"That's fair," I said softly.

He sighed. "I need a new chair."

I glanced over at the broken pieces. "Uh, yeah, how're you going to explain that one?"

"I'm going to tell them I've been feeding you too much, because you sat on it and broke it."

I pulled back and punched him in the shoulder. "Ha-ha. Look who has jokes."

He was smiling. Had I seen him smile yet? Not sure, but this smile was effortless—wide grin, big teeth. His eyes crinkled at the corners, and without thinking, I reached out and ran my finger over the creases.

His smile faded, but that look of affection didn't. In a soft voice, he said. "I think I like you, mate."

I dropped my hands into my lap. "I think I like you too."

As he clutched me to his chest, I closed my eyes. This truce between us felt tentative and a little weak, but he'd earned another kernel of my trust. I'd give it a little more time, but soon, I was going to have to make a decision. Trust Dare? Or escape?

CHAPTER FIVE

Dare

As Reese bounded around my room in his wolf form, I knew I was going to have to take him out soon. He couldn't be stuck here forever. I sucked on a piece of sugar candy as he barked at a fly on the wall. He was a pretty wolf, not that I expected him not to be. He still had those bright blue eyes, and his gray coat was much glossier now than when he'd first arrived a couple of days ago. The white patch at his throat was vivid, and made his neck look thick and his shoulders broad.

I'd already shifted to wolf and back to human to work out some kinks, but I was letting Reese play a little longer in his wolf form. When he finally shifted back, he rose to his feet and stretched his arms in the air. "Fuck, that felt good." He scratched his stomach and cocked his head at me. "Hey, what's that?"

"The novuses all call them pops. They are balls of hard sugar on a stick."

I held it out to him as he walked over. He lowered his head, lapping at the red candy. "Holy shit, that's delicious."

He snatched it out of my hand and plopped on the bed.

"Hey, thief."

"I'm skinny, remember? Gotta fatten up."

I crawled over him, so he was forced to lay on his back as he sucked on the candy. I ran a finger over his red-stained lips. I'd never thought about my previous partners' pasts, mainly because I hadn't cared. I cared about Reese's, though, wondering who else had gotten a taste of those plump lips. "How many wolves have you kissed?"

He pulled the candy out of his mouth with a pop and blinked up at me. "Kissed?"

"Yeah."

He squinted an eye. "One?"

One? "Wait…"

"Never been kissed before—is that what you want to know? My parents kissed all the time, but I rarely saw that in the Bluefoot pack. Wasn't something we did."

I pressed on the corner of his mouth. "What do you think about it?"

"What do I think about kissing?"

"Yeah."

He grinned. "I was missing out. Although I can honestly look back and say every person I fucked, I had zero desire to kiss."

Reese said he'd joined the pack at ten. I shuddered a little to think about his experiences. "Were you ever forced?"

He huffed out a laugh. "Sure, the first time."

The anger rose swift and sudden, surprising even me. Reese's mouth dropped open and he stuck the candy in my mouth. "Hold on there, Alpha Angry. It's not what you think."

I handed the candy back to him. "Then tell me."

He blew out a breath, and something churned behind his eyes. "I hate talking about this." After a shudder, he kept talking. "Okay, so when I was sixteen, a female from some other pack was in the labor force with me... I can't remember which pack now... She went into heat. Xan made me get her through it. And it was fucking awful. I was terrified of hurting her, and she was just plain terrified of me. She cried. I did what I had to do to get through it. She got pregnant and died six weeks later during complications from her miscarriage. The end."

He said it all in a monotone, which I sensed was a way of detaching himself from the emotions of it. But if I'd learned anything about Reese by now, it was that he felt emotions very deeply. The slight tremble in his lips and the tick in his jaw told me he was holding himself back.

I slipped my hand up his neck to cup his cheek, unsure how to comfort him. I pressed a kiss to his forehead. He peered up at me, his blue eyes a little glassy, and offered me a wobbly smile. "Thanks."

"I'm sorry."

He shrugged as he swiped under his eyes. "Yeah, me too. Anyway, after that, it was a couple of partners just to get off every once in a while. Now I'm here, and I'm obsessed with your dick, and that's my sexual history."

He grinned as I laughed softly. "I see."

"I'm assuming your experiences have been a little less traumatic."

I nodded as I sat up beside him. "Yes, but they were also about getting off. Nothing like this craving I have for you."

He waggled his eyebrows at me as he popped the candy back in his mouth. Watching him lay on my bed naked, half-hard cock laying against his thigh while he hollowed his cheeks to suck on the candy, was turning me on.

He glanced at me, and sat with his hand held out to me, his humor gone. "As much as my dick wants to stay here and let you ravage me again, I really want to go see my brother." He nibbled his lip. "Please."

His wide-eyed plea had me ready to cave in a nano-second. During the time we'd spent holed up in my room, we'd moved past the initial physical craving for each other and into the actual like stage. I loved the moments we'd shared, but outside the door was a whole other issue. I wasn't the only alpha in the Silver Tip pack, and there were plenty ready to challenge me and take my place.

I straddled Reese's waist and slapped the mattress on either side of his head. He gulped and kept silent.

"There are a couple of things we need to get straight before we leave this apartment. I'm the alpha of this pack. Xan runs a much different pack. But here? There's no shortage of pack members eager to challenge me, watching for weakness every damn day, hoping for an Achilles heel they can exploit." My sentence ended on a growl. "As the mate to an alpha, you're tied to me. If my throat is ripped out by a challenger, the same thing would happen to you. My self-preservation is in your best interest."

Reese swallowed, eyes wide, and nodded.

I took a moment to get myself under control before lifting a hand to caress his neck. "We came to a truce earlier, and I'd like to honor that. In here, you can challenge me within reason and question me. Out there?" I pressed slightly on his windpipe. "You must obey and show respect. Do you understand?"

He answered quickly with sincerity. "I understand."

I smacked his cheek lightly, then stepped off the bed to dress. After my pants and my shirt were on and I'd slipped my feet into my boots, I turned around. He hadn't moved from where he lay on his back on the bed, staring at the ceiling. I didn't deny that his life had drastically changed in the last couple of days. But that was the way it was on Earth since the plague that spawned the Noweres a century ago.

Life was hard, then you died.

Good planet motto, I'd say.

I snapped my fingers. "You want to see your brother or not?"

He jerked out of whatever thoughts he'd been in. "Yeah. Sorry." He scrambled off the bed and was dressed in seconds. I gripped his chin and angled his head to check out my bite. It was healing well. "Let's go then, my mate."

He ducked his head to follow me, but I caught the stain of a blush on his cheeks.

Reese

I WALKED BEHIND DARE WITH my head bowed. I didn't

want to look anyone in the eye or talk to them. Subservience wasn't something that came naturally, but after faking it my whole life around Xan, it wasn't hard to slip back into the role.

At least I didn't despise Dare.

Fuck me, but I actually liked him. Although legitimately terrifying, he was a good Were. He was a good mate.

It was going to suck if I ended up having to betray him.

My parents had traveled miles and miles to Eury for a better life for their family. For their trouble, they'd been killed and their children enslaved under Xan's rule. And just because Jude and I were safe, I couldn't leave my sister behind.

Fuck no. Fuck that.

I had to get Selene back. It wasn't an option to leave her with Xan. The reminder of my first time, and the fear in the female wolf's eyes as we'd been forced together, would always haunt me. I couldn't let that happen to my sister.

As Dare led me down a hallway with doors on one side and the balcony on the other, my stomach churned with the thought of leaving him. As much as my body craved him and my wolf ached for him, I had to close off my heart while I plotted how to rescue Selene. As alpha, his pack came first. And as a werewolf with murdered parents, my siblings came first.

He led me down a hallway full of identical doors, numbers above the frame the only way to tell them apart. He stopped at number 555, and rapped on the door. I shifted on my feet, eager to see Jude.

A deep voice inside grunted, "It's open."

When Dare turned the knob, I held myself steady when all I wanted to do was rush past him. That would be disrespectful, and I couldn't afford to let Dare be challenged. Not while Selene was still in Xan's grasp. I sure as hell couldn't rescue her if I were dead.

Dare motioned for me to go in first, and I shot him a grin of gratitude. I'd make that shit up to him later.

I rushed inside, immediately spotting Jude sitting cross-legged in the middle of a massive mattress, several plates of food around him. He gasped when he saw me. "Reese!"

He knee-walked to the end of the bed, where I grabbed him in a hug. Fuck, he smelled good. When I squeezed him, he moaned in pain, and I immediately went on the alert, pulling back to study his face. "You okay? Anyone hurt you?"

He shook his head immediately and gestured to the food behind him. "I overdid it."

One plate held the remnants of a whole chicken, another the tops of carrots, and yet another, the rind of a watermelon.

"Jude," I said with a laugh.

He grinned, although he did look a little sick. "G says I can have whatever I want. I always order so much and—"

"I get it, buddy. I had a steak the other day and ate it in thirty seconds."

His eyes went round. "They have steak?"

I shook my head. "I'm pretty sure you're in food timeout for a while."

A chair scraped the floor, and I looked up to see G shift

his position in a chair near the bed. I hadn't even seen him, I'd been so focused on Jude. G's gaze was solidly on Jude, even with his alpha standing beside him with his arms crossed.

"G," Dare said.

The man grunted, still not taking his eyes off Jude.

Dare pinched the bridge of his nose, muttering, "So fucking literal." He cleared his throat and spoke louder. "G, you can take your eyes off him for a minute and look at me."

G paused, then slowly turned his head and rose to his feet next to his alpha.

I lifted an eyebrow at Jude. "Everything okay?"

Jude nodded. "Sure. He doesn't talk much, and he won't take his eyes off me, but he's been good to me." He shrugged. "I feel safe."

His eyes were clear and his smile genuine, so I knew he was telling the truth.

"Any trouble?" Dare was asking G.

"None."

"Have you taken him out of the room yet?"

G shook his head.

"What's the word?"

G hesitated. "A little anxious. More curious than anything. Another day or two, I'd say."

I opened my mouth to ask what they were talking about, but Dare shot me a look, like he knew I was going to ask a question. I snapped my jaw shut, and he nodded in approval.

Jude tugged me to sit next to him on the bed. His fingers grazed the healed area around my eye and my jaw, then traveled down my body to test my limbs. "You're healed?"

"Yeah, I shifted."

He leaned against me. "You smell different."

"Yeah, well, I'm a Were mate now."

Jude heaved a sigh. "Right," he whispered.

I cupped his neck. "Don't worry about me, okay? Dare's taking good care of me. And I'm not just saying that because he's standing there listening to everything we're saying."

A Were snort followed my words, and I grinned.

Jude smiled at the sight of my grin. "Okay."

I had a lot of things to say to him, but none I could say in front of Dare, so instead I gestured toward his food. "Lot different from Xan's, huh?"

"They have chickens. And cattle and other animals," he said with awe. "G said I can have eggs tomorrow morning. And bacon!"

I whirled to Dare. "Bacon?"

Dare rolled his eyes. "I'll get you some tomorrow. Now it's time to go."

Jude's fingers tightened on my arm before releasing me. I wanted to protest, but again remembered the warning. "Okay."

I hugged my brother, who was now once again under the watchful eye of G. I decided I liked the big, silent guy. I'd misread his presence as threatening before, but now I realized he was on constant alert and observant. And best of all, he took the safety of my brother seriously.

After leaving G's apartment, I followed Dare down the hallway. I had my head down, thinking about Jude and how the hell we were going to get out of here, when I ran into Dare's back. I peered around his tense shoulders to see a Were standing about five feet away.

In his human form, this Were was the size of Dare, maybe a little older if the lines on his face could be believed. He wore leather pants, no shirt, and large boots that could crush my skull. His green eyes were right on me. "I heard you found your True Mate."

Dare's back straightened, and his voice was slightly garbled when he answered. "I did." The fur sprouting on his shoulders told me his canines were down, his Were near the surface. And holy shit, if these two went at it in this small hallway, I was as good as dead. Every instinct in me screamed to run, but I held my ground.

"A wolf?" Condescension dripped from the other Were's voice.

Dare didn't answer the obvious question.

The Were took a step forward, his head tilted. "You better hope you keep your pack—and your wolf—in line. Would hate to see his pretty little throat ripped out along with yours."

In seconds, Dare's jaw elongated, forming a snout with flared nostrils. His opened his massive jaws, razor-sharp teeth dripping with saliva, and *roared*.

The thunderous sound shook the walls, the floors, my fucking bones. The only way I stayed on my feet was to grab onto the wall and crouch for balance, covering my head with my other arm.

When the boom subsided, followed by the snapping of

murderous teeth, I peeked out from under my arm. The other Were was on his knees, head bowed submissively.

Dare stood over him, his face shifting back to human form. When he spoke, his voice was low and deadly, a reminder that I was in fucking Were territory. "I let your jabs slide, Gage. But make no mistake, you threaten me and my mate, and your throat will be the one I rip out. Final warning."

"Yes, Alpha." The Were's voice was strong despite his posture.

Dare turned to me and beckoned with his fingers. I stood on shaky legs and followed him, keeping my gaze straight ahead. But I felt Gage's eyes on me as I walked past.

I was sure that wasn't the last I'd see of that Were. No matter how much I hoped it was.

CHAPTER SIX

Dare

WHEN GAGE GOT UNDER MY skin, I usually shifted and went for a run. Now? I wanted my mate.

I forced myself to calm down. The last time I'd fucked Reese, I hadn't been able to control myself, and I refused to do that to him again. In the short time we'd been away from my room, he'd respected me, stood his ground in the face of Gage's wrath, and made me proud. Despite the power and energy it'd taken to half-shift and force Gage to submit, I was wired and hungry for my mate.

As soon as we were behind my locked door, I turned around. Reese stood with his back to my door, shoulders straight, his nostrils flared. He smelled my lust, just as I could smell his.

I advanced on him, and again, my wolf pleased me by lifting his chin rather than shrinking away. I took that as a sign he trusted me not to hurt him, and that made my chest swell.

I gripped his neck, rubbing the spot where I'd bitten him. "When we entered G's room, you didn't rush ahead, but waited for my cue." He swallowed and his tongue swirled across his bottom lip. "You didn't question me or defy me. And when Gage approached us, you held your ground." His eyes flickered as I pressed closer. "I know the mate call is fate, and we don't get to choose, but your behavior today made me proud. There are many Weres here who wouldn't have the strength you showed today." I tilted his chin up. "Do you understand what I'm saying to you?"

"I didn't—"

"You did. I could feel how badly you wanted to run when Gage stopped us. And when I shifted, you stayed put. Your instincts are good."

Reese's lips parted, and he spoke haltingly. "My instincts are to follow my mate and alpha. And that's you." He raised a hand and pressed it over mine around his neck. "I'm glad I made you proud."

I kissed his forehead and then shoved him away from me gently. "Now get your clothes off and get on the bed."

He stumbled away from me, removing his clothes with trembling hands while I shed my own. He climbed up on the bed on all fours, but I flipped him onto his back, where he landed with an *oomph*. His cock was already hard, and the smell of his slick was intoxicating.

I bent down until our lips were barely touching. "I'll take you on a tour, meet the pack, but your scent is driving me crazy. We might be here for a while." I licked the seam of his mouth. "Maybe a couple more days."

He arched his neck, trying to get closer to my lips as I pulled back. He made a frustrated growl. "Not going to protest that."

Reaching down between his legs, I circled his rim with a finger. His lids fluttered, then went wide as he suddenly jerked out of my grasp and slithered up the bed, a hand out. "Hold on."

"Reese…" I warned.

"No!" He hollered and pointed at the mattress. "See those giant puncture holes in the mattress? See those?" He now pointed at my hands. "They were caused by you. Your claws. So, imagine those in my ass and tell me why I shouldn't be afraid of you sticking your fingers there. Tell me, Dare!"

He stood up at the head of the bed, bouncing back and forth on his feet, face tight with fury.

I sat back on my haunches as he blew out puffs of air through wide nostrils. "Reese."

"What?" The word was sharp and angry.

"Sit down."

He crossed his arms over his chest and looked away. I waited him out until finally he sat down on his ass, knees drawn up to his chest.

"You'll sit here where I can reach you." I pointed to the spot in front of me.

Reese glared.

"I could overpower you and just take you. I'm not doing that, so I'm asking you to do one thing, which is sit here."

Finally, my wolf compromised. And with slow movements—which were on purpose—he crawled toward me until I could reach out a hand and pull him into my lap. He straddled me, his hands on my shoulders, but he still didn't look happy.

"The first time I was out of control. I'm sorry for that. But now that I know it can happen, I'll be much more careful. My claws will not come out while I'm knuckle-deep in your ass, making you come. I can promise you that."

He wanted my fingers, but he didn't want to show it. He shifted on my lap, his cock dragging against my stomach, as he stubbornly worked to maintain his glare. I reached around and circled his rim again. "Do you want this?"

His Adam's apple bobbed. "I guess."

I had to smile at that. "You only guess?" When I sunk in two fingers, Reese gasped and dropped his head forward onto my shoulder. His hips began to move. "Oh fuck, oh fuck," he chanted as I pumped in and out a few times before plunging back in to find his prostate. When I rubbed across it, he cried out, hands digging into my shoulders.

I grinned and pulled out.

"Noooo!" he cried, flinging his head back and smacking my chest. "Do not stop, you Were bastard."

"Tell me you want it, then. Tell me."

Fuck, he was still mad, eyes blazing, neck muscles tight, and I was close to throwing him onto his back and pounding home.

"I want it," he said through clenched teeth, grinding against me.

"What do you want?"

"I'm going to fucking smother you in your sleep."

"Tell me, Reese."

"Argh!" he yelled. "I want you in my ass. Your fingers,

your cock, your come. I want my alpha's smell in me and on me. Please Dare!"

I plunged my fingers back in, and he began to ride them, his eyes closed, head thrown back. This had better be quick, because I needed to be inside him about thirty seconds ago.

He was close, his muscles straining as he clung to me, as he slammed onto my hand when I shoved all four fingers inside. His growls went high-pitched and, when I tugged on his cock, he began to come, his hot release pulsing between us.

He was still dripping when I threw him onto his back and drove home. He clung to my waist with his strong legs, urging me on. "Fuck me, Alpha." He thrashed his head on the bed, hands in my hair. "Love your cock. Wanna feel you fill me up."

His pleas were what got me, because I didn't think many shifters heard Reese plead for anything. With a howl, I slammed into him one last time and came inside his body. I lowered myself to the bed, arranging us on our sides, still inside him.

For a while, we did nothing but breathe, the smell of our sex like a drug. I loved this, the after-glow of our mating. Reese began to root around my chest, burrowing his nose under my arms, between my pecs, all the places my scent was concentrated. He made soft whuffing sounds, and when I pulled his head back with a gentle grip on his hair, his pupils were dilated, just like the time he'd sucked me off.

He didn't speak, same as last time, even though he seemed to be trying to. So I let his head go, and he went back to sniffing me like an addict.

I ran my hands down his back, and his spine rippled beneath my touch. When my softened cock slipped from his hole, I gathered some of my come on my hand and began to rub it into his skin. Never in my life had I done this, but I needed Reese to be soaked with me. I needed it in his skin. Imprinted there. For all time.

He unwrapped himself from my arms, still rooting on my chest, I rolled onto my back as he made his way down my body, lapping at my abs before shoving his face into my groin. His moist breath coated my balls, and I closed my eyes as my mate basked in the scent of us. When his tongue began to clean me, I reached down and ran my fingers through his hair. He made a small sound of contentment as his tongue continued its way to my cock. My body was like stone, sinking into the mattress, and when Reese's ministrations stopped and his breathing evened out from his place between my legs, I closed my eyes and let sleep overtake me too.

Reese

I WAS ON MY KNEES between Dare's legs, mouth stuffed full of cock. Again. I couldn't get enough of him. One sniff, and I was dropping with a thud, mouth already drooling as I fumbled to rip open his pants.

I couldn't stop attaching myself to Dare's dick.

All we did was fuck, sleep, and eat. It was a cycle neither

of us could break. Dare kept saying he'd take me on a tour, and I wanted to meet his pack, yet we couldn't seem to actually keep our pants on and walk out the door.

I told myself this time spent bonding with Dare was necessary. The more he was attached to me, the more he'd be willing to help me save my sister. But I also couldn't deny that I was fucking happy for the first time since we left Astria. If I were telling myself the truth—which I didn't want to do—I enjoyed Dare's company. He had a sense of humor, and he *got* me. In a way, no one but my siblings did.

But this was getting to be a problem. I'd been here a week and hadn't managed to accomplish much of anything except a zillion orgasms. Dare hadn't even left to do...Were business or pack business or whatever he did all day before he met me and fucked me unconscious on the regular. I was starting to wonder how much this mate bond was affecting him too. Dare had made it clear that while I was his mate, his pack came first. But after that scene with Gage in the hallway, I wasn't so sure that was the case anymore. How much pull did I have on him? Enough to break the truce with the Bluefoot pack?

He let me set the pace, and I took my time, loving the feel of my mate on my tongue. I'd been working him now for ten minutes and could have gone another twenty, but his hands slipped into my hair, changing my rhythm, which was when I knew he was close. I let him fuck my mouth as I braced for his release. It came a minute later, the delicious come spilling down my throat.

I sucked until every last drop was gone, and I would have

kept going, kept my lips attached to his dick, if he didn't haul me up into his lap, my back to his front. I was boneless, my head swimming, so I let him arrange me so that my legs were spread over his thighs. I didn't give a fuck at the exposed position. I wanted to come. I turned my head and buried my nose in his neck on a whine.

He ran a hand down my chest and over my abs before gripping my cock in a huge fist. His other hand closed around my throat, squeezing slightly. "You're so gorgeous when you're like this." His voice was rubber-band tight. "So pliant, so needy for me."

"Yes," I panted, canting my hips, trying to get him to move his damn hand and get me off. "Need you so bad."

He squeezed my cock but didn't stroke it, and I moaned in frustration. Without warning, he plunged two fingers inside my slick hole. "This is what you need, right?" He worked his fingers in and out of me. "You need filled, right? My cock or my fingers, you don't care, you just need your alpha filling you."

"Yes," I said, riding his fingers shamelessly, my face still buried in the side of his neck. "Fuck yes."

He was hitting my spot with laser-like precision. My whole body was on fire, and I wondered what I looked like, writhing mindlessly on his lap. "Alpha," I whispered as my balls drew up while he relentlessly tortured my prostate. "I need—"

"This is all you need," he said. "Just this. You can come like this."

I wasn't sure I could, not without a hand around my

cock, but seconds later, I was proven wrong, because he added a third finger, increasing the pressure, and I was coming on a scream, shooting all over my stomach, thighs and groin.

I was boneless while Dare laid me down on the bed and leaned over me. His tongue licked up the side of my mouth. "Can you speak yet?"

I had to get my shit together soon, but when I was so damn drugged on sex, it was hard to even remember my name sometimes. I nodded. "Yeah."

He gripped my face, brushing my cheekbone with his thumb. His gaze searched my face in that tender way he'd been looking at me lately.

"We should probably do something other than fuck," I said. I wanted to get outside of his room and gauge the overall feel of the pack.

His eyes crinkled. "I agree, but this week has been important. We were able to get to know each other."

Well, we'd accomplished that, but I was still wondering if either of us was feeling any effects from the True Mate bond. "What do you know about True Mates?"

"Not much." He shrugged as he sat up on the bed, and I arranged myself cross-legged between his legs. "I wish I knew more, but I've never met True Mates."

"Really?"

"Since I've been alive, there been none in this pack." He nodded toward his bookcase. "I have a book you're free to read, but it doesn't have any records of cross species Tue Mates, like Were and werewolf."

"What does it say about Were True Mates?"

"There've been records of alphas becoming more powerful. Stronger. That some True Mates have been able to draw on each other to make themselves stronger or expand their power."

"What kind of power?"

"Well, I can order my pack members to shift. I can force them to submit. Remember when we met Gage in the hallway?"

"Yeah."

"I used my power to force him to kneel and submit. But it takes a lot of strength and power for that."

"Alpha werewolves are stronger and natural leaders. They don't have powers."

His grin was all teeth. Smug bastard. I resisted rolling my eyes at him. "So try to take some of my power."

He raised an eyebrow. "Reese, I don't know how to do that. And I don't want to hurt you. I'm going to do more research first."

"Okay." I flexed my bicep. "Well, I don't feel stronger." With a grin, I squeezed his arm. "Do you feel stronger?"

He huffed a laugh. "No. I don't think so. I also read that it can take time. It's not instant the minute we mate."

Fate was fucking weird. "Try to draw strength from me."

"What?"

"Try."

"Reese, I don't want to hurt you."

I rolled my eyes. "Come on."

"I don't know how. This isn't something I do." He

paused. "You said your parents were True Mates?"

"Yep."

"What do you know about their bond?

My parents had been peaceful wolves, like the entire Whitethroat pack. It was one of the reasons we'd been so thoroughly decimated. We were not fighters and our defenses against the Nowere horde were pitiful. We thought we were safe within our walls. "I don't know much. They could communicate without speaking. Why can't we read each other's minds?"

Dare scratched his stomach, yawning. "I don't know. Maybe because we're different species."

He had a point, but it was in my best interest to find out if he could read my mind. What if he could and found out about Selene? I needed to know if my own thoughts were going to betray me. "Maybe we have to…activate it."

Dare raised an eyebrow. "Activate it?"

"Yeah, I mean, have we tried it yet?"

"No, but—"

"So let's try it!" I readjusted my legs so my knees were touching him. Then I placed my hands on his thighs. "Touching might help, I don't know."

He still looked skeptical.

I didn't think this was going to work either, but at least I was making the effort. "Come on, Dare!"

"Okay, okay, fine. You think something."

I concentrated really hard on one single thought, repeating it on a loop.

After thirty seconds, Dare squinted at me. "You're hungry."

My mouth dropped open. "You heard me?"

Dare threw back his head and laughed. "No, I just guessed because you're always hungry."

I punched his chest. Hard. Which only made him laugh harder. "Why aren't you taking this seriously?"

He rubbed the area where I'd hit him, still smiling. "I'm sorry. It's not that I'm not taking this seriously, it's that I don't think sitting here trying to silently communicate is going to do anything."

I crossed my arms over my chest. "Well, now you're just making me feel stupid."

He grabbed me so that I was forced to straddle his lap. "Reese."

"What?"

He cupped my face, leaning so close that I could count the fine lines spreading from the outsides of his eyes. "You're my mate. I know this with every beat of my heart. If fate wants us to communicate, it'll happen. Okay?"

I slid my hands up his chest and curled them around his neck. "Yeah." I shifted slightly in his lap, then grinned. "You want to fuck, huh?"

He ran his tongue up my neck, then nipped my ear. "You read my mind?"

"Nah, you just always want to fuck. And your hard dick is pressed against my ass."

I laughed as he threw me back onto the bed, then he fucked me until I couldn't say anything but his name.

CHAPTER SEVEN

Reese

THE BED WAS WARM AND I didn't want to leave it. But Dare was bright-eyed this morning, already pulling on pants. "Thought I'd take you around the compound today. Give you a tour. Can't keep you shut in here all the time, no matter how much I want to."

I tried not to look too eager, but I was ready for this tour. I was enjoying the hell out of spending time with Dare—fucking him and getting to know him. For the first time I could remember, I was experiencing more than fleeting moments of happiness. But on the other hand, that happiness made me feel guilty as fuck, because my sister wasn't safe in front of me. I'd had to shove my worry over her to the side so Dare wouldn't notice, but it was getting harder and harder to hide my anxiety. I climbed off the bed. "Why now?"

Something flickered across his eyes, something that made my stomach turn over with dread. "They're starting to talk."

Right, his pack. Gage's words hadn't left my head, a constant worry that things in the Silver Tip pack were not all perfect. Dare had told me that Gage was his older cousin, but he'd quickly shut down any more questions. "Okay."

I was dressed in minutes and we headed toward the door. He turned around at the last minute. "Remember. Obey and respect."

"Yes, Alpha."

He nodded, flashing me a smile, and then we were out the door. After descending the stairs, he grabbed me around the waist. "We're going to make an entrance, so is this adequate warning?"

I peered over the balcony. "You're taking us all the way down, right?"

"Exactly."

I took a deep breath. "Go for it."

He didn't even have to get a running start. One minute, we were standing in place, and the next minute, the air was flying past my ears as we dropped down six flights, landing on the bottom floor with a loud *whomp*. Dare protected me from the impact, then set me on my feet. I gripped his arm to steady myself, so I didn't keel over in front of his pack.

Yes, his pack. Now that I wasn't terrified, beat up, and chained, I could get a better look at the main area of the Silver Tip compound. There were tables where some pack members were eating, another area where they were playing some sort of dice game. Through an open doorway, I spotted an arena-type place where some wolves appeared to be sparring. In their Were form.

Fuck me.

I quickly looked away, waiting for Dare's command. He began to speak to me, his voice a low rumble, authority dripping with every word. This was not the voice he used with me in his quarters. This was Dare, Alpha of the Silver Tip pack. Respect.

I kept my mouth shut and listened.

"We call this entire building the Hive, because it's kinda shaped like one. And this is the main meeting area," he said. "If we're alerted about an emergency like a Nowere breach, we gather here, in the Forum. The kitchens are over there." He pointed to a doorway near where many Weres were eating.

One major difference between the Bluefoot pack and the Silver Tip was the many shapes, sizes, and colors of the Weres in this pack. Pale skin, tawny skin, tan skin, dark skin. Everywhere I looked, I saw a range of people. While most of Xan's pack was lighter-skinned like me, my Whitethroat pack had been more like Dare's pack. "Is everyone here a Silver Tip?"

"Yes," Dare said quickly.

"No, I mean…" Some of the Weres fighting outside bore the same silver stripe Dare did, while another's coat bore gray stripes. "That one doesn't have the silver like you do."

"Ah," Dare said. "We've always taken in members of other packs who come to our gates needing a place to live. So they might not bear the markings of a Silver Tip, but they are pack. Novus markings vary based on the dominant gene in the parents."

A female Were approached us. She looked familiar, and I was sure I'd seen her before, but that first day here had been fuzzy. Her skin was dark, and she had her hair in dozens of long, skinny braids down her back. Her septum was pierced with a small piece of bone sharpened at each end.

She bent her head in deference to Dare, and he turned to me. "This is Rua. She's a member of my guard."

"Nice to meet you," I said, just as recognition hit. "Oh hey, you brought me water!"

She smiled. "I did. Glad to see you all healed."

That day I'd scrambled across the floor away from Dare felt like a lifetime ago. And it'd only been a little over a week. "Yeah, I was able to shift and got myself looking pretty again."

I grinned at her, then ducked my head when Dare turned a glare on me.

Rua laughed. "Ah, so you're like that."

Dare sighed heavily. Rua grinned back at me when Dare looked away, so I figured it couldn't have been too bad.

Rua approaching us broke the ice, because pack members began to materialize out of the shadows to meet me. They always dipped their heads to Dare first, and I liked that. He deserved their respect. He greeted each one by name, and asked them personal questions. He offered advice to a separated couple about their novus's custody, and told a young Were he'd meet him in the arena for a training session soon.

When the crowd thinned, a small novus came streaking through the Forum. Dare crouched and the little thing leapt into his arms.

"I missed you," the novus said, wrapping his thin arms around Dare's neck. Dare rose to his feet, holding the wriggling, dark-haired child as a petite woman with honey-blonde hair approached us. She smiled at me hesitantly before addressing Dare. "Sorry, he was excited, because it's been a little bit since he's seen you."

"I know," Dare said, setting the child on his feet. He couldn't have been more than five, with a thick mop of black hair and green eyes. "I meant to come see him but—"

She shook her head. "No, you were busy, Alpha."

With a slight bow to me, she said. "I'm Cati." She wore leather pants and a vest that showed off her slender arms and pale skin. She also wore an elaborate necklace—several strands of beads that stretched between her breasts. She was pretty, with large blue eyes and a small nose.

"And this is Mav," Dare said. "My son."

The eyes. I should have noticed the eyes right away. I'd never met anyone with emerald irises that vivid. But son? I glanced between Dare and Cati. "Um, were you mated?"

Dare tickled the boy, who giggled and hid his face against his father's hip. "When females go into heat in the Silver Tip pack, they get to choose who will get them through it. Cati and I had been friends for years, so she asked me. And I got a son out of it."

In my old pack, Xan determined who would help the females through their heat. Selene was about to enter her first heat, and Xan had chosen—himself. *Goddamn bastard.*

My face must have gone pale, because Dare leaned toward me. "Reese?"

I shook my head and pasted a smile on my face. Thoughts of my sister could be like a punch to the gut. I could at least be glad this pack had a great Alpha who treated them all with dignity. I bent down to greet the little one. "Hey there, Mav."

The boy was cute, wearing a gray T-shirt and black shorts "Hello."

"I'm Reese."

"Reethe," he lisped.

I laughed and ruffled his hair. "Close enough."

When I stood up, Dare grabbed my shoulder and squeezed. "Cati, I'll be by soon to visit Mav."

She smiled as she swung a squealing Mav into the air. "No problem. Nice to meet you, Reese."

"You too."

She walked away, still swinging the boy in the air.

"Again with the warnings, Dare," I muttered. "A son? That's a heads-up kinda thing."

He sighed. "My excuse is I'm not good at this. You're my first, last, and only mate."

Good point. I knew shit about this mating thing too. "It's fine."

I watched Cati as she spoke to another female Were, while Mav sat with another novus boy, playing quietly. I looked forward to getting to know the boy. If the Bluefoot pack hadn't been a hellhole, I might have tried to mate a female to have my own little novuses around. But if I had a say in it, I wasn't eager to rear a child there. With Dare as my mate, I wouldn't be free to sire a child with a female, which was fine. It wasn't like I didn't have enough to worry about.

But the more pack members I met, and the more I saw how Dare interacted with them, the more conflicted I became. Rescuing my sister as a lone escaped Bluefoot pack member was one thing. But if I arrived with Were backup and an alpha mate? The truce would be blown. And what kind of consequences would that have on this pack? On Cati and Mav and G? Other than Gage, the Silver Tip pack members were peaceful and happy. My heart ached, because this reminded me of Astria. Where we lived under an alpha we respected, who respected us, and we trusted.

What kind of harm would I be doing involving them?

I wanted to go punch something. Hard. But instead, I had to plaster on a smile and be the dutiful mate to the alpha. My acting skills were superb.

We met a couple more pack members, but no more secret babies, which was fabulous. I was thinking Gage was just a jealous loser until I spotted him on a balcony about three floors up, standing with four other men who all wore matching scowls aimed at Dare.

When there was a break in the crowd, I nudged Dare with my elbow and jerked my head up toward the Weres.

When he spotted them, his lips pressed into a thin line. He rolled his shoulders and shook his head. "Let's head outside." His voice was strained. Tired. The only reason I didn't glare at Gage and his band of Scowly McScowlersons was because I didn't think Dare would want me to provoke them.

So I glared at them with my mind. Really hard.

Outside, I shielded my eyes from the sun and stuck close

to Dare. Weres were everywhere and instinct raised my hackles. My impression of Weres in their Were form was that they were mindless predators, but the Weres training in the field were organized and disciplined. Still, I remained glued to Dare's side, knowing the only reason I wasn't being regarded as inferior was because I reeked of their alpha.

Dare gestured over to a Were in his human form who seemed to be a leader. "Every Were, as soon as they turn sixteen, is required to train for a minimum number of hours a day, which is determined by their age and position in the pack."

"What are you all training for?" I asked as two Weres slashed at each other with claws the size of my forearms.

"Protection from Noweres when we send our supply team outside the walls. And preparation to defend ourselves from other packs."

The smaller Were took the larger one out by his legs, and they crashed to the ground. They tussled until the smaller Were clamped his jaws down on the throat of his opponent.

"Bay!" Dare barked.

The smaller Were hopped up, his jaws snapping, and…was that a smile on his Were face?

He shifted quickly as he strode toward us, naked, dirty, and pretty damn hot with his green eyes and smirk. I waited for Dare to move closer to me, touch me in a way that was staking his claim, but instead he watched the approaching Were impassively.

Once he was closer, the family resemblance between him and my mate was clear. Ah, so that was why Dare didn't react to the smirk. "Yo, Dare. You saw me take down Vaughn, right? Tired of his yapping mouth."

"Fuck you, Bay!" came a good-natured jibe from the defeated Were.

Bay flipped a bird over his shoulder, and the other Were laughed.

He regarded me with amusement, but I sensed he was studying me beneath the jovial expression. "Hey there, little wolf."

"I was watching," Dare said. "Coulda been cleaner."

I thought he was being harsh on Bay, who'd managed to take down a larger Were, but when I glanced at my mate, his expression was affectionate.

Bay scoffed as he jerked his chin at me. "I'm Dare's younger brother. I can whoop Vaughn's ass and Dare's ass."

"In your dreams," Dare muttered.

"I'm Reese," I said. "Uh, Dare's mate."

Bay laughed, the sound booming and infectious. "No shit, you smell just like him." To Dare he waggled his eyebrows. "Finally let him out of your bed, I guess."

"Enough," Dare growled.

Bay seemed entirely unconcerned. "How's your new home? Heard Xan runs a pretty shit ship."

I cleared my throat. "You'd be right. Food's great here, and I'm not required to do manual labor ten hours a day." I gave Dare a look out of the corner of my eye. "Well, at least not manual labor I don't enjoy."

Bay cackled and Dare rolled his eyes.

The Were who was leading the training approached

Dare, waiting nearby silently for his cue to speak. Dare's relaxed posture changed immediately to what I had begun to think of as his Alpha Stance. "You need something, Nero?"

"Yes, Alpha. Can you take a look at Yare's training? She's really showing promise."

"She's eighteen, right?"

Nero nodded.

Dare turned to me, but Bay spoke up first. "Are you taking him on a tour?"

"Yes, I was about to show him the crops."

Bay clapped his hands. "You deal with your pack. I'll lead him around." He walked over to a nearby wall and reached into one of the small cubbyholes, pulling out a pair of pants. "Come on, little guy. I'll take you to the source of all our great food."

I tried not to take offense at being called little. I glanced at Dare, whose harsh gaze was fixed on his brother. "Bay."

"Yeah." He didn't look up as he finished adjusting the leather waistband of his pants.

"Bay!" Dare barked.

His brother jerked his head up, and once he caught Dare's tight expression, immediately bowed his head. "Yes, Alpha."

Dare walked over to him and clamped a hand on his shoulder, speaking quietly. "This is my mate, and you will guard him with your life."

Bay lifted his head, blinking up at his big brother. "I will take care of your mate, brother."

After holding his eyes for another thirty seconds, Dare

walked to me and gripped my chin, forcing me to look at him. "My brother will show you around. Respect him as if he were me. Okay?"

I nodded.

Dare's gaze fell to my lips, and then he swiped his thumb across them. "See you soon, Mate," he said, then pushed me gently toward Bay.

I followed Bay, and when I glanced over my shoulder, Dare was watching us walk away. Why did I feel like every step aware from Dare was the wrong one? Was this the mate pull? Because fuck, it was strong.

I took a deep breath, and shook my head, focusing on Bay's broad back in front of me. The sun was shining, and I was outside without being forced to repair a roof while the threat of a whip loomed over my head.

I kicked my feet through the grass, the long blades wrapping around my ankles. Dare had given me a pair of sandals, and I wriggled my toes, enjoying the breeze on my skin. I hadn't worn shoes since I'd arrived at Xan's gates. It felt a little odd to wear something on my feet, but it made me feel…more civilized.

This was the first time I'd seen the Hive from outside, and it was damn impressive. Six stories of solid stone. Most of the windows were barred, but there were several that were bare at the end of what looked to be hallways. We passed by a couple of novuses playing tag, while a group of elders stood in a shaded alcove, talking quietly and smoking something out of pipes.

I hurried ahead to keep up with Bay. Even though he

was smaller than Dare, he was still larger than me, his long legs eating up the ground much faster than mine.

We rounded a bend where the grassy field narrowed between the Hive and an outer wall, then set off down a small dirt path. Around the bend, the field opened up again. In front of me was a large fenced area. Bay made his way over to it, propping a foot on the bottom rung of the fence, folding his arms on the top. "So this is where we get you that fancy food you like so much. The Silver Tip Farm."

I approached the fence slowly, one foot in front of the other, barely able to believe what was in front of me. I hadn't seen a full farm since I lived in Astria. Inside the fence roamed a herd of cattle, off to the side I heard the snorting of pigs, and to the other side was a large coop of chickens.

"In this pack, the novuses start working our farm and crops at ten. They milk the cows, gather the eggs, and take care of the animals on rotating shifts of two hours each day. They go to school for five hours, and then train another two."

A young pair of Weres emerged from the chicken coop. One was a teenager and at the sight of Bay, her cheeks pinked, and she waved. "Hi, Bay."

"Hey there, Una. Liking your new shift?"

She nodded eagerly.

Bay slapped his hand on top of the fence and led me farther along until we reached the crops. The field was double the size of the Hive, and there were several Weres bent over rows of leafy vegetables while some picked apples from trees in the far corner. "Damn," I muttered. "This is incredible."

"Mom," Bay said quietly.

"What?"

"This is all my mom. She was the alpha before Dare. This was all her plan. She was brilliant."

"You say *was* like…"

"I say *was* like she's dead, because she is." Bay's voice was tight, his fists clenched. "Our uncle challenged her, because he thought we should be a war pack. Go on raids rather than work to sustain ourselves. He won the challenge. And he was Alpha for exactly one hour before Dare tore his head off."

I choked on my own tongue.

"You know about Gage?"

I nodded. "He said some shit to Dare in front of me that Dare didn't like too much. Dare partially shifted and gave him a warning."

Bay's eyes hardened. "Yeah, he has it out for Dare because Dare killed his dad. His father was a piece of shit just like ours, but Gage inherited the asshole gene, while it managed to avoid us. Thank fuck for our mom."

"Has Gage challenged Dare?"

He shook his head. "Not yet. Matter of time, though."

"Is Dare worried?"

He inhaled sharply. "Dare is stronger by far, but Gage…plays dirty. Who knows what kind of tricks he'll pull to win, just like his dad did to conquer Mom."

I was done looking at crops. I was done with it all. I wanted to get back to Dare, in his arms, on our bed. I didn't want to think about challenges and bloody throats. I'd told myself I'd check for escape routes on this tour, but I couldn't even think straight right now.

Bay must have sensed my stress. He cocked his head. "You all right?"

I rubbed my neck where Dare had bitten me. "Yeah, I'm all right."

He began to walk back the way we came. "It's okay to crave his presence. He's probably hurting a little right now."

"Hurting?"

Bay nodded as I drew even with his long strides. "Yeah, didn't you know? Were mates ache when separated from their mates."

This was absolutely new information to me. Dare was...hurting? "Wait, what? Like in pain?"

"Yeah."

"But, I've been gone for ten minutes. We're only on the other side of the Hive from him."

"Damn, did you two talk at all?" Bay shook his head. "The Mate Pain is sharper now when your bond is new. Once you're together longer, you can be separated for longer distances and time without him feeling too much pain. But right now, yeah, he's probably feeling sore."

My heart began pumping an odd staccato, and hot blood rushed through my veins along with what felt like needle pricks. I stopped walking and I rubbed my hands on my arms, trying to stop the feeling. The thought of Dare in pain shot off alarm bells in my brain. My instincts screamed for me to stop it, to ease his pain. *Mate. Hurt. Stop.* "I can't—" I sucked in a gasp of air. "I can't do this. I can't walk away if he's suffering. I—"

"Whoa, whoa," Bay crouched down, his face even with mine, kind green eyes less intense than Dare's. "It's okay. I swear. Dare knows he can't be around you all the time, so this is his way of weaning himself off you."

My stomach was queasy. This was...so not good. Me leaving would hurt Dare? "What happens if we're separated for too long?"

Bay studied me closely. "He'll be in pain. But he'll live as long as you do."

Wait... "What do you mean? What happens if I die?"

Bay's voice shook a little. "If an alpha's True Mate dies, so do they. Within hours."

Oh hell no. I tried to keep my expression blank even though I was panicking inside. How the fuck could I leave knowing if a member of his pack didn't kill him, he'd still live his entire life in pain?

CHAPTER EIGHT

Dare

I watched Yare spar with her training partner, and agreed with Nero that she was showing a lot of promise. I'd have to speak to her parents about giving her some additional training hours. I rolled my shoulders to ease the dull ache that had taken up residence in my muscles since my mate had left my sight. I'd have to get used to it, though. My absence had been felt by my pack the last week. They needed the presence of their alpha—my guidance, my leadership. The honeymoon with my mate was over.

A howl pricked my ears, and I knew immediately it was Reese. The howl was low, pained, and mournful. I whirled around in time to see a gray wolf with a white throat galloping around the corner of the Hive, Bay on his heels.

I took off on a sprint and met Reese halfway. He shifted mid-air as he leaped into my arms, his limbs wrapping around me tightly. He shoved his face into my neck, his chest heaving against mine.

I turned furious eyes onto Bay, wondering what had Reese trembling and terrified. My brother pulled up to a stop in front of me, breathing hard. "Dude, did you read that book? Or talk at all? He didn't know about the Mate Pain."

Oh. Shit. I closed my eyes and held onto Reese tighter. I hadn't thought to tell him. What did it matter? He wasn't affected by it.

I wasn't comfortable dealing with Reese when he was like this in front of my pack. "I'm going to take him up to my room."

"Sure, Dare. Hey, I'm sorry, I thought he knew."

I shook my head. "Not your fault. We'll talk later."

Bay's smile was wobbly. "Sure. I'll be around."

With my arms locked around Reese, I leapt in the air, landing on a large cutout window on the fifth floor. I climbed inside, then made my way down the hallway and up the stairs to my room.

The entire time, Reese didn't move, didn't speak, only clung.

There were a lot of things I hadn't told Reese, thinking it wasn't in his best interest to know, but his reaction to a surprise, to something that could harm me, was unexpected.

Once we were locked in my room, I sat down on the bed and attempted to pry him off me. Instead, he moaned, latching his hot, wet mouth onto my neck and grinding his erection into my stomach. He went from trembling with fear to panting with lust so fast, my head spun.

"Reese," I muttered, clenching my teeth from the feel of him rubbing against me.

"Fuck me, Alpha," he whispered against my skin as his nuzzled under my arm. He inhaled sharply. "I need you."

I shucked my pants, kicking them away from me as

Reese lifted on his knees and impaled himself on my cock. I spread my legs wider, letting Reese fuck himself on me. His mouth was open, stormy eyes locked on me as he moaned low in his throat with every thrust. His fingers curled into my shoulder, nails biting into the skin. "Alpha," he muttered.

"My wolf," I whispered back, my inner Were right at the surface. With a growl, I wrapped my fingers around his throat and tossed him off me. When he landed on the bed, he flipped onto his stomach, immediately pushing his ass in the air for me. I surged inside, pounding away, knowing the angle to make my little wolf squirm and cry out.

He writhed beneath me, until he came with a shudder. I fucked him through it, savoring his tight heat.

I wrapped my bicep around his throat, so he could turn his head into my arm to sniff. He was high on my scent now, his nostrils wide, his pupils dilated. With a final moan, I slammed into him and came.

He kept his face pressed into my arm, rooting around in my scent. I stayed on top of him, in him, and petted his hair as he worked his way down.

When he calmed down and watched me through slanted, puffy eyes, I unwrapped my arm from around his neck and made my way down his body. I sniffed at his back, the area under his ass, the back of his knees, as he sighed.

When I spread his legs and speared him with two fingers, he flinched, then groaned. Burying my face in the cheeks of his ass, I tongued his hole, cleaning him and savoring the taste of me inside of him.

He made small huffing sounds of happiness, and I continued my tongue bath until the sheet under him was drenched with my saliva.

Only then did I climb back up his body and draw him into my arms, chest to chest.

I thought he might have fallen asleep, but when I glanced down, he was watching me with alert blue eyes. I ran my fingers through his hair. "I'm sorry."

He blinked. "For what?"

"For not telling you about the Mate Pain."

"That was kinda shitty of you," he grumbled.

"Tell me what happened."

"I was watching a novus girl pick an apple while Bay was talking, then he mentioned that you would be in pain and..." His fingers squeezed my hip. "I freaked out. The thought of you hurting was actually painful for me. I had to get back to you, to end it. So I shifted and ran."

"I didn't tell you because it's not something you need to worry about. I'm in pain when we separate, but you're never far."

He was quiet for a while. "And if I die..." He let his voice trail off.

I nodded. "If you die, I die. The pain becomes too much."

He sucked in a breath. "Well that's a huge fucking checkmark in the con column for True Mates, don't you think?"

I couldn't help but laugh. "Yeah, I guess so. But the pros outweigh the cons."

"How, though? I don't feel any different, do you?"

"You think I have to feel different to know that finding you is a pro?"

His mouth gaped open. "Shit, you randomly surprise me by saying nice things."

I shrugged. He should know by now he made me happy. Sure, any physical side effects of the bond would be welcomed, but for now, I was enjoying Reese himself.

"So if the Mate Pain doesn't affect me…" he began.

"You'll be fine as long as I don't die in a challenge, because then the new alpha will usually kill you just for being my Mate."

"Thrilling," he muttered.

"The longer we're together, the less the pain."

"So right now it's strong when we part?"

I shrugged. "It's not pleasant."

He ran his tongue over his teeth. "How bad is it? Does it weaken you?"

I nodded. "Yes."

His eyes clouded. "Bay said you were trying to wean yourself off me."

"Yes, he's right.

"Does that mean no more shutting ourselves up here?"

I sighed. "Yeah, that's what it means. I have to get back to pack business. Handle things." Gage standing up on the balcony with his supporters flashed through my mind. He was up to something, and he wasn't being as subtle about it anymore.

Reese lifted himself to a sitting position and grabbed an

apple off the table beside our bed. He crunched into it. "So, there are a lot of things you haven't told me about, and they impact me."

I didn't deny that.

Reese chewed and swallowed. "Like Gage."

I grabbed the apple out of his hand, took a bite, and handed it back to him. He frowned at it, which made me smile as I sat up and leaned against the wall. "Okay what do you want to know about Gage?"

"Bay said you killed his dad."

I choked on my bit of apple, and thumped my chest. "What the fuck? Bay never could keep his mouth shut."

"I like him." Reese tilted his chin up with defiance.

"Everyone does." I blew out a breath. "Okay, so did Bay tell you what happened to our dad?"

Reese shook his head.

I laughed bitterly. "Right, left that one up to me, huh? Motherfucker." Talking about this shit always pissed me off. "When I was eight and Bay was six, our mom challenged our dad, who was alpha at the time."

Reese's eyes went wide.

"Yeah, she killed him, took over the pack."

His mouth fell open. "Wha-why?"

"He and his brother—Gage's dad, Veron—wanted to turn the pack into raiders."

"Bay mentioned that."

"Yeah. So my mom had been trying to get our farm and crops going, and she was making headway. They wanted to end all that, turn her pride and joy into another training field. Mom and Dad hated each other anyway. I think she relished ripping his head open."

I'd seen it all—when her claws held each of his jaws, pulling until she'd torn him apart.

Bay had cried. I'd felt nothing.

"Mom was a great alpha. But Veron plotted for two decades before challenging her. We suspect he used silver to weaken her. She lasted a long time, but eventually he tore her throat out." Bay had cried as we stood over her body. I'd felt a driving need for revenge.

"I'm sorry," Reese muttered. "My parents were killed in front of me too. It's not something you forget." He handed me the rest of the apple. "Bay said you challenged your uncle."

"Yeah, right away. Fight lasted twenty seconds. I tore off all his limbs."

"Fuck."

"I know it's easy to forget when we're talking like this, but I'm an alpha Were, Reese. It's what I do."

"I know," he mumbled, gaze cast down.

I lifted his chin. "But you trust me not to hurt you."

His eyes searched mine. "I do."

I let him go, polished off the apple and tossed the core in the trash can. "That was ten years ago. For a while, Gage was respectful. But the last year or so, he's found some Weres who've just had their first muto to look up to him, and I guess he thinks he's formed a small pack now. His doesn't hide his contempt for me much anymore."

"You can beat him in a challenge," Reese said quickly.

I smiled. "I can."

"So why don't you just provoke him and get it over with?"

"I can't be a leader that goes picking fights with his pack so they'll challenge him. It's what my father did and the pack lived in chaos and fear. I'll never be that alpha. Gage hasn't been bold enough yet to directly oppose me. I have my guards watching him." I reached out and pulled Reese toward me with a firm hand on the back of his neck. "One thing you need to know. Mates are allowed to participate in challenges. If he challenges me, you stay out of it. He's a Were, and as soon as he sees you enter the circle of the challenge, you're fair game. I can't be distracted because I'm worried about you, do you understand?"

"I can't help you? I'm trained to fight—"

"Are you trained to fight a Were?"

He swallowed and shook his head.

"Right, so let me handle the challenge. That's an order, okay?"

He didn't want to agree. I was learning my mate wasn't the best at hiding his emotions. Finally, he nodded. And I let him go. He slumped back onto the bed. I rose, intent on getting him some food. My hand was on the door when he spoke. "You're going to get me bacon, right?"

I grinned.

Reese

I STARED AT THE CEILING for a long time after he left. Selene's name was a constant echo in my brain. Every bite of food was seasoned with guilt. Every moment of happiness here eventually soured with the reminder that she was still back in hell.

I trusted Dare. If I told him about Selene, he'd find a way to save her. Dare was a great alpha to this pack, but his bond to me was strengthening. At the end of the day, I wasn't sure which he'd choose as his priority—me or his pack. And I wasn't sure which one I preferred.

But if I left? He'd be in pain. Constant pain. And that would be an opening for Gage to challenge him.

I rolled over with a groan, fisting my hands in my hair. This wasn't fucking fair. And this was all on my shoulders. Fuck, if I didn't die at the hands of some Nowere while trying to save my sister, then maybe I'd simply die of fucking agony over this decision.

I was so dramatic.

When Dare returned with food, I ate without tasting it. He raised an eyebrow at me, and tried to draw me into conversation, but when I was finished, I curled into a ball and closed my eyes.

I had over two weeks until Selene was expected to mate Xan. And I was no closer to figuring out a solution than the day I woke up in the Silver Tip cell.

LATER THAT DAY, AFTER WE'D eaten some dinner, I was kneeling in front of Dare's bookcase, scanning the spines of books. I hadn't seen any since I lived in Astria. Most of the Bluefoot pack couldn't read or write, which I suspected was a way for Xan to maintain control. Our parents had taught us before the Nowere attack, and I'd continued teaching Jude and Selene when I could.

"We're trying to build up a library," Dare said as he watched me from his seat on the bed.

"Really?" I looked at him over my shoulder before resuming my study of the books.

"Yeah, for now, most of the books that document our history are kept here in my room so they aren't ruined or misplaced. I loan them out sometimes, but I pretty much threaten life and limb if something happens to them."

I grinned. "That's the way to treat books."

"I have pack members who are working on writing children's books, some fiction, things like that. It meant a lot to my mother for the pack to be educated, and I want to keep that tradition."

"I wish I could have met your mom." I stood and stretched my legs, which had cramped because I'd been kneeling so long. "She sounds like my mom."

Dare stared out the window at the setting sun, his expression solemn. "Mom would have loved you."

I wasn't sure what to say to that. "My mom would have liked you too. I mean, initially she would have been completely terrified, but once she got over the Were thing, she would have loved you."

Dare's eyes immediately crinkled in the corners, and he laughed. "Yeah, that might have been a problem at first." He rose. "Come on, we're heading out."

"Out?" I was like a dog, excited every time he let me out of the room.

"Yeah, my guard is waiting for us. It's time for you to meet them."

Wait, no, that didn't sound super fun. "Um, what?"

He opened the door and gestured for me to walk out. "My guard. It's only four wolves. Don't be nervous."

"Uh."

"Reese, walk," he ordered.

I wasn't prepared for this. "You couldn't have warned me?" I stomped past him in a huff.

He snaked out an arm and clamped a hand on the back of my neck. "I didn't tell you on purpose because you would have fretted and paced the room for hours. I saved us both some energy."

He either could read my mind, or just knew *me*.

As we were heading down the hallway of the fifth floor, Dare said with amusement in his tone, "You know I'm right, and you don't want to admit it."

"Shut up," I muttered.

He laughed.

We walked past G's apartment and reached the end of the hallway. Dare raised a fist to knock, then paused. "When we get inside, I'll be explaining some pack business to you. You can ask questions in there. I know you're going to want to. Okay?"

Fuck, how did he know me so well already? "Yeah, thanks." I was nervous but also excited. Learning more about how the pack worked could help me figure out a plan to rescue Selene.

Dare knocked once on an unmarked door, then opened it up, walking inside. I followed and shut the door behind me.

The room was about the size of G's apartment. Standing in its center was a large table made of solid wood with deep grooves. Around the table sat Bay, G, Rua, and a wolf I recognized as the one Bay had been training with.

"You know Bay and G," Dare said. "You remember Rua, and the last member of the guard is Vaughn."

While the rest of the Weres were fully clothed, Vaughn wore only a pair of leather pants, his huge bare feet propped up on the table near Bay, who was pinching his nose. "Nice to meet ya, wolf," Vaughn said. G reached across the table with a massive hand and swiped Vaughn's feet off the table. "Hey!" Vaughn protested.

G ignored him, Rua snickered, and Bay stuck out his tongue at Vaughn.

Dare rapped the table with his knuckles. "Could we please behave in front of Reese?"

"No point in misleading him," Bay said with a grin, which softened. "You doing okay?"

I nodded. "Yeah, sure. Thanks for the tour this morning. Sorry I freaked out."

Bay waved a hand. "Nah, you were fine. Dare should have told you, but he sucks at using words."

Dare heaved a sigh. "Sit down, Reese."

I took a seat on one of the heavy wooden chairs, while Dare sat down next to me. "This is my guard. But when I say my, I mean they are mine to command, but they don't guard me, they guard the pack. They are the first line of defense in the case of any sort of threat. They are trained to fight and know pack rules and protocol. They are responsible for punishing any offenses committed by the pack and have the authority to make certain decisions on their own. They are also my council. We meet here biweekly to discuss the pack and make any changes to laws or regulations."

"The Whitethroat pack had a council of elders who met with the alpha and his family regularly. So is this kind of like that?" I asked.

"Yes, for the most part. We also have elders we consult. Many of them are pack law scholars."

"And who chose your guard?"

"The pack voted on six Weres they'd like to be in the guard. And I chose four out of that six."

"Why four?"

"I didn't want too many voices, and these are the strongest Weres in the pack. They are levelheaded." Dare glared at Vaughn. "Usually."

"Ah," I said. "And if you need to vote, then the four of them plus you equals five, so there are no ties."

Dare grinned. "Exactly." The guard remained silent during this exchange. Dare said, "Any more questions?"

I shook my head. "Not now." I shot him a small smile. "Thank you."

His eyes did that crinkle-at-the-corners thing, which meant the smile he flashed at me was genuine. Then his posture stiffened, and his voice deepened as he addressed his guard.

The four Weres in the room immediately straightened in their seats, full attention on their alpha, even Vaughn. In fact, all humor had vanished from his face. Vaughn seemed to balance on a knife edge. He'd play the joker, but I got the feeling that he didn't take shit when someone pissed him off.

As if sensing I was watching him, his gaze drifted to me for just a moment. He winked, the corner of his mouth kicking up, before focusing back on Dare.

That wink took me back to when I was beaten and in pain on the floor of the Forum. Vaughn had been the one who'd suggested Dare could *put us to work* and had taken interest in Jude.

At the time, I'd been full-on rage-monster protective, but now that I had a chance to study him, I thought those remarks had been typical Vaughn humor.

My mate called on each Were to make their reports. Rua was in charge of the scouting teams who ventured outside of the compound. She said a Were named Tan was heading out to scout soon. After she finished speaking, Dare held up a finger to his brother, then bent to me. "Do you have any questions?"

Why was my heart melting? "Um, yeah, what do the scouts look for while they're out?"

Rua answered. "We like to keep track of Nowere packs as best as we can. So the scouts report if they saw any packs, where they saw them, and the pack's size. We make sure there are no Weres or wolves outside the walls who need protection. We'll also send messengers to the other packs in the area to keep communication open."

"Okay, thank you."

Rua smiled and tossed her braids over her shoulder.

G was next. He was an expert on the novuses' education and work at the Farm. He spoke softly in that deep voice he had. The care they took in cultivating the young members of the pack reminded me of Astria. My eyes got a little misty.

Vaughn reported on the fight training. He wanted to introduce a new fight style he'd been reading about in one of Dare's books.

"Is the book still intact?" Dare asked.

"Seeing as you threatened to castrate me if I so much as breathed on it, yes," Vaughn said.

"Take a select group of the best fighters you have and train them first. See how they take to it. If they do all right, you can train everyone else."

Vaughn rubbed his hands together. "Consider it done. Thanks, Alpha."

Bay was last to report—he was in charge of making sure the Hive ran smoothly, that families were getting along, and Weres were doing their jobs. "We do need to make a supply run, soon," he said. "We need lumber."

"Let's arrange that for the next couple of days," Dare said.

"Will do."

When the guard had finished with their findings, Dare

leaned back in his chair. "Any other odds and ends to cover?"

Four voices murmured, "No, Alpha."

"Good. Reese will most likely not attend every meeting with me, but I wanted him here so he could see how the pack works. He also asks a lot of questions, and I'm tired of answering them all." I elbowed him in the side. He didn't even flinch.

When we left the meeting room, Dare was quiet, and I didn't feel like talking either. Because the longer I was here, the more I loathed doing anything to jeopardize this pack. It was run by a group of Weres who cared about the health and sustainability of the pack. They were peaceful and educated and all the things I'd once had in Astria.

"I wish the Bluefoot pack could see how others live," I said as Dare began to undress back in our room. "Most of them are brainwashed by Xan."

Dare sighed heavily. "If it wasn't for the truce, I'd storm the gates."

I straightened. "Really?"

"How you and your brother were treated is unacceptable. And not giving you a proper death and burial is unheard of."

He had a point. I should have been killed and my body burned, not left for Noweres to desecrate.

Dare shook his head. "But I can't go back on the truce. I can't risk lives here, disrupt this pack, in order to save people who might not even want to be saved."

My heart sank. I knew this. And it crushed my remaining hope that I could ask Dare's help in rescuing Selene.

Of course he wouldn't risk his pack. And if he knew I

wanted to leave, what would he do? Why would he let me leave knowing I'd be risking my life—and his?

That was why telling him about Selene was a risk I couldn't take.

The weight on my shoulders was crushing. I told Dare I was tired and needed to rest. His brow furrowed but he left me alone, retreating to the corner and pulling out one of his precious books.

I closed my eyes, but I didn't fall asleep for a long time, my mind turning over and over again how I was going to save Selene and ensure a happy life for my family.

They were all I'd had for so long. And now, fate had given me...so much more. But with a price tag that I didn't know how to pay.

CHAPTER NINE

Reese

IT'D BEEN ALMOST TWO WEEKS since I became Dare's mate, and I hadn't quite been given the freedom I'd hoped.

If I wasn't walking the compound with Dare or another guard, I was locked in our room. I knew it was for my own safety, but that didn't stop me from wanting to shove everyone away and take off. Time was ticking by, and no matter how much I knew I was falling for Dare and this place, I couldn't forget Selene. That pull in my gut to make my family whole again was still there, strong as ever.

I sat at a table in the Forum, eating with Dare, Jude, and G. Jude watched me carefully, eating his chicken with small bites. We hadn't had a chance to talk privately, and it was killing me, because every time I saw Jude, his anxiety was worse.

He was thinking about Selene. Well, so was I.

Dare scraped his empty plate with his fork and pointed at my roll. "You going to eat that?"

"Of course I'm going to eat my roll. Get your own." I snatched it off my plate and took a massive bite.

He grinned at me and squeezed the back of my neck.

I rolled my eyes as I chewed and swallowed. When I glanced at Jude again, he bowed his head, avoiding my eyes.

The bite of roll dropped into my stomach like lead. Dare was affectionate with me around the pack, which was common for shifters. And I was affectionate back, because I liked him. A lot.

And he was my mate. This was allowed. But yet of course I felt guilty. Because Selene wasn't here—and wouldn't be—unless I got my head together and figured out a plan quick.

I pushed my plate away as a squeal sounded on the other side of the Forum. Mav ran toward us, grabbed the rest of my roll off my plate, then hopped into Dare's lap.

I gasped in mock outrage. "Thief!"

Mav screeched and took off, looking over his shoulder to see if I was chasing him. And of course, I had play along, so I raced after him across the floor of the Hive. He was a quick little thing, and dashed outside, finding his mom talking with another female Were.

Mav hid behind her long skirt, peeking out at me, as Cati placed a hand on his head absentmindedly. She smiled at her friend, who walked away with a wave.

Cati turned that smile onto me, raising an eyebrow. "What's going on here?"

Mav giggled loudly, and took a bite of my roll.

I pointed at him. "That little guy has committed carb theft, and we all know that's just about the worst theft there is."

Cati gasped dramatically. "Mav, you didn't!"

"I hope you find a fitting punishment," I said gravely.

She nodded. "Of course."

"It's just a roll, Reethe!" Mav said, holding it out to me in a panic.

I grinned and ruffled his hair. "We're just kidding, buddy." I leaned down. "But if you steal my pop, we're going to have problems."

Mav shook his head. "I won't!"

I straightened as a novus called to Mav, and he took off on a sprint to join his friends. Cati watched him go, her expression wistful. She sighed and turned to me. She was beautiful, and I might have been jealous if I hadn't known Dare was completely committed to me.

But I did know. Deep down to my bones. I knew.

"I'm sorry," she said. "For what you've been through. Dare told me. And while none of us have had perfect lives, yours has been exceptionally harsh."

It had been. And I had many fears it would get worse. "Thanks for that. Although, I know it hasn't always been happy here."

She shook her head. "No, which is why I understand how you were willing to risk all to get away from a horrible pack." Her eyes clouded for a moment before clearing. "It's a blessing to live here now, under Dare. He's a selfless alpha who cares about this pack and is committed to helping it thrive." She sighed. "Sometimes, behind these walls, I can pretend everything is fine, that the world is ours and not overrun by Noweres." Her smile was wobbly. "You know?"

I knew so fucking well what she meant. I had fleeting

moments of that too, before I remembered my sister. I swallowed around the lump in my throat. "I do."

She patted my shoulder. "I'm glad you're here, Reese. You're good for Dare."

Fuck, I was going to cry, just have a mental breakdown right here, right now, while Cati confirmed to me that this pack's way of life should be preserved at all costs.

I couldn't let Dare break the truce, or help me rescue Selene in a way that left this pack vulnerable.

A tentative plan formed in my mind, and I knew I had to talk to Jude. I nodded to Cati, as that was the only reaction I was able to make without losing it. With a quiet goodbye, she made her way to her son, skirt swirling around her long legs, blond hair blowing in the breeze. Mav ran to her side, grabbed her hand, and that was the point I had to look away.

I waited until I gathered my composure before joining Dare in the Forum. The smile Dare turned on me made my belly warm. None of this was wrong. It couldn't be. It was just a shitty situation that I didn't ask for. I wanted to cross my arms and pout about it, and I would have if my sister's life didn't depend on me figuring this shit out.

Dare greeted me when I returned. "I see you have no roll."

"Nope, I'm roll-less thanks to your son."

He laughed softly. "I need to run out and speak to Cati for a minute. Is that okay?"

"Sure."

"G," Dare said. "You're in charge of my mate and his brother."

"Yes, Alpha," the big man grunted.

As Dare walked outside, Jude bit his lips, his gaze darting between me and G. He was plotting something, and I hoped he was smart about it. Dare was good to me, and he'd moved past the initial mate call into caring about me. But I didn't want to test what kind of punishment he'd mete out if I disobeyed him in front of his pack.

My brother turned to G, who watched him steadily and with what I noticed was a little bit of affection. "Hey, I remembered I forgot my journal in our room. Would you get it for me?"

G began to shake his head, but then Jude turned a megawatt smile on him, and holy fuck, when did my brother turn into a manipulative little shit? "I wanted to show Reese what I've been working on, and I'm not sure when I'll get to see him again soon. Please?" He laid a hand on G's arm, and I did not miss the big man's shudder. "We'll wait right here. The Forum is full of pack members. We'll be fine."

G swallowed and looked at me. I played along, smiling as well. "Totally. Rua's over there in the corner. We'll be fine." I hoped those weren't famous last words.

G heaved himself to his feet and pointed a thick finger at my brother, his voice low. "Don't move. I'll be back in five minutes. You need anything, you yell."

Jude nodded, again with that smile. "Of course. Thanks, G."

In two strides G was in the air, leaping to the first balcony, then to the next. Jude turned wide eyes toward me. We were both a little speechless during the first moment we'd been able to talk alone since arriving here. He leaned in to speak quietly. "So honestly, are you okay?"

"Yeah, I'm fine. Dare treats me well." "Well" was an understatement. "We could be without throats right now, you know?"

Jude sighed. "Fuck, I know. G dotes on me."

"Brother, I think he's in love with you."

Jude blushed and ducked his head, then heaved a sigh. "So what're we going to do about Selene?"

I closed my eyes briefly. "I've thought about this every day. Every hour. My original plan was to escape and rescue her myself. But the Mate Pain complicates things."

"Mate Pain?"

"When Dare and I are separated, he's in pain. Actual physical pain. And if I die...he dies too."

Jude looked like he was going to cry. "Are you serious?"

"Yep. And what worries me is that if I leave, Gage will challenge him. The Mate Pain will make him weaker. I can't do that to Dare, let alone this pack."

"Do you think we can tell Dare and have him help get Selene? Do you trust him?"

"I do, with my whole heart."

"Then—"

I sighed. "I think if I told Dare, he'd drop everything to save her. And that's why I don't think I can tell him."

Jude blinked at me.

"What'll happen to this pack if we break the truce?" I said. "You know Xan wouldn't let that stand. I see Mav and his friends playing, and the elders relaxing outside, and I'm not sure I can live with being the one who fucks that up."

Jude's face fell. "I know. I-I love it here."

"Me too, buddy."

"So what're we going to do?"

There was no choice that wouldn't have lasting consequences. But I had to choose what would result in the least amount of impact. If I had Jude's help. "I have a plan, but I need your help."

Jude placed his hands on the table, face flushed. "Of course, anything."

"I've been watching the scout schedule. Dare is giving me more freedom, so I'm going to sneak out when they open the gates. I'll give you a heads up ahead of time, and once I'm out of those gates, you have to tell G. Dare's going to be in pain, and vulnerable, so G and the guard are going to have to protect him until I get back. I should be gone four days, tops. They can make excuses for him until I get back."

Jude nodded solemnly. "Of course. I can do that."

"I don't like this plan either. The thought of Dare in pain..." My stomach rolled, and my mouth went dry. "It's unbearable. But we have about two weeks until Selene goes into heat and Xan claims her. Time is running out." I reached out and gripped his hand. He curled his fingers around mine. "I almost died for you both once. And I'll do it again in a heartbeat. You know that, right?"

"I do," he said softly. "And that's what worries me."

I frowned, wanting to ask what he meant, when a thump alerted us to G's return to the Forum.

His expression on Jude was intense, but since that was

his default look, I didn't worry too much. I drew my hand back and tried to act like I wasn't on the brink of a nervous breakdown.

G dropped the notebook on the table in front of Jude, then sat down on the bench heavily beside him. He went back to finishing his lunch.

"Thanks so much, G," Jude said, recovering quickly to smile at G. I was starting to wonder if his affection for G was actually real. He opened the book, bound crudely with leather, the homemade paper inside thick and uneven. He flipped through the pages, and I caught glimpses of pencil etches. The Silver Tip pack made writing instruments out of ground-up stone and natural dyes, kind of like chalk.

My stomach flipped, and my heartbeat sped up. It'd been a while since I'd seen Jude's drawings. Back at the Bluefoot compound, I'd back-talked my superior a couple of months ago—because I just couldn't help myself sometimes—and as punishment, they'd taken away Jude's pencils and paper. The worst part was they'd thrown away every single drawing he'd tacked to his wall. Jude had maintained a stone face as they left with his prized possessions, and he'd had to calm me down while I'd screamed and flung myself around the small room we shared.

I was pretty sure he'd rather have been caned again.

Jude finally settled on a page and slid it over to me. He'd sketched a picture of a young novus feeding the chickens. She wore a dress down to her knees and was barefoot. Her arm was in mid-throw, the feed in an arc as it was thrown on the ground.

The chickens were surrounding her, and the best part of the picture was that she was smiling.

Jude's drawings at Bluefoot had always been happy, a way for him to escape our life, but they'd been fantastical. Made up.

Here, he could draw something happy and it was *real*. My throat closed and I had to breathe deeply so I didn't burst into tears.

"G took me on a tour and let me sit at the Farm for three hours so I could draw." The pleasure in Jude's voice nearly broke me. We deserved this happiness. Me, Jude, and Selene.

"It's beautiful, Jude." I ran my finger over the girl's smile. "She's cute."

He took the book back and closed it. "She's G's daughter."

I blinked. Did everyone have offspring here? "Oh, I didn't know that."

G's gaze remained on his plate as he chewed slowly, while Jude talked with a low voice. "His mate died on a gathering expedition outside the walls."

Fuck, that meant he or she had probably been killed by Noweres. "I'm sorry, G."

"Una is so sweet," Jude said, his face brightening. "You'll have to meet her sometime, Reese."

I ignored the ache in my chest, the awful feeling that my future wouldn't be long, and because of that, Dare's wouldn't be either. "Yeah, I'd love to."

I had begun to sense my mate before I saw him, and that was the case now. I knew immediately he was back in the

Forum, so I glanced up to see him striding toward me. He rolled his shoulders to loosen up the soreness he told me he always felt away from me, and stretched his mouth into a grin.

He slid into the seat beside me and said to G, "Any problems?"

"None, Alpha."

Dare's eyes slid to Jude's notebook. "Can I see?"

My brother handed it to him, and Dare paged through it silently. Jude had only filled a quarter of the book so far, and when Dare reached the blank pages, he handed it back. "You've very talented."

"Thank you." Jude's cheeks flushed.

Dare's hand closed around the back of my neck. "You ready?" His voice was a rumble in his chest, and immediately, I craved his skin.

"Yes, Dare."

"Say bye to your brother then."

I hugged Jude, not daring to whisper anything that Were ears could ear, but I pressed my nose into his neck and inhaled, gripping him extra hard. Jude's body trembled slightly within my embrace, and when I pulled back, he discreetly wiped away a tear.

I hated this plan, but it was the only one I could see working. At least, I sure as hell hoped it would work. I had a lot of people depending on me.

I LEANED AGAINST THE FENCE to the cow pen, watching the animals graze. One stretched its neck and mooed. The sound, foreign yet comforting, echoed off the stone wall of the Hive behind us.

It'd been a couple of days since I'd seen Jude and he'd shown me his sketches. Now, he sat behind me cross-legged in the grass, his sketchbook in his lap, his dark head bent as he drew. G stood over him, eyes on Jude's paper. My brother squinted up at his guard. "Come sit down next to me. Your shadow is blocking the sun."

G moved quickly, the first time I'd ever seen him uncomfortable with his bulk. He took a seat next to Jude, who smiled at him and went back to sketching. After a few minutes, G pulled a small knife and block of wood out of his pocket and began to whittle it.

I'd seen the various animals G had carved, clutched in sticky novus fists by just about every young member of the pack. Dare told me G was born outside the walls, in Nowere territory. There were still small families of Weres and werewolves who preferred to live as nomads. And G had been one of them, one of the lasts descendants of the Greatwolf pack. His parents died from a Nowere attack when he was still a novus. He'd manage to survive on his own until he'd shown up at the gates of the Silver Tip pack. Dare said G was the most independent Were he'd ever met. My respect for G had grown so much since the first time he appeared in the doorway of our cell, when I'd been convinced he was there to kill me.

Resting my chin on my hands, I eyed Dare, who stood with his arms crossed beside me. The breeze ruffled my hair, the sun warmed my skin. And goddamn, I was so happy.

And with that came the ever-present guilt, which gnawed at my stomach like a hunger pain. Although I planned to escape, the thought of leaving Dare made me physically ill. Of course I didn't want him in pain, but I also didn't want to leave *him*.

I held my hand out as a cow lumbered up to the fence. My fingers brushed her soft nose and whiskers, the velvet skin smooth on my palms.

A sound from Jude's direction drew my attention, and when I glanced at him, my body went rigid.

He gasped for breath, face red and quickly turning blue. He clawed at his face, eyes rolling, while G leapt to his feet and hauled him upright.

I shoved away from the fence and sprinted to my brother. In all the confusion of mating and a new pack, I'd completely forgotten how close Jude was to his muto.

G knew what was happening and murmured in a low voice, instructing Jude to breathe through it. When I reached them, I tore my brother out of G's arms. His eyes were round and terrified, his mouth flapping open as his hands began to sprout fur.

I held them at his sides while his body began to spasm. "It's your change, Jude," I said in a loud, firm voice. "I know it hurts the first time, and you think you're going to die. But you're not. We talked about this." I was furious at myself for losing track of the date, but there was nothing to do about it now.

Jude's chest heaved. "Reese," he hissed through a locked jaw.

I kept one arm wrapped around his waist and used the other to massage his neck. "Don't fight it. This is good, Jude. Your first muto." I smiled, wishing Selene was here to see this. "You're going to be a beautiful wolf, Jude, okay?"

His lips twitched, and I knew he was trying to smile.

When his back bowed, I drew us to the ground, and the first sounds of his bones snapping sounded like the crackling of flames. He cried out, and G started, his face pained. I glanced at Dare, who stood nearby, his silent nod telling me I was doing the right thing.

"Only a little longer, Jude." His face was changing, jaw elongating. Tears leaked out of his eyes as his tail grew, and his ears shifted from the side of his head to a set of furry ones on top. His shape changed in my arms, and with a heavy thud, a light gray wolf with a white spot on his throat slumped to the ground at my feet. I peeled off the tatters of his torn clothes.

His chest heaved and his paws twitched. I ran my fingers through his fur as he whimpered, tongue lolling out of his mouth.

I let him lay there for a moment as his tail flopped on the ground like a dead fish. "Okay, Jude. Time to get up. You gotta walk."

He peered up at me, as if to say, *fuck you.*

I laughed. "I know you're sore, buddy, but you have to get up and work out the kinks in your muscles, okay?"

"Stand up," Dare barked, and I turned furious eyes on him. I could handle this; I didn't need him yelling at my brother.

But when I glanced down at Jude, the command had worked, because he was slowly clambering to his feet, his paws flapping awkwardly in his new joints as he got used to them.

Finally, he stood on four wobbly legs, and took one halting step forward.

As he turned his head to me, eyes losing the haze of pain, I smiled, my chest swelling. "Proud of you."

His tail wagged, and he took another step, then another, until he walked around me in circles, then trotted around Dare. By the time he made it to G, he was sprinting, his body low to the ground as he took a wide berth around the large Were.

G was smiling as he watched his charge bound around the field. The cows were not happy, sensing a predator in their midst. Their alarmist moos were amusing, and seemed to rile up Jude more as he ran up and down the length of the fence, yapping at the confused animals.

"Hey, leave them alone." I laughed, and Jude ran up to me, sitting down about a foot away.

"You want to shift back?" I asked.

He licked his wolf lips.

"Okay, all you gotta do is think of your human form. Might take a couple of tries. Don't panic. Just give it a shot."

His wolf eyes flickered. A minute went by, but he stayed calm, until finally, he began to shift back.

First his paws morphed into hands, then his human limbs took shape. When he fell to the ground in a heap of nakedness, the fur was slowly receding from his skin.

He panted on his side, skin slick with sweat.

I knelt down and gathered him in my arms. "I'm so proud of you."

"Scared the shit of me," he gasped. "One minute I was drawing, the next my skin felt like it was being flayed from my bones."

"That gets better."

"I sure as hell hope so. Fucking wolf body," he muttered.

I patted his back. "You did good."

"I can't move," he said quietly. "My entire body is sore. My teeth are sore. My eyeballs are sore."

G gathered Jude's sketch pad and supplies, tucking them safely into a felt bag he'd given Jude. After crossing the strap over his chest, he bent down and carefully drew Jude into his arms. My brother went willingly, snuggling up against his guard's broad chest.

The man stood up without even a grunt. "He needs to rest. I'll take care of him."

I nodded. "I know you will."

G's gaze flickered, then he was off, striding toward the Hive to take Jude to their room.

I stood up, brushing the grass off my clothes. Dare watched me carefully, his green eyes intense. Fuck, that look made me hard. I knew the minute he smelled my arousal, because his nostrils flared, and his eyes flickered black.

He licked his lips and stalked toward me. I backed up, allowing him to push me against the stone wall of the Hive. The Farm was between shifts, so we were alone.

He braced a hand over my head as the other gripped my

hip, thumb digging into the skin.

"What got into you?" I asked.

"I like watching you take care of people," he said. "You're good at it."

"I'm glad you think so."

He licked a wet stripe up the side of my neck. "I like seeing my pack prosper. Your brother successfully shifting makes me want to celebrate."

I arched my back, rubbing my hard dick against his, wishing we were naked. "Oh yeah? How do you like to celebrate, Dare?"

"By taking my mate." He shed his shirt in one fluid motion, and then mine was next, along with my pants. He rucked down his pants, hard cock now visible. With a strong grip on my neck, he turned me around and pressed me up against the wall. I leaned my cheek against the hard stone, closing my eyes as he sniffed and rooted around my neck.

I waited to feel his hardness at my hole and curled my fingers into the crumbling rock, but instead, his heat left my back. I was about to turn around to see what he was doing, when something wet and soft probed me.

"Oh God," I muttered, my knees going weak. "Oh fuck, Dare."

I peered over my shoulder to see my mate, my alpha, on his knees, face buried in my ass as he speared my hole with his long, expert tongue.

I whimpered as his teeth scraped the sensitive skin. I was leaking slick and my cock was dripping with pre-come. The wall was the only thing keeping me upright as Dare ate my ass like he needed it to survive. He was growling, the vibrations entering me and driving me further into bliss. His big hands massaged the cheeks of my ass, occasionally slapping the flesh with hard smacks of his palm.

I was crying, whining, needing to come but not able to let go of the wall for fear my body would completely fail me.

Finally, Dare pulled away with a growl, and in the next instant, I was impaled on his cock.

I couldn't move, couldn't even speak. I was my mate's to fuck right now, and that was perfectly fine with me. His dick speared my prostate, sending my body into the stratosphere with all-consuming flames of pleasure.

A fist closed around my neglected cock, and it took a couple of tugs until I was painting the wall with my come. When Dare came a minute later, he did so with a bite to my shoulder, which had me emptying whatever was left in my balls.

After that, I was done for, my body slumping to the ground. Dare caught me, neatly settling me in his lap while he sat on the grass, back braced against the wall.

I buried my nose in his neck, breathing him in, needing as much of my skin touching his as I could. I opened my mouth on his shoulder, craving the taste of him too. He ran his hands over my back soothingly, occasionally massaging my scalp as I came down from my high.

When he pulled my head back and quirked an eyebrow, I nodded. "I can speak now."

He smiled, caressing my chin with his thumb. "You okay?"

"Why is it always this intense?" I asked. "Is that the mate thing?"

He was quiet for a moment. "I thought at first, yes. But now I'm not so sure. Because…that would have faded by now, I think."

"So that's just…us?"

His lips brushed mine, so tender in contrast to the brutal way he'd just fucked me. Not that I complained. "I care for you very much, little wolf."

I slid my hand up his chest and brushed it along the stubble on his jaw. "I care for you too, Alpha."

"You make me more determined to control and maintain a healthy pack."

"I do?"

"You do." He smiled. "My mother used to tell me that I was a good leader, but I'd be a great one if I was ever lucky enough to find my True Mate."

"I never thought I'd have a True Mate. If it wasn't for my parents, I would have thought it was a myth."

His expression hardened. "Mine were not True Mates. They hated each other. They only married because they had me after she went into heat."

"Didn't she choose your father?"

Dare laughed bitterly. "No. She chose no one. My father found her in heat and raped her."

My stomach flopped and my skin prickled. "Oh shit. I'm so sorry."

"She went into heat another time, and she used my father so they could have Bay." He shrugged. "Six years later, she killed my father."

For a peaceful pack now, they'd sure had a violent inception. But maybe that was what it took. "I wish you hadn't had to go through that."

"It's why stability in this pack is so important to me. My father was alpha and he took what he wanted, challenged enemies on a whim. I'm determined to be an alpha that my pack trusts."

"They do," I said. "It's clear when you walk into the Forum—they look at you with respect, they come to you for advice. They love you, Dare. As they should."

He pressed me tighter to his chest and tucked my head under his chin. "Enough pack talk. I want to enjoy the sun with my naked mate."

I huffed a laugh against his skin and stuck out my tongue to tease his nipple, then wriggled my ass against his now-hard cock. "Round two is always less intense. We can do that. In the sun. Naked."

He spread his legs wide and let his arms fall from around my body. "Go on, mate." His mouth turned up on one side in a filthy smirk. "Start round two with your mouth."

Yesssss. I slipped to my knees between his legs and wasted no time sucking one of his balls in my mouth. Dare moaned and leaned his head back against the wall.

Round two commenced.

CHAPTER TEN

Dare

I WALKED DOWN THE HALLWAY to our underground storage facility, Mav skipping beside me, while Cati and Reese walked behind us.

"So is he okay?" Cati was asking about Jude.

"Yeah, we just checked on him," Reese said. "Tired and a little bit sore, but he's eating a lot."

In a span of a day, Jude had filled out, looking less like a wiry novus and more like a full-grown wolf. "He might even eat more than you," I said over my shoulder, smiling at Reese.

He narrowed his eyes at me. "Don't start."

"Reese, I told you that we didn't have any more pigs left, and you actually believed me. And then you cried."

"I did not cry!"

"Your lip trembled."

"Bacon is delicious, and you're being a jerk."

We reached the door, and I grabbed the back of Reese's neck, tugging him to my chest. He remained stiff. "I'm just kidding. Feeding you is one of the greatest joys of my day." He relaxed beneath my palm, then tilted his head back, his lips slowly stretching into a grin. "Does this mean I get more bacon?"

I rolled my eyes and shoved him away. He laughed, and I shook my head, hiding a smile as I spun numbers on the lock to the correct combination. Once the door was unlocked, I ushered them inside.

Cati, who was in charge of providing clothes for the pack, needed supplies, and everything worth anything to the overall health of the pack was kept under lock and key. She was the boss to a group of Weres who were experts at sewing and, in a pack where clothes were often ripped during shifts, Cati was kept busy.

Most of our clothes were made from leather—provided by our cattle—but we had fabrics we traded with a nearby wolf pack who grew cotton. They gave us fabric, and we provided them with lumber we scoured from Nowere territory.

Mav, who usually remained attached to me or Cati at all times, was glued to Reese's side, clutching Reese's much larger hand. He'd taken an immediate liking to Reese. My mate had tried to explain it away. *It's only because I'm new.*

I didn't argue with Reese, but I knew that wasn't the reason. He was likable and treated Mav less like a novus and more like a little brother.

"Wow," Reese said, his head swiveling as he took in the ceiling-high racks of supplies. "This place is incredible."

Cati knew where we kept the fabric, which the Striped Tail pack made for us. Ever since she'd been placed in charge of clothing a couple of years ago, our pack had been given a makeover. Cati made beads from stones and used them to embellish leather pants, shirts and vests. She studded belts and had begun designing jewelry too. For many decades, we'd been all about survival, but the tide was turning, and we were focusing more on living. Cati's influence had improved the overall confidence in the pack in a way I never would have anticipated.

Today she wore a short leather skirt and a vest, her hair braided with a blue-dyed leather wrap. Her slender fingers touched each roll of fabric, and her brow furrowed as she studied the thickness. Striped Tail gave us different thread-counts of fabric, which we used for different products, like bed sheets and towels.

Reese and Mav had wandered down a different aisle, and from the sounds of it, they were where we kept emergency stashes of our seeds. I could hear Reese reading off the names on the labels.

"How are you?" Cati asked, tugging down a bolt of fabric with a grunt and leaning it up against the shelf.

I used to wish Cati wanted a mate, because I gladly would have made her mine, back when we'd had Mav. But she'd made it clear she didn't want a mate, at least not anytime soon. She was happy with her son and her friends and her job. So I respected that. "We're good. But it's been an adjustment."

"From what I've seen, you're not the mate I thought you'd be."

"Oh? How so?"

She chewed her lip. "You're going to take this the wrong

way."

"No, I'm not."

Her eyebrows lifted, then she laughed softly. "Okay, well I thought you'd be uncompromising. Cold. When you interact with your guard, it's all business. Even with Mav and Bay, sometimes I think you keep them at a distance."

The comment cut a little deep. "I don't—"

"It's okay," she cut me off. "I'm not saying it's a flaw in your character. It's just how you are. Yet I see you with Reese and..." She lifted a shoulder. "I'm surprised. In a good way."

I wasn't sure if she was being vague on purpose or because she couldn't define what she was feeling. "What do you mean?"

"I thought you'd keep your responsibilities as Alpha very separate from your mate. And from what I see, that's not the case. Reese is your equal. You include him and consult him. Rua said he's come to guard meetings."

"I don't really have a plan for this. I'm going off what feels right."

"That's not even what's most surprising." She ran her tongue over her bottom lip. "You're...affectionate."

I blinked at her. "You didn't think I'd be affectionate?"

"You joke and smile and laugh with him. And touch him. It's all a new side to you, Dare."

I'd never really thought about how the pack viewed me, including Cati. "To be honest, I wasn't sure what kind of mate I'd be either, Cati."

"I mean..." She shrugged. "If I'd known this was the kind of mate you'd be, maybe I would have agreed when you asked."

I snorted. "Now you tell me."

She laughed. "I'm kidding. I think it's not about being mates, but it's about the fact that you actually like him."

"Of course I like him, he's my mate."

"Uh-huh," she sassed. "Sure. It's not noticeable at all that you two are clearly into each other beyond the mate hormones."

I glared at her.

She smiled and patted my arm. "Anyway, I imagine if your mom had a mate she cared about, she would have acted a lot like you."

I swallowed around the sudden lump in my throat as Reese and Mav drew closer. "Thank you for saying that."

My mate rounded the corner, carrying Mav on his shoulders. Mav giggled, his hair flopping as Reese bounced him. I quickly shoved Cati's words out of my mind and plastered on a smile. "Hey, you two."

"I could live down here," Reese said. "I can't believe how well supplies are stored. The more I learn about this pack, the more I cannot understand how Xan plans to sustain his."

I was still concerned about the state of the Bluefoot pack. And I was going to have to make some decisions soon regarding it. "We've worked hard to get to this point." I handed him the bolt of fabric. "Could you two take this up to Cati and Mav's room? I want to talk with her a minute."

"Sure," Reese said. "Come on buddy."

"Vaughn is in the Forum if you need anyth—"

"We'll be fine," Reese called over his shoulder, still

bouncing Mav.

I waited until they'd left the storage room before turning to Cati. "So have you heard any rumors about Gage?"

Cati crossed her arms over her chest. "Rua is worried, said he's been discontent lately. And I overheard one of my seamstresses say that her son has been hanging around Gage a lot and it's making her nervous. Apparently he came home the other day talking about how we should be taking over the Striped Tail pack rather than trading with them."

I held in a growl. The Alpha of the Striped Tail was a no-nonsense female who thrived on peace. Her pack was small but well-equipped. "Gage is a fucking idiot. Just like his uncle."

"I'll keep my ear to the ground," she said. "Anything else, I'll let you know."

"Thanks. And you know if anything happens—"

"Come in here, move the shelf in the far-left corner, enter the code and hide in the bunker with Mav."

"Good."

"I would never trade him or regret choosing you to get me through my heat. But I never forget that I have the Alpha's kid running around, and sometimes his blood feels like an albatross around my neck."

I cupped her cheek. "I understand. But you've got the strongest neck in the pack, right?"

She grinned at that. "Damn right."

"All right." I led the way to the door. "Let's make sure those two didn't take a detour."

"Yeah, it's nap time soon for Mav, and Reese always gets

him riled up. If I lose out on me-time because of your mate…"

I closed the door behind us and locked it. "You have my permission to smack him. Lightly. No permanent marks."

Cati's laugh rang out down the hallway in front of us. "Deal."

Reese

LATER THAT DAY, I BOUNCED on the balls of my feet at the front gate, eager to see beyond the stone walls.

Dare gripped the back of my neck. Hard. "Calm yourself."

I was stir crazy from being inside the compound for so long. "Sorry, I'm excited."

"This isn't a party," he growled. "We need to get supplies and manage not to get eaten by Noweres. It's the farthest from a party you can get."

I huffed. "I know, I know."

He dropped his clothes as we waited for the rest of our group to arrive at the gates. "I'm trying to keep us alive. Be glad I'm letting you come with us."

He was right. "I am."

We were heading out to gather some wood and do a general check of the surrounding area. After replacing the chair Dare broke, and a couple more pieces of furniture, we were running low on lumber.

Bay trotted toward us, naked except for a huge grin.

"Hey, little wolf," he said, patting me on the shoulder. Any other Were who said that to me—other than Dare—would get a nut punch, but Bay's tone held nothing but affection. The best part about Bay was that I knew he had my mate's back.

"G's staying back with Jude," Bay said. "He's not comfortable leaving him alone with Gage acting like he is."

Dare nodded. "That's fine."

Dare introduced me to Tan, who was one of his scouts. Also along for the scavenging party was Vaughn. He wore that ever-present smirk, which he aimed at me as he stretched his limbs.

So our total group consisted of four Weres and a feisty werewolf. Dare said he didn't often leave the walls, preferring to remain with his pack. But sometimes he liked to see for himself what was going on outside the walls and not solely rely on scouts.

It'd taken some major convincing and a lot of time on my knees to get him to agree to take me. It'd been three days since I'd spoken to Jude about my escaping, and this was my opportunity to work on my plans—to see how the gates worked, what the terrain was like right outside the walls, and if any Noweres were around.

I planned to leave the next time Tan left to scout. My instincts were at war, some pulling me to rescue my sister, some tugging me to stay with Dare. I wasn't sure how my body wasn't ripped apart yet. My heart sure felt like it was being torn in two.

"So." I tried for casual. "Have you ever had a problem

with anyone outside trying to dig under your walls?"

Dare lifted an eyebrow at me. "Our walls go ten feet underground. They'd be digging for a while."

Okay, well through the gate it was, then.

Dare signaled for the gates to open. My gaze followed the rope and pulley system to the two Weres who strained to raise the heavy wooden door. There was no way I could get out myself, which was why I had to wait until they were opened for Tan. But directly inside the gate was a large storage facility. I could hide in there and slip out. The gray walls should help disguise me in my wolf form so I could slip out undetected. The Weres lifting the gates couldn't actually see the opening. They relied on voice commands to tell them when to lift and lower. So as long as I stayed hidden from Tan, I should be okay.

Okay being a relative term.

With my nerves bunched like vipers in my chest, I tried to focus on what I needed to do next, which was shift. Dare had already shifted to his four-legged wolf form, and was looking back at me expectantly along with Tan, Bay, and Vaughn.

So I dropped onto all fours as I shifted, shook out my fur, then followed the Weres as they bounded outside.

The Silver Tip compound was surrounded by dense woods, which was where Noweres liked to roam. Xan's compound was in a several-mile-wide clearing, so venturing a short distance outside the compound was a little less risky.

That didn't mean I had ever been allowed to leave. Hell no. The only time I'd been out of those walls since I arrived with my parents was when I escaped.

Even though I didn't feel trapped in the Silver Tip compound and there were plenty of places to run, my wolf knew I was caged within walls. And he hated it. None of us were ever meant to live like this, but we had no choice. Now, unrestricted by walls, with the sky big and blue above me, I stretched out my body and I ran and ran and ran, the scent of my alpha providing security, the absence of Nowere stench spurring me on.

At one point, Dare slowed down and tipped his nose up to scent the air, then he lowered it and continued on.

Maybe I should have been scared, but it was hard when my heart was singing with freedom.

Eventually we reached an area that had clearly been harvested for lumber. It was littered with wood dust, and stray branches surrounded tree stumps. Some axes lay nearby too.

Dare shifted to human, and we all followed suit.

Bay and Vaughn immediately picked up axes and began to chop trees at the edge of the clearing. The trunk Vaughn worked on was twice the size of me. Vaughn's massive shoulders bulged as he hacked away, and when he caught me staring, he blew me a kiss. I gave him the finger and turned away with a sneer.

Dare stood at the center of the area, hands on his hips as he glanced around. Tan climbed a tree and crouched down on a sturdy branch to scan the distance.

I walked over to Dare. "What do you want me to do?"

"Stay here with me. Listen and scent for Noweres."

The memory of the stomach-curdling Nowere stench

made me nauseous. "Does the chopping draw their attention?"

Dare's jaw clenched. "Always."

Shit, okay. Running was fun, but this was serious business. I wasn't about to get eaten by a Nowere today.

Dare roamed the perimeter, sometimes leaving my side as he weaved in between the trees and stayed on high alert. I remained in the center, doing my best to be a good lookout.

Vaughn slammed his axe into the trunk one last time and then whistled to give us a heads-up as it crashed to the ground. Bay's wasn't far behind.

They chopped down two more each, and just as I was getting confused about how they were going to carry all this shit back, they shifted to Weres and picked up three trees each. "Wow, okay, you guys are fucking handy," I muttered.

Dare and I walked ahead of them, alert for any undead Weres. Tan ran ahead of us in wolf form.

"You're happy to be outside," Dare said. It wasn't a question.

"Of course."

"I'm guessing Xan never allowed you to leave."

"Hell no." I lifted my head so the sun warmed my face. "The sky looks different when you're not behind walls. Brighter, bluer." I smiled. "Don't you think?"

He was watching me closely. "Sure. I do think so."

"I hate walls," I said. "I think sometimes about what it would be like if there were no Noweres. What would life be like? I haven't known any different."

Dare shook his head. "Me either."

"What do you know about the virus?" I'd learned the origin of the Noweres was a tale that varied per pack, a legend with a dozen variations.

Before the virus, Weres and werewolves lived among humans. We kept our true natures a secret, remaining in human form, working everyday jobs alongside the other species. We still met with our packs, but the connection was looser. At the time, there'd been small pockets of Weres who sought to take over civilization, but they were outnumbered and never gained the strength needed to overthrow the human leaders.

Until the virus, which wiped out humans, depleted Were numbers, and sent us all scrambling away from cities and into the country where we hid behind our stone walls.

Many records were lost in the early days of the virus. All we knew for certain was the human race was wiped out completely, unable to defend themselves from the slaughtering Nowere packs. Were numbers were greatly dwindled as they became infected with the virus, adding to the Nowere numbers. As for werewolves, we were immune to the virus, but Noweres could—and would—kill the fuck out of us.

Dare glanced over his shoulder at Bay and Tan. "You tell me what you know first."

"Well, in Astria, we were told a Were found some sort of bite on him. A day later, he was dead and, an hour after they moved his body to have it be burned that night, he woke up and tore apart his whole village, turning every Were into a Nowere."

Dare nodded. "I've heard that one."

"Xan told everyone that Weres were too welcoming of anyone, and let visitors mingle with everyone else. And in doing so, let in a virus. It's why he's crazy about outsiders. That entire pack is inbred as fuck. I was one of the last groups of wolves he let in." The only way to survive was to fortify packs in compounds, so Xan's paranoia was free to breed.

Dare snorted. "Well, in this pack, we're aware there are a lot of stories. The one we believe the most is that a Were leader created the virus for population control, but it didn't quite work the way he wanted."

"Holy shit, so they think this was…created on purpose?"

"Yes."

"Who would do something like that?"

He tilted his head. "You have a hard time believing in the evil of Weres and werewolves?"

I kicked a root. "Shit. Good point."

"I guess it doesn't matter now how it started. No one knows how to stop it, and that's all that matters. And as far as we know, these things aren't dying."

I didn't know much about Noweres. In hindsight, one of the mistakes my pack in Astria made was thinking they were safe behind their walls. The Whitethroats didn't educate about the Noweres. So when we were breached, no one knew what to do. "Xan's only caution against Noweres was to stay within the walls. He said they'd made humans extinct and would do the same to us if we weren't careful. How does a Were get infected?"

"It's through blood transfer. So a bite. A scratch alone

won't kill us but if any Nowere blood gets in the wound? We're done for."

"Have you ever seen anyone get bitten?"

His answer was low. "Yes."

"What's it like?"

He was quiet for a long moment. "It's the saddest, most helpless feeling, to see a Were with a soul fall, and then come back to life as a mindless predator." There seemed to be a story there, but he clamped his lips shut and glared straight ahead. "The Were population now isn't big enough to fight the Nowere numbers, and we can't afford to lose Weres to strengthen the Nowere packs."

"So you've thought about a solution?"

"Rua's scouts have been gathering as much information about them as they can. I've been interviewing pack members to see who'd like to study the Noweres extensively. I'm not content for my legacy to be that I kept the status quo against our greatest threat."

I blinked up at him. His face was set in lines of determination. If only every pack had an Alpha like Dare. Maybe this world wouldn't suck so bad. "That's amazing, Dare."

He smiled tightly. "We'll see, Reese. We'll see."

We soldiered on, and made it back to the Silver Tip gates in one piece. Dare whistled and the gates opened for us. Tan ran in, while Vaughn and Bay trudged inside, dropping the lumber at their feet before shifting to human.

I turned around to watch the gates close, mourning a little at the loss of freedom. Every day I looked at those gates from Dare's window, and it was time to admit that my only way out of this compound was through them.

My heart warred with itself, because the thought of leaving made me nauseous, but the thought of not trying to save my sister was unacceptable.

I wasn't sure if that made me a crappy brother, or a good mate.

Either way, I wasn't any closer to figuring out how to be good at both at the same time.

CHAPTER ELEVEN

Reese

MAV SAT ON THE EDGE of Dare's bed, kicking his legs while he gnawed on a chicken leg. Cati was off doing whatever single female Weres did when they didn't have a novus underfoot. I'd been taking up a lot of Dare's time lately, and Mav looked happy to be in his father's presence again.

And it made my heart ache for my own family which would never be complete again. My parents sure as hell weren't coming back to life.

Dare stood at the far side of his room putting away our clothes, which had just been laundered. I sat on the floor, eating a cookie. Because I was an adult wolf, and if I wanted a cookie for lunch then I could have one.

"Hey, Dad," Mav said, green eyes round in his small face. "Kep said if you cross your eyes for longer than twenty seconds, then your face will stay that way."

"Who's Kep?" I asked.

"My best friend," Mav answered.

Dare closed the door of his bureau and leaned against it with his arms crossed. "Oh yeah? Try it."

Mav gasped. "No way."

"Why not?"

"Because I don't want my eyes to stay crossed."

Dare shook out his hands and cracked his neck. "Okay, I'll try." He crossed his eyes and said, "Count for me, Reese."

I leaned back against the wall and laughed. "All right, here goes. Twenty. Nineteen. Eighteen."

"Dad!" Mav jumped to his feet. "No! They'll stay that way forever! Stop!"

This was so mean, but I had to admit, it was fucking hilarious. As I counted, Mav began to paw at his father's legs.

"Twelve. Eleven. Ten."

"Uh oh," Dare mumbled. "Something's happening."

"Dad!" Mav ran in a circle around him, beating him with little fists.

"Five. Four. Three."

"Nooooooo!"

"Two. One."

Mav stopped in front of his dad, hands curled at his mouth, eyes wide. He didn't move, and Dare blinked his eyes. He held out a hand and said in a trembling voice. "I guess Kep was… he was…"

Mav started whimpering.

"He was…" Dare uncrossed his eyes. "He was dead wrong."

"You're mean!" Mav pulled back a fist and slammed it into his father's stomach.

I toppled to my side in hysterics as Dare made an *oomph* sound and buckled over laughing while Mav continued to holler.

Finally Dare scooped up a scowling Mav and hugged him. "I was just kidding with you. I'm sorry. But now you know not to believe everything Kep tells you."

Mav went slack in his arms. "Yeah, you're right."

"You can always ask me, and I promise not to tease you next time."

Mav rolled his eyes. "You always tease."

Dare began to tickle him, and Mav giggled and writhed in his arms.

My face hurt, and when I lifted my fingers to touch it, my lips were still stretched into a smile. I wasn't sure how long it'd been since I laughed that hard and smiled that long. My stomach flopped as I remembered the way my father used to tease me, the way he tickled me right in the ribs and squeezed my kneecaps, which would always send me into a fit of giggles.

Fuck, I missed them. The way they loved their kids, the gentle way they disciplined us, determined that we grow up to be good and kind wolves. I hadn't let myself mourn for ten years, and now all of a sudden the grief was rushing up like a tidal wave.

There was a knock at the door, which distracted me from letting that wave drown me. I opened the door, and Vaughn poked his head in. "You guys doing anything fun in here?"

Dare set Mav on the ground. Mav waved at the guard. "Hey, Vaughn."

"Hey, little man."

"What do you need?" Dare asked.

"Hate to interrupt, but Bay asked me to fetch you. He

has some things he wanted to go over with you."

Dare ruffled Mav's hair. "You okay here with Reese while I'm gone?"

Wait, what? "Um…" I began.

"Sure." Mav turned a big smile on me.

Oh goddamn. What was I going to do with this kid? I'd never really been alone with him for more than five minutes or so. "Uh…"

Dare didn't catch on to my anxiety. "Be back soon." He grabbed my chin, kissed me hard on the lips, then disappeared out the door. Vaughn followed, closing and locking the door behind him.

I stared at the closed door, then at Mav, who was bouncing on his toes, looking at me expectantly like I had plans.

I had zero plans.

"So, what do you want to do?" I asked, my gaze searching the room.

Mav hopped over to the corner where Dare kept his bookcase. He ran his fingers over the spines, and I walked over to stand behind him, squinting at the words. I still hadn't studied Dare's entire library, mainly because I wasn't into reading a whole lot, and also because most of the time I was in this room, I was eating, sleeping, or getting fucked.

"This one!" Mav snatched a gray book off the shelf and shoved it at me, then gently guided me to the chair near the window. He sat on the floor and peered up at me, waiting.

Oh, he wanted me to read to him. Right, he probably couldn't read yet. "Uh, you want me to start somewhere in particular?"

He shook his head. "Dad said we could read that next, so I haven't heard any of it yet."

I ran my hands over the cover. In relief were the words, "A Silver Tip History." The book was bound in leather with real paper pages. I couldn't stop touching them, running my hands over their smooth edges.

"That was made before the virus," Mav said, pride in his voice. "Dad has the only pre-Nowere books in the whole pack."

Yeah, and Dare had made it clear these books were to be treated like precious babies. I was scared to touch it for fear of breaking the spine or ripping the page. Mav must have sensed my hesitation. "It's okay," he said softly. "Dad said books are made to be read and worn edges and tears are okay as long as it's because you learned from the words inside."

Mav was watching me expectantly, so I opened the first page and began to read. At first, I thought it was kind of tedious, but then I began to get into it. The Silver Tip pack was one of the oldest, descended from the Gauls. They had a history of strong alphas who formed solid alliances with nearby packs. They were also fierce fighters, which led to frequent challenges.

That made me gulp.

I paused after the first chapter and glanced up. Mav was asleep, curled up on his side on the carpet at my feet. He was sleeping so deeply that small snores escaped his lips. I closed the book and leaned back in the chair.

My eyes strayed to the bookcase, to the books that appeared to be post-virus. The bindings weren't as tight, the edges of the pages uneven. I tilted my head to the side to read the spines.

One word stuck out to me, and after standing slowly so as not to wake Mav, I crept over to the bookcase. After slipping the Silver Tip pack history back in its spot, I slid out the book labeled *Astria*, the word written on the spine in crude etching.

On the front was a picture of a wolf with a white throat. I lifted my hand to my own throat self-consciously, then crept back over to the chair and placed the book on my lap.

For a while, I did nothing but stare at the cover, remembering the way Astria used to be, before the breach and the screams and the blood.

In the Whitethroat pack, there'd been no central building like the Hive. We'd lived as a village within the walls we'd taken for granted. We worked and farmed and learned and loved. Every year, we'd celebrate Feast, which was our way of thanking our Whitethroat Alpha for protecting us.

The last Feast I remembered had been right before the Nowere attack. Selene had sung songs, Jude had painted a landscape for the alpha's daughter, and I'd gotten in trouble for trying to look up a female novus's skirt. *Oops.* In my defense, she was my first crush. I hadn't let myself think of Piper in a long time. Had she survived the Nowere attack?

I steeled myself by clenching my jaw and opened the front cover of the book. I began to read, all the words on the page in front of me taking me back to another time. Another place. One that no longer existed. As a child, the threat of Noweres was nonexistent. Thinking back on it, I wondered if that was intentional on the alpha's part to reduce panic. She led us to believe the virus was a thing of the past. I had no idea it would affect my entire future.

After the confusion of the attack, my parents felt as though they didn't have any option but to leave Astria. But not a day went by that I didn't question whether any of my pack had lived. Whether they'd rebuilt. The constant gnawing in my gut had lessened now that I was away from Xan and mated into the Silver Tip pack. But it was still there, and I hadn't forgotten.

When the words on the page began to blur, whether from tears or fatigue, I knew I'd had enough reminiscing. I placed the book back on the shelf and walked to the window, where I had a view of the front gate. Tan was outside the walls now. I'd missed my chance when he left, and kicked myself for it. I'd eavesdropped on some conversations and learned another scout planned to leave in a couple of days. That was my chance, because time was running out.

I turned away from the window and carefully picked up Mav. He didn't wake up as I transferred him into the bed, just immediately curled around a pillow I pressed to his chest. Then I crawled in next to him, falling asleep myself to the rhythm of his snores.

Dare

VAUGHN WAS BEING A PAIN in my ass. "Don't get pissed off. I don't need details. I just want to know what it's like to fuck a werewolf."

I glared at him, and held it until he dropped his gaze submissively.

"He's my mate. So of course fucking him is amazing," I explained. "It has nothing to do with him being a werewolf."

Vaughn thought about that for a minute. "Oh, that's a good point."

I rolled my eyes.

Bay strolled into the meeting room, shirtless and covered in dirt. He grinned at me, white teeth in a mud-streaked face. "Hey, bro."

"Couldn't you hose off?"

Bay glanced down at himself. "Oh shit, I forgot."

"You forgot you're completely covered in filth?"

"Oh, how dare I see the alpha in this state, right?"

I shoved him, laughing. "I don't care about that. I don't want you getting everything dirty."

He sank down on a chair in a cloud of dust. "Too late."

I leaned on the table as he plucked a carrot from the center bowl with dirt-caked fingernails. "What do you need? I left Mav alone with Reese, so I'd appreciate making this quick."

There was a slight noise behind me, and I glanced back to see G waiting by the door. I turned back to face my brother just as he swallowed a bit of carrot. "So Dal is back."

Dal was one of Rua's scouts. She'd been gone for weeks on a mission to report on the Nowere packs to the south of us. "Great, she okay?"

"Oh yeah, she's fine. But she had some interesting news."

"You going to tell me or draw this shit out for dramatic effect?"

"She made it the whole way down to Astria." Bay's gaze slowly lifted to meet mine. His next words were spoken slower and with great care. "She didn't get close, but she saw activity there. Particularly around the Whitethroat pack compound."

I slowly dropped into the empty chair next to me. Astria. Reese's home. His pack. I closed my eyes, remembering how my mate looked when he talked about his home. How his face grew soft, his voice wistful. I shouldn't keep this from him, but I also didn't want to get his hopes up.

I swallowed. "Could she confirm it was members of the Whitethroat pack?"

Bay shook his head. "She smelled werewolves and that was it."

"We should confirm," I heard myself say, my voice sounding distant. "For Reese's and Jude's sake. We should confirm."

Bay nodded. "I can talk to Rua about getting together a team. It'll probably be a couple of weeks before they leave."

"That's fine."

Bay was silent for a moment. "You going to tell Reese?"

I shook my head. "Not yet. I think I'll wait until after the team leaves. I can picture Reese wanting to go, and I can't let him make that journey."

"Right, of course."

"Any other news?"

Bay launched into a detailed update on our supplies, and

I leaned back in my chair, happy to have my mind off of my mate problems.

By the time our meeting concluded, I was sure I'd been gone too long. I sped my way back to my quarters, and when I opened the door, silence greeted me.

After I closed the door, my gaze fell on the bed, and tension leached from my muscles. Reese lay on the bed on his side, fast asleep, with Mav cuddled up next to him. They were both snoring.

I ran my hands through my hair and glanced over at my bookcase. The history of the Silver Tip was out of place, and I smiled because I was sure Mav convinced Reese to read to him. I plucked it off the wrong shelf and placed it where it was supposed to go. Another misplaced book caught my eye, and all the lightness I'd felt a minute ago was now replaced by a heavy weight on my shoulders.

Reese had taken a look at the book on Astria. I imagined him sitting in the chair, biting his lip, blue eyes filling as he remembered what his life was like once upon a time. His hometown would always be in the forefront of his mind.

What if Dal was right and the Whitethroat pack was revived? I could take Reese to visit, but he wouldn't be able to stay.

If he had the choice, would he stay or go?

I didn't want to think about that. Whether fate had chosen him for me or not, the fact of the matter was that he *was* mine. I wanted him. I liked him. I craved him.

The sudden urge to hold him surged up through me, and

I crossed the room in several strides before sliding into bed behind Reese. I wrapped an arm around his waist and tugged him back to me, burying my face in his neck to inhale his scent.

He murmured something, and I lifted my head to see him blinking at me groggily. "Oh hey, you're back," he mumbled, rubbing his eyes. "Wow, I fell asleep."

He turned his head to see a still-sleeping Mav, then flashed me a bright smile. "He's cute when he sleeps."

I cupped Reese's cheek and pressed a kiss to his lips, wishing I could take him now.

When I pulled back, his brow was furrowed. "You okay?"

"Fine."

"What was the meeting about?"

I couldn't tell him yet, especially not with a sleeping Mav beside us. "Boring pack stuff."

He yawned. "Glad I got to nap instead. Nap beats boring pack stuff any day."

I laughed. "I would have rather stayed here and napped with you two."

He grinned. "Next time."

I didn't answer, and his eyes drifted shut.

In a couple of minutes, he was asleep again. But I didn't sleep. I stared at the ceiling and I clutched my mate to my chest and I wished I could see into the future.

CHAPTER TWELVE

Dare

NOWERE PACKS WERE UNPREDICTABLE. THEY were mindless, and changed direction based on the thinnest hint of a scent. Receiving these reports from the scouts on the location of Nowere packs was my least favorite part of being alpha.

Tan had shifted to his human form and his shoulders heaved while sweat dripped down his chest. "Something's got them sticking close," he said breathlessly. "They were also dormant, moving really slow and sluggish."

"How big?" Bay's dark brows were drawn in, his expression tight.

"Maybe fifty?" Tan squinted. "I'm sorry I don't have an accurate number. I had to take off—"

"You're a worthless scout if you die," I said. "You did the right thing. Good job."

Tan's shoulder sagged in relief. "Thanks, Alpha."

"The rest of the day is your own." I clapped him on the back.

He nodded at me, then trotted off, probably eager to clean the stench of Nowere off his skin.

Bay blew out a breath and rapped his knuckles against the stone wall of the compound where we stood on the south side. "Glad we got these."

I frowned. "Still makes me uneasy."

"Mom said sometimes there was no reason for what the Nowere packs did."

"Yeah, but sometimes there is a reason. She also said they seemed to have some sort of weird intuition."

Bay was quiet for a moment. "Where's Reese?"

"Farm. With his brother and G."

"You didn't tell him the scout report yet, did you?"

I shook my head. "Not yet. He finally seems settled here. Jude too. I want to give him some time before springing that on him."

Bay raised an eyebrow. "Oh yeah? Your reason isn't selfish at all? Wondering how he'll react?"

I didn't answer, and Bay's gaze bored into the side of my head before he turned away with a sigh. "I get it, brother," he said quietly. "I understand what it's like when things are good and you don't want to wreck them. And I also know what it's like when they are wrecked."

Bay's voice was low and a little raspy, the way it always got when he thought about Nash. His childhood best friend—and I suspected more—disappeared outside the walls one day when they were novuses. We assumed he either ran away to find his home pack—he wasn't born a Silver Tip— or he'd been the victim of Noweres. Either way, Bay certainly hadn't forgotten about him.

"I'm sorry about N—"

"Whatever," Bay cut me off. His cheeks flushed, like he knew it'd been rude to cut me off, but I let it slide.

I had a sudden desire to see Reese. To hold him. To prove to myself he was real, and he was whole, and what we had was better than I could have ever hoped for with a mate. "I'm going to go check on Reese. Want to come?"

"Sure."

I began to walk, Bay at my heels. When I turned the corner of the Hive to reach the Farm, a low growl immediately raised the hair on my shoulders.

Bay stiffened at my back as G held a Were by the throat, pressed up against the wall, his lips pulled back and teeth bared. I recognized the Were as one of Gage's cohorts, Kin.

Jude was standing next to Reese, whose face was twisted into one of fury. "Fuck you, man," Reese spat from behind G, rising up on his toes. "Gage would run this pack into the ground. Dare is the best alpha, and everyone knows it except your little band of assholes."

I saw the moment Reese sensed me. His nostrils flared, and his head whipped to the side. Blue eyes blazed as his fists clenched at his sides. Then he fell silent, waiting on his mate, his alpha.

He was such a good wolf.

"G," was all I had to stay for my guard to release Kin's throat. He stepped back, and I waited while Kin gasped for breath. "What happened?"

"Reese said he had to take a piss. While he was out of my sight, Kin approached him."

Reese whined low in his throat. I turned to my mate.

"And?"

My mate opened his mouth, but I was beyond listening.

Because I smelled blood.

My body tensed, and he noticed the change in my behavior, because he fell silent.

The iron tang was like waving a red flag in front of my face. My canines punched through my gums, and my claws elongated, fur sprouting on the backs of my hands. "Where?"

Reese went pale for a moment before he held up his arm. Five deep grooves were etched into his arm, blood dripping to color the grass at his feet. "Kin?" I asked.

Reese nodded.

The act took two seconds. One second, Kin was standing against the wall, the next he lay at my feet, throat pulsing with blood, life leaving his brown eyes. The scent of his blood mixed with Reese's was making my head spin, the rage I felt swirled with the protectiveness over him. Aggression toward my mate was the same as aggression toward me, and the consequence was death. Every time.

I stared at Kin's body at my feet, gulping deep breaths as I willed myself to return to human.

When I turned, G was standing with a shell-shocked Jude, while Reese stared at Kin impassively. Bay rubbed his temples like he had a headache.

"What?" I asked my brother.

"Just…how stupid was that for him to attack Reese?" He kicked at Kin's body. "Idiot."

Reese was picking at his wounds, dark head bent. Gripping his chin, I forced him to look at me. "Tell me what he wanted."

Reese's expression was clear, and his voice was firm. "He was asking questions in a way devised to trick me to reveal things about you. He wanted to know your habits. Your favorite foods. Things like that."

Favorite foods? The only reason that would be relevant was if Gage thought to poison me. Coward. "What did you tell him?"

"Nothing."

"Nothing?"

"Well, actually I told him you eat novus brains for breakfast, and that you have a nasty habit of wrestling with Noweres before bedtime. He didn't enjoy my sense of humor."

"That was when he slashed you?"

"Yeah."

I glanced up at G. "When did you come over?"

"When Kin was questioning him. I thought Reese could handle it, and he did, until Kin slashed him. Then I stepped in."

I slid my hand to the back of Reese's neck and tugged him to my chest. He was breathing hard, inhaling my scent, and I needed to get him alone, let him shift, then fuck him.

Gage's response to me killing Kin would be unpleasant, but the pack would understand Kin needed to be dealt with. That I'd done what I had to do to protect Reese. But I worried there'd come a time where I'd have to choose him over my pack.

Every day with my mate made that choice more and

more murky.

Reese

MY ARM HURT, BUT I didn't care, because Dare's Were scent was strong since he'd partially shifted. I was drugged on it, so I was grateful I heard him murmur that he was taking us to our room to shift.

Yes, my brain screamed. Shift. Scent. Fuck. Mate.

The rush of air surrounded us as Dare leapt up the side of the Hive. He carried me to our room and ordered me to shift before he'd even shut the door behind us. I did, bounding around him and shaking out my fur.

When I shifted back, my arm was healed.

And I was hard.

Dare had undressed while I'd shifted, so he stood in front of me, gloriously naked, his erect cock jutting out from between his thighs, large balls enticing me.

Dare said he loved when I acted on instinct, so I dropped to my knees and immediately rooted around his groin, breathing in his scent, lapping at his balls and nuzzling his cock.

He ran his fingers through my hair, and when he'd had enough of my playing, he wrenched my head back. "Good wolf," he said softly, and I whined. I wanted his dick in my mouth or my ass. One or the other. Soon.

He held the base of his cock and smeared my lips with the sticky pre-come leaking from the tip. I stuck my tongue out, catching a drop, and he took that opportunity to plunge himself into my mouth.

I planted my hands on his thighs and stared up at him as he fucked my face.

His eyes were swirling, which used to scare me, but now only turned me on, because it meant he was losing control a little bit.

And Dare on the edge meant he fucked me the best.

Even now, his mouth was twisted into a grimace, like he was in pain from keeping his Were at bay.

I did this to him. *Me.*

Before he came, he pulled out of my mouth and hurled me onto the bed. I bounced on my back, and then he was between my legs, thrusting his dick into me.

My back arched as I screamed, the sensation too much when he hit me at just the right angle, sending fireworks of heat up my spine.

His canines were out, mouth open, as he muttered, "Mine. My mate," in a garbled chant.

"Yes. Yours," I said back, along with some other gibberish as he continued to fuck me to within an inch of consciousness. I stared at his teeth, remembering the sharp pain and then immeasurable pleasure when he'd bitten me the first time we'd mated. "Bite me," I whispered. I'd be leaving tomorrow night, and I needed him, needed this reminder of where I belonged. "Make me bleed. Remind me I'm yours."

He growled, long and low, a rumble in his chest as his hips stuttered. I was coming, my eyes rolling back into my head, as his teeth sliced into my skin. I wasn't sure how long the orgasm lasted, but it was a fuck of a long time. When my body went limp, and Dare had collapsed beside me, my voice was hoarse. He gathered me into his arms, his fingers at my hole as he began to massage his come into my skin.

My brain wasn't online yet, so my only instinct was to remain attached to my alpha. I snuffled under his arm, rubbing my face on his skin, wanting to bathe in his scent. He ran his hands down my back and over my ass until the room smelled like concentrated sex.

His hands cupped my head and pulled my face back. "Can you speak?"

"Barely," I murmured. My body felt heavy, my eyelids like five-pound weights. "So tired."

"Sleep." His fingers sifted through my hair. I was almost asleep when I heard him say, "Fate is not always right. A lot of times she's a wrong bitch. But she was right with you, my mate. She was so right when she gave me you."

A warmth washed over me, a smile curling my lips, until I remembered that fate was an evil bitch. She gave me Dare, and she seemed determined to take him away.

THAT NIGHT, I LAY ON my back staring at the stars, hands behind my head. The night air was cool, but the massive bonfire the Weres had erected on the training field, plus the heat of hundreds of Were bodies, warmed my skin.

Dare sat beside me, gazing into the flames while Mav sat on his lap.

Kin's body was somewhere in there. Dare had made an

announcement to the pack at dinnertime that Kin had challenged his mate and was killed for it.

Kin had a been a loner, a transplant from another Were pack out west, so he had no family. Gage was nowhere to be seen after the announcement and during the mandatory-attendance cremation.

Dare was distracted, rubbing his hands idly over his son's back as Mav played with a set of small wooden wolves. I knew Dare was thinking about his pack.

"I'm sorry," I said.

Dare jerked his head to me, brows drawn in. "For what?"

"This is my fault, isn't it? Gage sees me as a weakness for you and is trying to exploit it."

Dare's lips twisted. "No, this isn't your fault. Gage has been like this for years. He's stepping it up now, but I think even if it weren't for you, he'd make his move sometime soon."

I leaned up, bracing myself on my hands. "So he'd turn this into a raider pack?"

Mav made a growling sound as he smashed two of his wolves together. Dare smiled at him before his brow furrowed. "Yeah. He thinks we should be growing in numbers, conquering packs until we have an army that can defeat the Noweres."

A land without Noweres sounded great, but I shuddered to think of the amount of casualties it would take to get there. The Silver Tip pack was self-sustaining and peaceful—for the most part. In one corner, by the light of the bonfire, several novuses kicked a ball back and forth.

A group of female Weres were laughing uproariously as Rua stood in front of them, telling some sort of story that required a lot of hip swaying. Beads at the end of her braids caught the light of the fire, so she looked like she had dozens of fireflies around her head.

And everywhere I looked, families were happy, smiling, and most of all—*safe*.

"He's fucking crazy," I said softly. "I've been behind walls that were a prison. I've been part of raider groups, because Xan couldn't provide enough food for his pack. It's a horrible way to live. Yes, you have threats—" I gestured around the bonfire. "But this is a pack where we can live and hope and not live in constant terror. This is a pack where futures are created."

I crossed my legs in front of me and tore a blade of grass into pieces. When I peered up at Dare, his irises were swirling, and I couldn't tell if it was from the flicking flames of the fire, or his Were.

He reached out and squeezed my knee silently, then returned his gaze to the fire.

A scout would be leaving tomorrow at dusk. I planned to make an excuse during dinner time in the Forum, tell Dare I was going to my room, when in fact I'd hide out in the storage facility near the gates waiting for them to open.

There was no other option anymore, and there wasn't time left.

Mav leaped into my lap, shoving his toy wolves in my face. I smiled and pretended to eat one. He squealed, then curled up in my lap, his wolves tucked under his little arm, green eyes watching the flames.

I fingered his hair, his little ear. I'd miss him so much when I left, and I hoped like hell he'd be okay. What would happen to Dare's son if Dare fell to a challenger?

What would happen to Bay?

Fuck, what would happen to this whole pack?

Anger swirled in me along with despair. I hadn't asked for this, and now I was faced with an impossible choice. Was my sister's life worth the stability of the Silver Tip pack?

Off to the side of the fire, Jude sat with G, his head on the big Were's lap. Our eyes met, and I forced a smile on my face. I'd told him earlier that I planned to leave tomorrow at dusk, and he knew what he had to do to help keep this pack safe.

Jude waved and blew me a kiss.

I cocked my head. He'd never done that before. But then he closed his eyes, and Mav began snoring in my lap.

The flames climbed higher, and my heart was heavy.

CHAPTER THIRTEEN

Dare

REESE TWITCHED IN HIS SLEEP as a small whimper escaped his lips, and I squeezed him tighter against my chest. The last couple of nights, he'd had nightmares. They didn't wake him up, but they woke me. His all-body shudders, his cries of pain, all of it tightened a vise around my chest.

Something was bothering him. I'd asked him several times about it, and he'd waved me off, then distracted me with sex.

I let myself be distracted.

He jerked against me, his arms clinging to my biceps. I shushed in his ear, and he took a couple of halting breaths before settling.

Kin's burial had been hours before, and Reese had passed out almost immediately. I was still awake, staring at the moon through the windows in the ceiling. I was already eager for morning, to see my mate's blue eyes, the radiant smile he always turned on me first thing.

I'd always been indifferent about mates, but that was because I hadn't known about late-night talks and lazy morning fucking. I hadn't known what it was like to hold my mate in my arms and run my hands over his warm skin.

I hadn't known how much it healed my soul to drop my guard and let someone else in.

Footsteps thundering up my steps shook me from my thoughts and had me bolting upright in bed, while Reese snuffled under the sheets as he came awake.

A pounding started, followed by G's alarmed voice. "Alpha!"

G never, *ever* spoke like that. I leapt out of bed while Reese muttered, "Who is that?"

When I flung the door open, G's fist was raised to knock again. His jaw was clenched, veins in his neck bulging. He swallowed and said with a barely restrained voice. "Jude's gone."

A thump came from the bed, and I turned to see Reese fully awake now, scrambling from where he'd fallen off the mattress. He surged forward. "What did he say about Jude?" He smacked into me as he rounded on G. "What's wrong?"

G's gaze darted between the two of us. "He's gone. Disappeared." He held out a piece of paper with handwriting on it. "He left this."

Reese stared at it like it would bite him. "What does it say?"

G's expression flickered. "I don't read."

Reese snatched it and squinted at the letters. I tried to read over his shoulder, but before I could catch any of the words, Reese's knees buckled.

He collapsed to the floor on his hands and knees, the paper fluttering to rest on the wood beside his hand. His body shook, his breathing raspy. I dropped to a knee, concerned what could make Reese react so drastically. I picked up the paper and read in precise handwriting:

I'm going back to Xan's, or I'll die trying. This time, my brother, it's not all on your shoulders.

Love, J

The words blurred in front of my eyes.

Jude heading back to Xan's alone was a recipe for a disaster. He was barely a week past his muto. The Nowere packs were close, our scouts had said, and Jude alone…

I stared at the paper again. *I'm going to back to Xan's.*

Bay's caution when I'd first mated Reese came back to me in a rush. By now, Reese and Jude knew how the pack worked, what kind of resources we had, and where exactly in the compound those were located.

That knowledge getting out would leave my pack vulnerable. The alpha in me shut off the emotions concerning Jude and Reese, and focused on the safety of my pack. I lifted the hand that had been soothing Reese's back and clenched it in his hair. I jerked so he was forced to sit up on his knees. He gasped, eyes glazed with fear and anxiousness. "Hey—"

"Why is your brother going to Xan's? What's this about your shoulders?" My tone was harsh, because the thought that my mate could be deceiving me left me cold as ice.

Reese swallowed and winced in pain at my grip on his hair. "Dare."

My name fell from his lips on a lone cracked syllable. My

inner Were raged. I tightened my hand, and he cried out. All my instincts screamed at me that I was hurting my mate, but my anger was drowning them out. "Bay told me I needed to be cautious with you. That you could be a scout or a mole sent by Xan to infiltrate our pack."

His entire body trembled, as his face paled and lips thinned. "Dare, I'm not a mole." He held onto my forearm with both hands, digging his nails into my skin. "Please listen to me. I'm speaking as Reese. As your mate." He spoke over the growl rumbling in my chest. "There *is* something I haven't told you, but I'm not a mole."

I roared and shoved him away from me. As he sprawled onto his back by the bed, I whirled to G, knowing my Were was too close to the surface to deal with Reese right now. "We need to talk."

"Dare!" Reese yelled, lurching forward and grabbing for my leg. "Wait, we have to follow Jude! He can't be out there on his own!"

I turned on him. "You must have forgotten that you don't make the pack decisions."

Reese reached for me again, but I was already out the door.

"Dare!" he screamed, and the last thing I saw before I slammed the door was his tear-stained face lunging for me.

I locked the door behind me as the banging started, along with muffled yells. I motioned to G to descend the stairs and he did. On the fifth balcony, he began to pace, twisting his hands in agitation.

"Stop," I barked, and he froze.

I was on edge and needed G's default calm demeanor to help me from reaching the boiling point. "Tell me what happened. How did Jude get out?"

"I think he'd been planning it, Alpha. I admit I'd been lax with him. He seemed happy and always obeyed me. He asked me to make him a wooden wolf, and he knew I didn't have any more wood in our room, that I would have to get more from storage. When I returned with a couple of blocks, he was gone. He'd picked the lock on the door." He ducked his head. "I'm sorry."

Goddamn it. "You're a good guard, G. And I know it was asking a lot of you to stay on him full time." I propped my hand on my hips. "What do you think? Are they deceiving us?"

G was quiet for a long time. "No, I don't think so. Sometimes Jude would get real quiet. And one time I asked what he was sad about. And he said he missed his family."

"Reese said his parents were killed."

"Yeah, and when I mentioned that, he shook his head, like that wasn't what he meant."

I frowned at that.

The banging from my door had stopped, and I hoped Reese hadn't taken to wrecking my room. "I need to get Bay. He can help me question Reese, because I can't be impartial with him." I thought G would nod, and return to his room, but instead he gazed at me steadily, waiting. "Is there something you want to tell me?"

G took a step forward. "If you decide to go after Jude, I'd like to be on the team."

"You don't think he's a spy, do you?"

G shook his head. "No, I don't, Alpha. I think there's a reason they both need to go back to Xan's, and neither of them are happy it has to be done."

I wanted so badly to believe my mate wasn't deceptive that I was willing to take any scraps I could. "Thanks for your observation, G. I'll let you know what we decide."

When G turned to walk away, I took a leap over the balcony. Time to get Bay and interrogate my mate.

Reese

BY THE TIME I HEARD footsteps returning to the sixth floor, I was out of my mind. I'd shifted and thrown my body against the door. I'd clawed at the wooden window panels which were closed with a padlock. The only result was severely scratched-up window frames and bloody paws.

Jude had no idea how to defend himself from Xan and his men, let alone Noweres he encountered on the trek to the Bluefoot compound.

Why had he thought he could do this himself? As much as I'd hated having this on my shoulders, I never wanted to pass off the responsibility to Jude.

If my wolf could have cried, I would have shed a river of tears by now, because I was convinced I'd never see my brother again. Or my sister. I couldn't even blame Dare. I'd kept this a secret from him on purpose.

When the door opened, I was on the floor in my wolf

form, panting, bleeding, and battered.

Dare cursed when he saw me, while another voice said, "Wow. You're lucky he didn't get out, brother."

Great, he'd brought Bay. I closed my eyes, knowing the gentle life I'd known as Dare's mate was gone. He couldn't kill me, but he sure as hell didn't have to treat me well.

"Shift," Dare said on a growl.

I didn't want to, but he was my mate, and my body still obeyed his command. I didn't move other than to whimper as my damaged body morphed into human form.

Rolling onto my back, I blinked at the ceiling, testing out my limbs. They all worked. Well, I had that going for me.

Footsteps drew closer, then Dare's face filled my vision as he leaned over me. "As Alpha of this pack, I'd like to believe I could be impartial, even with my mate. But this is all too new for me to trust myself. So Bay is here."

I stayed silent, even though my instinct was to shout in his face to let me follow my brother.

Dare glanced over his shoulder, then back to me. "I'm going to ask you some questions, and you have to tell me the truth. If I get even a whiff of a hunch that you're lying, I'll chain you back up in the basement." Something flickered over his eyes, before he pursed his lips. "I don't want to do that. Don't make me." His voice cracked, and he cleared it. "So tell me the truth, Reese."

I could do that. I had to. I had nothing to lose anymore. Tears leaked out of the corners of my eyes as I nodded.

A chair scraped out across the floor, then creaked as a

heavy body descended on it. Dare's gaze tracked his brother's movements before focusing back on me. "Are you a mole sent by Xan's pack to spy on us?"

"No," I said quickly.

"Why did your brother leave?"

"To rescue our sister."

Bay made an odd sound, and Dare tilted his head. "What did you say?"

I slowly raised my body into a sitting position, Dare still crouched over me. I needed to look him directly in the eye, so that he saw I was telling the truth. "I'd always wanted to leave the Bluefoot pack. They killed our parents, for fuck's sake. But it wasn't until Xan said he planned to mate with my sister after her first muto that I knew I had to get my family out. I've seen the mates he's chosen. They last maybe a year."

"Fuck," Bay muttered.

"So, I made a plan. I got Jude out, hid him away, and I was heading back in for Selene when Xan's men caught me, beat me and...you know the rest."

"Why didn't you tell me this?" Dare demanded.

"Because I knew you had a truce with Xan. Why would you break a truce and risk the whole damn pack for one wolf you've never met?"

Dare didn't argue with that. "Then what was your plan?"

I blew out a breath. "Well when I first found out you were my mate, my plan was to obey and play nice so you'd give me freedom that would allow me to escape." He sucked in a breath, and I hurried on. "Did you give me enough freedom to escape if I'd really wanted to? Yes. Did I do it? No. First, because of Mate Pain. The thought of you...suffering because of me was inconceivable. And what if Gage took advantage of me leaving to challenge you, using your lack of control over your mate against you?" Dare's teeth were grinding, his eyes swirling. "I couldn't come up with a good plan. One that saved my sister and didn't put you at risk. But I was running out of time, so I'd planned to leave today—sneak out the gates at dusk when the scout left. I didn't want to do it, you have to believe me, but I couldn't leave my sister there. Jude was going to tell G, so he and the rest of the guard could protect you while you were hurting." Saying this out loud was killing me. "Jude knew I didn't want to leave, that the thought of you in pain was making me sick. I guess...he decided to take the choice out of my hands.'

Dare held my gaze for a long time, before turning to his brother. Bay was watching me, his elbows resting on his knees, fingers in a steeple in front of his face. Finally, he leaned back and crossed his arms over his chest. "So I was wrong. He's not deceptive, but he's not smart."

"Hey!" I protested.

"Bay," Dare growled.

He threw up his hands. "Reese, you should have told him. I get why you were holding that in your back pocket. As soon as you told Dare, your element of surprise would be gone if you ever wanted to escape. But you played this all wrong. And now your brother is out there all by himself and your sister is...what? Days from being mated to some crazy wolf?" He tsked. "Not smart."

I jumped to my feet with my fists clenched at my sides. "Fuck you, Bay. I was beaten to within an inch of my life, chained in the basement of a Were compound, then found out I was mates with the alpha. I wanted to keep myself alive, as well as my brother. I made the best decision I could at the time. I see how this ended up, but you know what? It could have ended up a lot fucking worse."

Bay shrugged. "Fair enough." Then he grinned at Dare. "I like hanging out when it's just the three of us. He's much feistier then."

I started toward the joking Were, intent on pummeling him, but Dare grabbed me around the waist and pulled me back. "Let me at him!" I yelled.

"If you want your brother back, you'll calm down," Dare hissed in my ear.

I went limp.

Dare set me down and turned to his brother. "Form a rescue team of a dozen Weres. Include G, Rua, and Vaughn. You'll stay here as interim alpha."

I nearly fell to my knees. "What did you say?"

Dare ignored me. "We leave in two hours, so make it quick."

Bay saluted his brother. "Consider it done, Alpha. Although, fuck me. I never get to see any action."

"You're needed here."

"Yeah, yeah. You gonna rescue Selene too?"

"Yes. As the sister of my mate, she's within my right to possess," Dare said. And I got tingles at the sheer bad-ass alphaness in his tone.

"Dare," I whispered. "The truce."

He responding by gripping the back of my neck, his gaze still on his brother. "We meet at the front gate in two hours. Go."

Bay took off running, slamming the door behind him. I crumpled in Dare's arms, clutching his shirt and snuffling against his chest. "I'm so sorry. I'm so so so sorry."

Dare didn't move, didn't wrap his arms around me, and when he spoke, his voice was tight. "I know."

I pressed closer. "As much as I don't want to say this, Bay's right. I should have told you. But at the time, I didn't think it was the right decision."

He was quiet for a moment. Then his fingers slipped into my hair, and he yanked my head back so I'd have to look up at him. "You lied."

I searched his face for a glimmer of affection. I saw none, and my heart dropped onto the floor. "Because I thought this would happen. Tell me, Dare. If I'd told you, what would you have done?"

His voice was tight. "I would have organized a team like we are now and gone after her."

"Exactly," I said. "And where does that leave this pack if something happens to you? To me? I was trying to prevent you from choosing me over your pack." Fuck, my eyes were filling as Dare continued to glare at me stonily. "I'm sorry if I made the wrong choice. You have to understand why I did what I did!"

He pointed a finger at me, and for a second, hurt flashed

across his eyes. "You didn't trust me to save your sister."

I shook my head violently. "No, I trusted you too much. Your pack—"

"My pack will be fine," he spat. "Bay's in charge, and we won't be gone long."

"But—"

"This decision isn't yours to make!" He roared, and the sound shook my bones. If I hadn't been his mate, I would have cowered. "Instead of having the luxury of time to form a plan, now we'll have to rush out in the middle of the night."

"I'm sorry," I whispered.

His nostrils flared. And this was Alpha Dare. Not my mate, not the one who cuddled me and called me his little wolf. "I'm risking my pack for you. Tell me this is the right call, Reese. Tell me I'm not being drawn into an ambush."

"I swear to you, on Jude's life, I'm telling you the truth."

He shoved me away from him, his features hardening as he strode toward the bureau where he kept his clothes. "We'll make the journey as wolves. Pack some clothes to take with you."

"Dare—"

He whirled around. "Say my name one more time like that, and I'll leave you here. I don't want more apologies or excuses. I want to get home with every Were I take, plus your brother and sister, and then I want to learn to trust my mate again. Do you understand?"

I was sufficiently cowed. "Yes."

"Now pack."

I packed, my eyes blurred with tears. I'd taken for grant-ed Dare's affection. Now that he was withholding it, I was very aware how much I'd grown to love it. Somehow, while I'd been learning about the Silver Tip pack and plotting ways to escape, our bond had become much more than fated mates.

And I'd blown it all.

CHAPTER FOURTEEN

Reese

I was ready to shift.

The night air was cool, and a dewy mist stuck to my skin, settling in little drops on my arm hair.

We wore special packs that would stay on our backs after we shifted. Inside were clothes, food, and water.

I bounced on the balls of my feet, stifling a whine in my throat. My mind was already on the run to chase after my brother and rescue my sister.

Dare's presence was both a source of comfort and guilt. He didn't show me the affection he normally did, where he dipped his chin and held my gaze, silently asking me if I was okay. Instead, he mostly ignored me as he rallied his team. I didn't fault him for it, but I couldn't deny it stung.

When he turned to me, his eyes were hard, mouth tight. "We're going to head in the direction of the Bluefoot compound, since we know that's where Jude is headed. Explain the compound's security to me."

Hey, I could actually be useful. I told myself to stay calm, and focus on telling Dare everything I knew. No more lies. No more surprises. "Xan's guards work in shifts. There are a dozen posts on the top of the wall, which are manned all the time. And then there are patrol guards. There are three of those, and each handles a small section outside the wall. It typically takes them fifteen minutes to canvass their area before they start again or are replaced by the next shift."

"How often do the shifts rotate?"

"The wall guards rotate every six hours. The patrols every four."

"Entry points?"

"Locked gates. There are two of them."

Dare's jaw worked. "And how did you get caught?"

In my head, I heard the howl that went up when I'd been spotted. I'd never forget the sharp spike of fear that lodged itself in my ribs at the sound. "There is a twenty-foot area on the south side of the wall that is a blind spot for the wall guards. Whenever we could, Jude and I snuck there to loosen a chunk of stone. I'd observed the guard who patrolled there, and he'd begun to shorten the distance he canvassed out of laziness, I guessed. The day I escaped, he'd been replaced without my knowledge. And the man who took his place did a much more thorough job."

Dare's lips twitched, and I thought for a minute he'd give me that amused smile, but then he turned abruptly to Rua. "When we get close, we'll secure ourselves in a camp and send scouts to find weaknesses in their security."

She agreed and they began to talk about the details. I had been dismissed. I ducked my head, not wanted to piss off Dare any more than he was already.

Standing at the gate, G ignored us all, nearly blending in

with the darkness. The moonlight glistened off the damp skin of his naked body. His shoulders were massive, his back like a sculpture. I walked over and stood next to him, but he didn't acknowledge my presence, until he held a crumpled piece of paper in front of my face.

I reached out cautiously and plucked it from his fingers. After smoothing it out, I gazed at one of Jude's drawings. It was a sketch of G in profile, wearing an expression I'd never seen. His head was tilted down, and he wore a small smile. A *gentle* smile.

I couldn't look away from it. Was this Jude imagining G with that expression? Or did G actually make that expression? Because I'd sure never seen it. I blinked and turned the paper over, surprised to see Jude's writing on it. I glanced up at G, who was watching me silently. "Do you want me to read this?"

He nodded.

Feeling like I was intruding on something private, I squinted at the paper in the dark. "'Gav...'" I stopped and glanced up at G with an eyebrow quirk. He didn't react. *Okay then.* I returned my eyes to the paper. "'I broke my promise to you, and I'll carry that guilt forever. I'm not sure how long forever is, but know that you'll be in my thoughts until the end. You never broke your promise to me. Not once. You deserve someone as loyal as you.'"

I knew shit was going on between Jude and G. But this...this indicated something much deeper than surface affection. Of course I was protective of my brother, but he was smart, and this note showed that whatever they had between them was reciprocated. I cleared my throat as I finished reading. "It's signed, 'yours, Jude.'"

G's entire body was vibrating. I had no idea what that meant, but I backed away slowly, hoping he didn't shift and tear me apart.

A yell went up behind me. Dare's voice.

With a low creak, the wooden gates swung open.

Snarling, G snatched the paper from me, shoved it into his pack, then shifted. A second later, a massive black wolf leaped through the open gates and took off into the darkness. A couple more flew past me, and I stumbled forward when something smacked me on the shoulder. I glared at Vaughn, who grinned at me before shifting midair and racing out the gates. I shook myself, shifted, and did the same.

As we galloped into the wilderness of Eury, I looked over my shoulder. Bay stood at the entrance, his hand lifted in a wave. The gates closed and blocked him from view.

Head down, I plowed forward, knowing I was going to have to work extra hard to keep up with the larger wolves. My energy was high, though, from the adrenaline of Jude's disappearance and the hope I was getting my sister back.

Teeth nipped at my tail, and I jumped to the side. Rua's eyes met mine amid black fur, and she flicked her head to the front of the pack, where G ran along Dare's left flank. *Oh, right.* I was Dare's mate, even if he hated me right now. I sped up, passing the wolf pack and taking my rightful place at Dare's right flank.

He glanced over his shoulder at me, and then continued on at a fast pace. I squared my shoulders, dug in my paws, and kept going.

IN A COUPLE OF HOURS, we'd covered half the distance to our goal, but the pace wasn't going to be sustainable. The back of our pack was starting to lag, and Caro, a Were who often farmed with his younger brother, was limping.

Dare took a sharp left at a grove of trees, which led us up a steep slope and into a small clearing. I was surprised he chose this place, as we were penned in. The only way out was the way we came or...off a cliff. But I didn't question my alpha. He came to a stop, circling the area as we all collapsed onto the ground. G stood at the edge of the clearing on four paws. His sides contracted with heaving breaths, but other than that, he didn't look tired. He pawed at the ground near Dare, who snapped at him. G ducked his head, and sat down, his tail curled around his hind legs.

G didn't want to stop, but the pack wasn't going to make it at this pace without some rest.

This was Nowere territory, and every single tree branch snap had us on edge. Once Dare seemed content with the perimeter, he shifted. After a sharp order from him, we all shifted too. Dare immediately went to Caro to examine his leg. They murmured to each other quietly.

I reached into my pack and drew out an apple, as well as a handful of peanuts. Everyone else was digging into their packs for some provisions. I was halfway through my apple when Rua settled next to me, braids secured at her neck with a tie. "You doing okay?"

I nodded. "Yeah." I squinted at her. "So what's everyone

think about this mission?"

Her brows drew in as she crunched on a carrot. "What do you mean?"

"They think we should just let Jude go?"

"What? No. Why would they?"

"He's just a wolf, and if I had told Dare—"

"Look, Reese." She leaned closer. "You're our alpha's mate. That means something to us. And Jude is your brother. You're a part of us, our pack. We consider it an honor to be on this mission."

I watched as Dare went from Were to Were, checking on them and overall being a fucking awesome leader. Like he'd proven since I'd been taken in by the Silver Tip, and then I went and rewarded him by being a lying liar who lied.

In that moment, I hated Xan even more, for being a shitty leader who enslaved his people and half-starved them.

And as Dare clapped G on the shoulder and murmured words to him, the big man finally began to relax. My chest tightened, my apple forgotten as my brain confirmed what my heart had been feeling. I was falling for Dare—for the person he was—independent of our mate bond.

Fuck my life. I rolled the half-eaten apple in my hand before offering Rua a small smile. "Thank you. This means more than you know."

"Should have known Dare would do anything he could as soon as you mentioned a sister. He's been mourning his for a decade."

"Wha—"

"Rua!" Dare called from across the clearing. "Need you

over here."

She hopped up immediately. "Talk later, Reese."

I stared after her, blinking. Dare mourned...a sister? Now who was keeping secrets?

<center>~~~</center>

Dare

I KEPT ONE EYE ON Reese the entire time we rested. What if he snuck off to warn Xan? What if all this had a been a ruse to bring down the mighty Silver Tip pack?

What if I was making a huge mistake?

Bay believed Reese was telling the truth, and I did too, but the logical part of my brain told me to remain aloof, to keep my distance. That was hard as fuck, especially when his scent drifted on the breeze as he sat alone, back hunched and head bent, on the outside of camp.

Fuck this situation. I wanted to be back in my compound, working out how to deal with a lying mate, not out here on high alert for Noweres and about to ruin a decade-long truce.

Reese's words nibbled at the back of my mind. I didn't look at it as choosing him over my pack. He *was* my pack—and that included Jude and Selene. But it was clear he didn't look at it that way. Did he not feel a part of my pack? Insecurities began to swell inside me as I remembered him reading about Astria. Did he want to go home? Especially if he knew about surviving Whitethroat pack members...

Reese lifted his head and locked eyes with me. Lust

surged in my gut, as it always did. As it always would. Reese could hold a knife to my throat and cut slowly, laughing gleefully. I'd still want him even as I bled out as his feet.

True Mates was a curse and a blessing.

I left Rua to talk to the pack and made my way over to Reese. He watched me approach, his gaze hungrily taking me in as I stalked toward him.

When I reached him, his eyes dropped. I squatted down and gripped his chin to force him to look at me.

His eyes were a little wild, his cheeks flushed. If we were safe, I would have taken him right there. And I was half thinking of doing it anyway, when he parted those sinful lips and said, "Why didn't you tell me you had a sister?"

I jerked away and nearly fell on my ass. "What did you say?"

"Rua said you had a sister."

Fucking pack couldn't keep their traps shut. I sat down beside Reese and bent my legs in front of me, resting my wrists on my knees. Already Lee's face swam in my vision, with our mother's laugh and Bay's eyes. They'd been twins. "What do you want to know?"

"Uh, I don't know. Why didn't you tell me?"

The last question was easy. "I didn't tell you because it didn't affect you in any way. She's gone and there's no bringing her back."

He blinked at me.

I ground my teeth together until my jaw ached. "Remember when you asked if I'd ever seen someone turn at the hands of a Nowere?"

Reese's face collapsed. "No," he whispered.

"She snuck out with a supply group and got separated from them. By the time they realized what had happened, and they fetched me, she had already been bitten. We watched as her body came back to life as a Nowere. And I'll never forget it as long as I live."

He was silent for a long moment, face drained of color. "What was her name?"

"Lee." The one syllable was like a flower petal with an acid chaser on my tongue.

Reese didn't speak for a long moment. Then the warmth of his body coated my arm, and the soft hair of his head tickled my neck. "I'm sorry," he said as he rested his head on my shoulder.

I was too. I stayed silent, trying to swallow the bile that always rose when I thought about the sight of my sister, unrecognizable as a Nowere.

A faint breeze wafted over my skin, and as soon as I inhaled, the hair on the back of my neck rose. Reese's head went up, and I sniffed again. Yep, the breeze was carrying downwind the unmistakable stench of Nowere. I lurched to my feet and hauled a confused Reese with me, growling a danger warning low in my throat. My pack immediately gathered their bags, leaving no trace, and surrounded us. They were becoming alert now, sniffing the air and shifting restlessly. It was hard to fight the immediate instinct to flee at the smell of our predator. But we had to be smart.

I walked to the edge of the cliff and grabbed Reese's arm. He stifled a yelp as I gripped his wrist and flung him off the edge, swinging him back under the cliff to the small ledge below. He landed with a stumble and glared up at me. I ignored him, because he was safe and that was all that mattered.

From behind us came the sound of Nowere chatter—the bone-chilling clack of gnashing teeth. It spurred me on, the safety of my pack members my primary concern.

G stepped up next to me, and while the stench grew stronger and the sounds drew closer, we dropped the entire group onto the ledge below, where they retreated into the cave. One of my first duties as alpha was to send out pack members to map the nearby land so we always had an escape route from Noweres. This cave was why I'd chosen this spot to rest.

I helped G down, then glanced back, seeing movement among the dense brush about a hundred yards away. Fucking Noweres. Reese shouted my name and when I swung down, he was at the edge of the ledge, peering up at me.

"Get out of sight," I hissed.

"Well, excuse me. I can barely breathe from Nowere odor, and you hadn't dropped down yet. Fine, I won't worry about you."

He stomped off into the cave, standing at the side with his arms crossed over his chest, pointedly ignoring me. I didn't give a shit. I was trying to keep my pack alive. I didn't need to deal with his bullshit. With a sharp growl, I crowded everyone back. G's body was tense, his jaw locked and nostrils flared. His meaty fists were balled at his sides, and I knew he'd battle one hundred Noweres himself if he had to.

Especially because I suspected this rescue mission was very personal because of Jude.

Footsteps sounded above and, despite Reese's posture, I went right to him, shielding him with my body. He huffed against my chest, then settled his hands tentatively on my hips.

Noweres smelled like rotting corpses left out in the sun for five days. Even protected by the small ledge above us, the stench surrounded us, and I had to bury my nose in the crook of my arm. All around me, my pack members gasped for breath and blinked through watery eyes while trembling at the sounds of the chatter above us, the roars and growls, all which swirled to deafening levels. I couldn't hear myself think, couldn't do anything but press closer to Reese, whose entire body was shaking. He clung to me tighter, pressing his forehead against my chest.

By the sounds of it, the Nowere pack was large, maybe fifty to seventy-five strong, and we'd be no match for them, even if all of us shifted. My little wolf would be overpowered in a second, no matter how much I tried to protect him.

The Nowere brain had one function and that was to detect living things and consume them or turn them. They had a keen sense of smell and poor eyesight. Their frustrated grunts and stomps above, which rained dirt and stones down on our heads, told me they smelled us.

Noweres were dumb, but I wouldn't put it past them to somehow slip off the cliff and land right on our little ledge. I wasn't sure how long we were there, huddled together as the Noweres stomped above us. But eventually the chatter began to retreat and the footsteps lessened. I was breathing easier when a fist-sized rock crashed to the ledge floor, then four-foot claws curled over the edge of the cliff right near my head.

I held up my hand to signal silence, never taking my eyes off those claws. The panic was welling up inside me, for Reese, for my pack. For myself. I stuffed it down, calling on every bit of alpha I had in me.

A gust of air blew a cloud of dirt in front of the ledge, a Nowere exhale, which brought with it another cloud of stench, then the chattering started. I glanced at my pack, who were staring at the claws and at me, like *do something*.

The air heated from the Nowere body and our breaths. Fear swirled in the air like a dust cloud, and I hoped like hell it didn't tip into panic.

The foot claws uncurled and disappeared. I held my breath for one second, two, and then in a shower of dust and rotting fur, a Nowere crashed to the cliff in front of us.

I shoved Reese back into the cave and shifted immediately to my Were form as the Nowere flailed, trying to gain its balance as it scrambled for purchase on the edge. Its teeth chattered in time with my racing heart as my bones morphed. Just as it regained its footing, I finished my shift.

The Nowere threw his head back on a roar, and we met on the ledge in a clash of claws.

I didn't think; I didn't feel. My only mission was to protect my pack and my mate. The Nowere slashed at me, but I evaded his razor-sharp claws with a quick duck of my head. One bite, and I'd be a mindless killing machine like the thing in front of me.

Luckily, I had gravity on my side. With two hands in its sunken chest, I shoved, and the Nowere fell back with a grunt. For a second, he hung suspended on the edge of the cliff before he dropped out of sight with a screech.

I raced to the edge and looked over to see the body slam into the rocks below.

When I turned around, my pack members were shifted and standing in a line, protecting...Reese. Through their bodies, I could see him pacing back and forth in his wolf form, snarling and snorting.

I heaved a sigh of relief and shifted back. My pack followed and parted the line. I touched each one, thanking them and checking on their welfare, before attending to my agitated mate. He hadn't shifted yet, and I wasn't sure if it was because he couldn't or because he didn't want to.

I kneeled down and placed a hand on his furry head, tensing when I felt his trembles. "Shift," I said quietly.

He did after a moment, and when he peered up at me from where he knelt on the ground, his eyes were wet. "Fuck," he said, swiping at them furiously. "I thought I was going to have a heart attack when I saw him take a swing at you."

I tugged him to me, and he clung to my shoulders. I glanced back at G. "Let's rest here for the night. I'm going to head back farther to talk to Reese."

When G nodded, I dragged Reese deeper into the cave. We went around a bend so we were out of sight, and only a small sliver of light let me spot Reese's blue eyes. I sat down along the damp wall of the cave and pulled my mate into my lap.

He clung to me, zero hesitation, and huffed into my neck. His fingers flexed on my shoulders. *Squeeze. Release. Squeeze. Release.*

Then his tongue began to lap at my skin.

"Reese," I growled.

"Need you," he said, his voice muffled as he pressed closer to me. "Please. After everything... I know you don't want me right now, but I need you."

I grabbed his face. "I never said I didn't want you."

He blinked glassy eyes. "I lied to you. You're risking your pack for my brother—"

"I'm angry at you. But I still want you. I'll always want you." I didn't wait for him to respond. My mate needed me, and fuck if I didn't need him too. With a low growl, I surged forward, flattening Reese on the ground under me as I ground on top of him, plunging my tongue into his mouth. His hard, leaking cock rubbed against mine. He moaned and scrabbled at my back, fingernails scraping my skin.

I flipped him over onto his stomach. He arched his back on a whine as I positioned the tip of my cock at the entrance of his slick hole. With one thrust, I sank into him. He moaned, long and low, his hips working as he fucked himself on my dick.

"Is this what you needed?" I growled in his ear as I pinned him down and took control. He squirmed under me, panting and writhing as I fucked into him.

"Yes," he panted. "Yes, Dare."

"You needed to be reminded that I'm your alpha and you belong to me." My speech was garbled as the orgasm began to build in my spine. "You're mine to protect. Mine to take care of. You understand?"

"Alpha," he keened beneath me, his nails scraping the cave floor. "I'm yours."

My punishing thrusts were moving us across the floor. As my balls drew up tight and my orgasm slammed into me, I yanked his head to the side and sank my teeth into his neck.

He muffled a scream into his arm, and his body shuddered, his inner muscles milking me. After the last of my release pumped into him, I braced myself with one arm, and rolled him over. He was boneless, half-lidded eyes gazing up at me. I lay down beside him, and he immediately burrowed into me, his face pressed into my bare chest, his arms wrapped around my waist.

After several minutes, Reese stirred. "The last time I saw a Nowere, I was a kid and they were killing my entire pack," he said, his voice muffled against my skin. "I keep thinking about Jude. What if he ran into one of those fuckers?" He shuddered.

"G said he can still smell Jude, that we're on his trail."

"Really?" Reese said. "Wow, Weres track scents better than wolves." He was quiet for a moment. "All I've ever wanted was to be safe, happy, and free with my brother and sister, like we were back in Astria. I've always had this pain in my chest, this ache that never goes away, because I'm not home."

Free. I latched onto that word and rolled it over and over in my brain.

He sighed heavily. "I wonder all the time if there are any members of the Whitethroat pack still alive other than us."

The guilt swamped me. I still hadn't told him what the scouts reported to me about Astria. I couldn't imagine my entire pack wiped out. They were my family, my strength, my world. For them to be decimated in one fell swoop was unthinkable. I would always want to know if they still lived, if they needed me, if my pack could be rebuilt.

I glanced down to see Reese fast asleep, his nose pressed into my armpit. Well, there was no telling him now, but he deserved to know. I pulled him on top of me, so his head was pillowed on my chest. Despite the sex, I was restless and unsettled. I'd thought my future and that of my mate's was determined, but now none of that seemed possible or *right*. He'd spent his life a prisoner under Xan, and then went directly to being chained in my compound, then chained to me. He had no knowledge of his old pack, his old home. And I wasn't entirely convinced he considered the Silver Tip pack home either.

Was a life with me what he wanted? He could never be truly happy without his pack, knowing there could be some alive. The mate instinct drew him to me, made him want me. But was that what he wanted out of life? He'd risked his life to get out from under Xan's thumb, to be free, to go home. And now he was mated to me.

Somewhere along the way, watching Reese's courage and charm, I'd grown to like him, maybe even love him. What did I do when the best thing for my mate might be to let him go?

CHAPTER FIFTEEN

Reese

WHEN I WOKE UP, MY head was on Dare's lap. He sat with his back against the wall, gnawing on some dried fruit. When he noticed my eyes were open, he held a ring of dried apple to my lips. I opened my mouth so he could drop it inside. The sweet softness hit my tongue, and I chewed as Dare rested his hand on my chest, right over my heart.

His face was impassive, devoid of the soft expression he wore when we were alone. The one I hadn't seen since before Jude ran away. "Hey," I said, stretching.

He didn't answer, continuing to chew his fruit.

Voices echoed from the front of the cave. I turned my head and glimpsed some shadows in the morning light. "Everyone up?"

"Yes," he said, holding another piece of fruit to my lips, then a canteen of water.

I drank greedily. "Never thought I'd sleep so well on the floor of a cave."

"You slept on me."

"Oh."

Something was off. I sat up and kneeled at his side.

"What's going on?"

His eyes were in shadow, so I couldn't see much of them. Only his tight jaw. "Once we rescue Jude, you're free to go."

I blinked as my stomach twisted painfully. "Free to go?"

He leaned forward, so the green of his eyes shown neon in the dim light of the cave. "I've thought a lot about why you kept this from me. I think it's because you always wanted the option to escape and go home to Astria. Am I wrong?"

I dug my nails into my legs. Did I? Did I want the freedom to take my brother and sister home?

"You spent your life with no freedom. I don't want to keep you from it when it's something you wanted so badly that you risked your life for it. You can return home and help to rebuild your pack."

"Dare." I grabbed his arm, but he didn't move. I didn't know what to say. The idea of freedom, of choosing *where* I wanted to live, *how* I wanted to live, definitely had its appeal but I'd be leaving my mate. I couldn't imagine him not touching me again, or gorging ourselves on food in his bed, or playing with Mav. Then there were the consequences for Dare to think about. "What about the Mate Pain? I can't leave you like that."

That must have been the wrong thing to say, because Dare's eyes narrowed, and a muscle in his jaw ticked. "I'll be fine." He stood up quickly, shaking off my grip on his arm like I was a fly.

"What do you mean you'll be fine? You'll be pain, and vulnerable, and—"

"Then I'll challenge Gage as soon as get home. Problem solved. I can live with the pain after that."

I stared at him. "But you said you didn't want to challenge him unprovoked, that you didn't want to be like your father—"

"It's for the good of the pack. My pack." He blew out a harsh breath. "The pack I now see you never saw as yours, even though I saw you as a part of it. A crucial part."

His words were a physical blow. "Can't you understand how torn I've been? She's my sister, Dare. I spent my whole life protecting them. I couldn't just leave her."

"You had options, Reese," he said firmly. "It's telling which one you chose." He rolled his shoulders and glanced away. "We need to get going."

I scrambled to stand as he began to walk toward the front of the cave. "Dare, hold on. Can't we talk about this?"

He turned around. "Can you look me in the eye and tell me you don't dream of being free?"

I clamped my jaw shut, and I wished like hell I could lie to him. But I couldn't. Not again. So I shook my head.

He nodded. "Right. So when we get back, you're free."

He walked away, leaving me standing in the middle of the cave wondering what the hell happened. I was so tired of shit being decided for me. When would I get to decide how my life went?

BY THE TIME WE HAD shifted and were once again on the route to find Jude, my anger toward Dare had built to critical levels. I didn't want to cause problems with his pack, so I ran at his flank, but I did so while shooting eye-daggers at him. He seemed unfazed, back to the Dare who had calmly stalked me while I'd crawled away from him in chains.

How dare he decide my life?

So fine, I'd rescue Jude and my sister and we'd leave. We'd find a new home and a new life, and he could sit in his compound with a sore body and think about what he'd done.

I was acting like an immature novus but I didn't even care. Freedom was within my reach now, and while that ache was still in my gut, I was one step closer to home. To peace.

If Dare didn't want me, if he decided that I'd broken his trust in an irrevocable way, then fine. Screw him.

We ran for hours, until my paws were sore, and my tongue lolled out of my mouth. There was no sign of Jude except a faint whiff of his scent on the breeze.

Dare pulled us to a stop out of sight of Xan's compound and we shifted. We were so close I could smell the pack, but we were downwind so they shouldn't have scented us yet.

He sent Rua ahead to scout the condition of the pack and its walls, while my anxiety ratcheted to intolerable levels in my body. I alternated between freezing to listen for any sound I could and pacing.

Finally, Rua raced back toward us, her ears back, and shifted as she skidded to a halt. Her shoulders heaved as she gulped in breaths, and her wide-eyed gaze darted to me before addressing her alpha. "Something's going on."

My spine stiffened as my heart beat double-time, a resounding bass in my chest. "What? What's going on?"

She didn't look at me, her eyes on Dare. "There's a lot of smoke coming from within the walls."

I had to brace myself on a nearby tree so I didn't fall over.

"Did you hear anything?" Dare's voice sounded far away as I gasped.

There was a pause. "Yes, there was a lot of shouting. And screaming."

Selene was in there with that fucking monster, and Jude could be in there too. I didn't question my next action, or say a word. I shifted and took off at a dead sprint toward the compound. I was probably racing to my death, but my instincts were screaming at me to get to Selene.

A shout rose up from behind me. Dare was saying my name, but I didn't care, because I had to get to my family. He wanted me to be free? Well I was making my own damn decisions then. All I had left were Jude and Selene. They were all that mattered.

When I crested the hill, the Bluefoot compound rose before me, all gray stone and iron spikes. Sure enough, thick gray smoke billowed into the sky from the center of the compound, fed by licks of flames. A thunder of paws followed me, so I knew Dare and his pack weren't far behind. The front gate was open, and a body lay on the ground. As I drew closer, I recognized one of Xan's guards. I knew the smart thing would be to hang back, bide my time and figure out what the fuck was going on, but with the fire, I didn't have time. I had to get inside and find Selene. I shifted to human as I entered the gates, and turned to see Dare and his pack, also shifted, following me. Dare's face was thunder, the veins in his neck protruding, as he glared at me.

"I have to find them," I explained as he drew closer. "The fucking Column is on fire."

His gaze drifted away to take in the burning building in front of us. He seemed to want to protest, but in the end, he jerked out a nod. "Then let's go."

Xan's compound was comprised of one main building, the Column, which housed Xan and the elite members of the pack. The rest of the pack lived in small huts surrounding the building. Among the huts were wolves, some shifted, some in human form, running amok. Despite the way I was treated here, this was my surrogate pack and my heart hurt at the chaos and hysteria.

Along the far wall, I spotted Xan's two sons, armed to the teeth with knives, facing off against a small group of Xan's guards. Ah, so that was the source of this anarchy. As I'd long predicted, there'd finally been a mutiny. Zin and Zen had no love for their father, and I'd always suspected if anyone was going to challenge him, it would be them.

The brothers hated my guts, so staying out of their sight was preferable. They'd only be a distraction from the reason I was here.

Something crashed to the ground, and we all glanced up to see a chunk of the Column's roof had broken off. It looked like the entire top floor was on fire.

Weres among their midst sent the panicked wolves into a

bigger frenzy. Werewolf novuses screamed, and adults fled from the Weres as well as the rapidly spreading fire. Some larger wolves shifted, acting on instinct to protect their pack and family, but the Weres, even in their human form, easily fended off any advances. The open gates were a huge security breach, and I was eager to get the fuck out of here before the noise attracted Noweres.

A familiar form burst out of a side door of the Column and ran toward me. "Reese!" Gale, my sister's best friend, grabbed my arm and tugged, eyes wide, face blackened with ash. "Is it really you? Am I seeing things?"

She was frantic, blood trickling from a cut in her lip. "No, it's really me. Gale, what the fuck happened?"

Her nails dug into my arm. "Zin and Zen. They aren't daddy's little boys anymore."

"How did this start?"

"I don't know, but Xan thinks his guards will win. He's locked himself in his quarters." She swallowed and her next words were spoken through clenched teeth. "With Selene."

I tore my arm out of her grip and took off into the building as my entire body lit up like the flames above me. Dare was at my back, his solid presence giving me more courage than I'd have on my own. I took the stairs two at a time, dodging wolves as they fought and snarled at each other along with way. The scent of Weres made members of the Bluefoot pack cower or flee, both of which were excellent choices, because I didn't have time to fuck around with them.

When we reached Xan's door, Dare pushed me aside.

With a roar, he kicked the door open, splintering it on the hinges. I took one step inside and stopped dead.

In the center of the room stood Selene, holding a knife dripping with a dark red liquid. Her long white dress was torn, covered in ash and blood. And at her feet lay the motionless body of Xan, the former alpha of the Bluefoot pack.

At the sound of the door, her head jerked up, and she brandished the knife in front of her body, ready to defend herself from intruders. Her jaw was set, eyes glowing. When she saw it was me, her entire body slumped, like her muscles gave out. She dropped the knife to the floor with a clatter, and sobbed out, "Reese."

"Selene." I rushed toward her, and she fell into my arms, gripping me tightly as she sobbed into my neck.

"I thought you were dead!" She wailed against my skin. I squeezed my eyes shut, inhaling her scent. "I'm right here." I gripped her face. "Let me look at you."

She didn't want to meet my gaze, and I soon saw why. Her throat was red, fingerprints visible where someone had tried to cut off her air. Her jaw was bruised and her eyes were swollen and purple. With a raspy voice, gaze darting at me, then away, she said, "He tried, Reese. He tried, but he didn't succeed." Her voice cracked and in spite of that, she jutted her chin out and met my eyes. "I fought like you taught me."

My heart cracked open in my chest, blood pumping poisonous fury throughout my body. I'd never wanted this for Selene, that she had to see the worst of wolves, that she had to be treated like property, like a breeder to carry on

Xan's line. *Fuck. Him.* With a growl that scratched like sandpaper up my throat, I picked up the knife, and fell to my knees beside Xan's body. With two hands, I slammed the knife into his bloated belly. "You motherfucking bastard!" Again, and again, I stabbed the man who was already dead, the man who'd killed my parents, ruined my life, and brutalized my sister. For the last goddamn time, I screamed into his lifeless face.

Hands closed around my biceps and hauled me up and away from my mutilation. Dare's voice was firm in my ear. "Stop."

I went limp in his grip. My arms were sore. My throat hoarse. I threw the knife across the room, and braced myself on my knees as I caught my breath.

Selene watched us closely, her gaze darting between Dare and I, then taking in the dozen Weres behind us. She took a careful step backward. "W-why are you surrounded by Weres?"

Waving a hand, I said, "I'll explain later. We need to get out of here."

"And go where?" Despite the dirt and blood, she looked regal standing there, her long dark hair flowing past her shoulders.

"Back to the Silver Tip pack. Just trust me, all right?"

She nodded, her expression still wary. "We need to get Jude first."

I started. Oh shit, in all of this, I'd forgotten Jude should be here too. "You know where Jude is?"

"Yeah, they caught him sneaking around the compound

and threw him in a Hole."

"Is he okay?"

She nibbled her lip. "I'm not sure."

"Shit." I turned to see Dare and his pack in formation at the door. Gale was there too, clinging to Rua, who'd wrapped her arms around the wolf's shoulders. The crackling of the fire was louder now, a dull roar above us, and I wondered how long the ceiling would hold. G jerked, then held his ground, but his gaze was darting to the door, his hands fisted at his side.

"We need to get Hans too," Selene said. "He's also in a Hole."

"Hans?" He was a quiet wolf about Selene's age.

"Yes," Selene said. "He risked his life to get me that knife. We have to save him too."

I was already on my way out. "Sure, I'll save whoever, I just want to do it and get the fuck out of here."

With Dare striding at my side, Selene's hand clutched in mine, and the Weres flanking us, we made our way back downstairs. The screams were fainter now, and I wondered what would happen to the Bluefoot pack. Zin and Zen were not any better men than their father was. They were just a different kind of evil.

***

Reese

REESE LED US TO THE first floor of the Column. Bodies littered the floor and I nearly slipped in a pool of blood.

Werewolf fools. The Bluefoot pack had a real enemy outside their walls, yet they were fighting and killing each other.

Once outside the building, Reese took off at a sprint down a narrow path between some stone buildings. We followed him until we reached a clearing. At first, I couldn't understand how Jude would be here, until I saw the metal grates in the ground, about five of them spaced ten feet apart.

"I helped dig these fucking holes, so I know they're about eight feet deep." Reese peered down into an empty one. "There's enough room to sit down in a ball, and that's about it. Guards have the keys, and those metal grates are silver." He cupped his hands over his mouth. "Jude!"

A strangled cry went up from a Hole in the far corner.

A streak of black fur flew past us, and then a shifted Were came to a skidding halt ahead of us. With a ferocious growl, he gripped the gate with his clawed hands and ripped it open, sending it flying into the far wall where it crumpled like it was paper. G shifted into human form, then reached inside the Hole, hauling out a body. He clutched Jude to his chest like the wolf was made of gold.

G stroked his hair and ran his hands over his back, while Jude blinked up at him with adoration. "Jude!" Reese screamed. I cringed at the sight of Jude's face, but he managed a bloody, lopsided smile for his brother.

Reese fell to his knees beside them and tugged Jude into his arms. "I'm so mad at you," Reese said, shaking him slightly. "I'm so fucking mad at you, and I love you so fucking much."

Jude gripped his brother tightly. "I love you too." His gaze went past Reese and widened. "Selene!"

She was a blur of white cloth as she raced to her siblings, and they fell into a heap of limbs. There were apologies and whispered promises, and they ignored everything around them. My heart pounded in my chest at the sight of the reunited family. Reese had spent the last couple of weeks as an outsider with my pack, and now he'd finally found his home. He deserved it. I'd made the right decision letting him free.

I turned away to see Rua at another Hole, lifting out a wolf who looked even worse off than Jude. Selene gasped and tore herself out of her brothers' grips, running to brace the injured wolf as he stumbled. His skin was a deep, dark brown, and it wasn't until he stretched his lips, showing off bloody teeth, that I realized the liquid glistening on his skin was blood, not sweat.

When the wolf lifted his head, he smiled at Selene and raised a mangled hand to her face. "You're okay," he said in a broken voice.

She wiped a drip of blood from his chin. "Thanks to you."

I checked the rest of the Holes, finding them empty. I was walking away from the last one, when a chain rattled. I sniffed the air, having trouble picking out scents because there were so many around me. But there it was, the scent of a Silver Tip pack member, but mixed with something foreign.

I leaned back over the Hole and peered inside. A foot

moved into a small patch of light, and I ripped open the grate, ignoring the burn of the silver on my palms.

The scent was stronger now, and a silver chain attached to an emaciated leg rattled.

I yanked it out of its bolt in the wall, and tugged slightly. "Hello?"

A form dragged itself into the light, then a face peered up at me, green eyes sunken into its skull. His cracked lips moved, and his scent hit me. He was a Were, and definitely a Silver Tip. How the hell did he get here? "You're a Silver Tip," I said.

He nodded.

"I'm your alpha, and I'm going to take you home."

His lips moved again, and finally a raspy voice rumbled out. "Dare."

I smiled as I reached inside, and lifted out the bare-bones Were. "Yeah."

In the sunlight, he looked even worse. Dirty, brown, stringy hair, and bones protruding sharply against thin skin. He blinked at me and said even more softly, "Bay."

I tilted my head at him, pushing his hair out of his face. Those eyes. I remembered those eyes. "Wait, are you... Are you Nash?"

His lips moved, like he was trying to smile, and a bit of blood trickled out of a crack. "Yeah."

I cupped his face, unable to believe it. Nash—my brother's long-lost best friend—was actually alive. "I can't believe it's you."

"Me," he said, then coughed.

Right, we needed to get the fuck out of here. I handed Nash off to Vaughn and rose to my full height. "Time to move out. Weres, we form up around the wolves. Protect them at all costs."

In seconds, my pack surrounded the werewolves and Nash. Vaughn supported Nash, while Selene and Reese walked with Hans between them, his arms thrown over their shoulders. Jude stuck close to G's side, and Gale matched strides with Rua.

That was it, our party was full, and I was ready to get the fuck out of here and back to my pack. Reese directed us back to the front gates, and we walked quickly, on alert for attackers.

A werewolf raced toward us on four legs. I wasn't sure if he was friend or foe, but the answer became apparent when he launched himself into the air toward Jude with a snarl. G didn't even bother to shift. He snatched the wolf with a hand around its throat and with one twist of his wrist, the wolf lay broken at his feet.

From behind me, Hans sucked in a breath. "Who are these guys?"

"They're Weres," Reese answered. "And they don't like anyone fucking with their pack." There was a hint of pride in his voice.

"But we're not—" Selene began.

"We're their pack," Reese said quickly. "The alpha is my mate."

There was a stunned silence. "I have so many questions," she muttered.

Reese snorted. "You and me both."

When we reached the gates, I glanced back and met the brown eyes of a wolf. He stood watching me, a spear in his hand, head tilted. Behind him, a group of wolves were kicking the motionless body of a wolf bearing the tattered remains of a guard uniform.

Something brushed my arm. I smelled Reese. "That's Zin," he said, pointing to the brown-eyed wolf.

Zin's expression remained hard to read, and his gaze took in the group behind me. When his expression hardened, I followed his sightline to Selene. His lips curled back in a sneer. "Taking our females? That's breaking the truce, Alpha Dare."

"Consider it broken," I growled back. "But I think you have enough to worry about within your own walls and directly outside of them. Good luck."

I urged my pack out the gates, bracing myself for an attack from the back by the wolves. But none came. And when the gates closed and shouts went up from behind the wall, I knew the brothers had chosen to deal with bigger problems than losing a couple of female wolves.

Reese walked with his head down, trudging forward. Selene faced forward, chin up, dark hair billowing around her face, and a steady stream of tears flowed down her cheeks.

"We're free, Reese," she whispered in awe.

My mate's eyes met mine, and he didn't look away as he said, "Yes, we are, baby. We're finally free."

CHAPTER SIXTEEN

Reese

I WANTED MY EYES ON Jude and Selene at all times. I wanted some part of my body touching theirs. Any minute, I expected them to be snatched away from me, but the farther we walked from the Bluefoot gates, the more I could grasp the fact that they were alive, and real, and we were together. And at the end of this journey, we were *free*.

Xan was dead. His sons let us go. We were under the protection of some badass Weres.

We were *free*.

I would have danced if I could, or laughed at fate—that bitch. But I was too busy holding up Hans who seemed to look worse and worse with every step.

Dare, ever aware of his pack, could tell we had too many injured to make the entire trek back in one stretch, so he led us to a small clearing, well away from the Bluefoot gates but not quite in Nowere territory.

The scent of blood surrounded us to the point of being nauseating, so hopefully it didn't draw the Noweres to where we were. As Dare checked on his pack, Selene and I lowered Hans to the ground. I barely remembered the guy, but

Selene said he'd risked his life to save her, so I was going to do what I could to repay him.

Hans lay on the ground panting. His dark skin was ashen, his lips a dull gray, and the whites of his eyes were bloodshot. I dug in my pack for a canteen of water while Selene knelt beside him, running her hands over his body, taking stock of his injuries while speaking in low tones.

He was gritting his teeth, trying to shift. But I knew he wouldn't be able to, not in the state he was in. Selene held the canteen to his lips for him to take a drink, then she tore off a piece of her dress and began to use the dampened strip to clean his wounds.

I blew out a breath as I watched the poor wolf struggling. *Shit.* His breathing was off, something wheezing in his chest that made me suspect one of his lungs wasn't working.

I chewed on my thumbnail, unsure what to do, until Dare walked over to me, his brow furrowed in concern. "He okay?"

I shook my head. "He's gotta shift, and he's too weak to do it. I think he's got a couple of cracked ribs and some internal damage. They really worked him over."

Dare crouched down next to Hans, who watched him with wary, bloodshot eyes. "You need to shift," Dare said.

"I know." *Wheeze. Wheeze.* "Can't."

"Please, Hans," Selene pleaded. "You have to."

I was so damn proud of my sister. She'd been through so much, and yet she managed to stay strong and keep fighting. I wasn't sure I'd ever forget the image of her standing over Xan's body, knife in hand, pure fury on her face.

Dare rose to his full height, and a pulse in my body pulled me toward him. His gaze was intent on Hans, his entire body so tense the veins in his neck looked like they'd burst. He inhaled deeply, like he was gathering power, and my body was responding, my muscles coiling, blood pumping. *What the fuck?*

His canines descended, and his claws sharpened. He stared down at the dying wolf below him and with a voice that echoed off the trees surrounding us, he boomed, "Shift."

Hans's mouth opened, but no sound came out.

"Shift!" Dare shouted.

Something snapped inside me. My legs buckled, and I fell to the ground on all fours, muscles shaking. My energy was zapped, like it'd been sucked out of me.

Hans cried out, and began to writhe on the ground, back arched painfully. His nose and mouth formed a snout; his arms and legs shifted to furry ones.

Selene fell back and crawled away quickly as Hans's body was forced to do what he couldn't make it do. He screamed throughout the shift as the change healed his injuries.

I felt for him, knowing he was in agony right now, but it was necessary.

When he was finished, he lay at Dare's feet, his dark gray, furry sides heaving, his tongue rolling out of his mouth. Selene scrambled back to him, running her hands over his fur.

Dare turned to me, jerking when he spotted me on the ground. "Shit." He hauled me upright and gripped my face. His gaze searched my face. "Are you okay? I—" His brows lowered. "I drew on you, didn't I?" He blinked. "Shit."

I breathed in slowly and exhaled. My face warmed where Dare touched me, five points of energy returning much-needed fuel to my body. He'd taken it away, but now he was giving it back. My heartbeat returned to normal, and my chest loosened, making breathing easier. I nodded. "Yeah, I, uh, think I'm all right. Did you do something different?"

He set me on the ground, but kept a hand on my hip. "No, I was gathering my own power like I've always done. I could feel the drag, then like a rubber band snapping, more power slammed into me. I've never felt anything like that before."

"Yeah, I felt that snap, except, uh, it didn't feel quite so good."

"I'm sorry," he said quickly. "I hadn't realized I was doing it."

I shook out my limbs. "It's okay. I feel all right now."

He gripped my neck, peering into my face. "You sure?"

"Yeah." Did the power exchange go both ways? Unfortunately, this wasn't the time to investigate this new fancy True Mate bond feature, as much as I wanted to ask questions and see what else we could do. I glanced at Selene, who was watching us. "How's Hans doing?"

"I think he's sleeping now."

Dare pointed at her. "You need to shift too."

She nodded and, after a quick look at me, dropped her dress to the ground and shifted to a small gray wolf. After a small shake of her fur, and a couple of circles around Hans, she curled up in a ball next to him.

Happy with Selene's condition, I searched the pack for Jude. He was shifted into wolf form too, and was lapping happily at G's face, who batted him away with a…a smile?

Selene was fast asleep, next to a healed wolf who'd saved her. Jude was smiling in G's arms and I…needed a fucking moment. I excused myself from Dare and retreated to the edge of the clearing to get my head together.

I'd never had an anchor, not since Xan slashed my parents' throats in front of me. Not since I saw their blood mix with the dirt and stones. No anchor, no home. Just a constant gnawing in my gut, an ever-present awareness that I wasn't where I was supposed to be.

When I'd been with Dare back at the Silver Tip compound, I'd nearly forgotten about that ache. It was back now, and it had been since Dare told me I was free. Was this fate calling me home to Astria?

Heat rose in my face, and I rubbed my eyelids as the familiar prick of tears threatened. Alone, away from the eyes of the pack, I let the tears fall. Before I showed up in Dare's basement, the only time I'd cried was when my parents were killed. I locked away every single emotion, refusing to let Xan have anything.

Now I couldn't hold back. I had my family again, and they were safe—well, they would be as soon as we made it home.

Wiping away my tears, I turned to see Dare sitting on the ground next to G, and a smiling Jude—now in his human form—who sat with his back against a tree, munching on an apple.

I walked over and sat down next to him. I grabbed his water and took a swig. "You're lucky you're alive."

Jude sobered immediately, and his head dropped. "I'm know."

"That was a stupid fucking plan."

"It was."

Dare leaned forward. "I hope you understand what you put your brother through. And the pack."

I wanted to snap at Dare, to tell him that Jude was my brother and I'd discipline him as I saw fit. But as of now, Jude was still a member of Dare's pack. And Dare still outranked all of us. It'd always been hard for me to see my brother and sister disciplined by someone who wasn't me. Dare had a point though, so I kept my mouth shut.

Also? I didn't need to be an ungrateful asshole. My family was alive and together. Dare was to thank for that. He'd risked a lot to rescue Selene.

"I'm sorry," Jude said, sufficiently ashamed.

When I met Dare's gaze, he was studying my face, his head slightly tilted, lips thinned into a grim line. Was he…trying to read my mind? "Dare?"

He blinked a couple of times, then with a slight shake of his head, he said, "I'm going to go check on Nash." He stood up and, with stiff movements, walked over to the thin Were. Nash had shifted, but even in his Were form, he looked sickly.

G was watching them, and turned to me with sad eyes. "I don't know if he'll make it."

"Who is that?"

"A Silver Tip."

"Really?"

"He left before I ever joined the pack, so I don't know the whole story."

Dare ran his hands over the Were, who stared up at him with a little bit of adoration. Something shifted in my chest. I turned to Jude. "So give me details. You got caught?"

"I tried to go in the same way we came out. Guard saw me struggling with the stone."

"Damn, Jude."

"I'm sorry! I was so desperate to get to Selene. I didn't think my scent would be strong enough for them to detect me. I was wrong. As soon as they realized who I was, Xan went batshit. Asked me about you. I told him you were dead, but he didn't believe me. Beat me to get me to talk about you, and when I wouldn't talk, threw me in the Hole. Last thing I heard was that he ordered someone to bring him Selene, so I was sure I screwed up."

"Fuck," I muttered.

"I knew it was a matter of time before they pulled me out and went to work on me again—" A low growl cut him off, and we turned to see G with his lips curled back. Jude smiled at him and squeezed his leg. "—but then I heard some sort of crash. I think the brothers saw me as a distraction, and that's when they started the fight for power. I thought I'd die down there in the Hole."

I looked over his shoulder at Hans and Selene huddled together. "What happened with Hans?"

Jude chewed the inside of his cheek. "I don't know. I was

in the Hole the whole time. I heard them throw someone into the Hole near mine, but that was it."

"Hmm. I'll have to ask Selene."

"How's Hans doing?"

"I don't know. He's in his wolf form now, so we'll see when he shifts back."

Jude muttered something to G, but I wasn't listening, my attention on Dare as he spoke in low tones to Nash.

I was so confused about where I stood with Dare. There was so much change and uncertainty that I was off-kilter. The security of my relationship with my mate was eroding like a flooded riverbank. I was still grasping for it while it slipped through my fingers.

He'd come to mean the world to me in a month. I'd thought all I needed was Selene and Jude to make a home, but now I wasn't so sure I could ever be home without Dare.

He'd told me to go. But what if that wasn't my choice?

Dare

NASH HAD SHIFTED, BUT EVEN as a Were, his body was emaciated. He lay on his side, jaws gaping as his sides heaved. I'd instructed Vaughn to give him some water and a bit of food. My guard stood over him, clearly distressed and unsure what to do.

I clapped Vaughn on the shoulder. "I'll take it from here. Go get some rest."

Vaughn held my gaze, zero humor in his brown eyes,

then he nodded and walked away with slumped shoulders.

I knelt next to Nash and ran a hand over his furred head. His large eyes rolled to me, and with a shudder, he shifted back to his human form.

"Why did you shift back?" I frowned.

He shrugged his shoulders, a weak jerk. "Doesn't matter, Dare. We both know it."

"That's not true," I said. "We have healers back at Silver Tip. They can take a look at you."

With a groan, he rolled onto his back, knees bent. He stared up at the sky, and licked his cracked lips. He was silent for a long time before he said with a shaky voice. "How's Bay?"

The question caught me off guard, but talking about Bay wasn't a hardship. I was eager to get home to see him. And maybe the change of topic would take Nash's mind off his health. I settled down on the ground beside his head. "Bay's good."

Another long pause. "Tell me more."

I squinted up at the sun. "Well, he's grown up like you. He's not as tall as me, but he's solid. He's funny, just like he was as a novus. The pack loves him. He's my second-in-command. In fact, he's back taking care of the pack while I came to rescue my mate's family."

Nash squeezed his eyes shut. "That's good. I'm glad to hear it."

"You can see him for yourself when we get you home and healed up."

His laugh was hoarse. "Right."

I didn't know what to make of his responses. I hadn't known him that well as a novus. "What happened, Nash? How the hell did you end up in the Hole at the Bluefoot compound?"

Nash coughed and his face paled. "Another time, Alpha. If that's all right? Another story for another time."

"Sure." I squeezed his shoulder. "We're going to get moving soon. I want to get home as soon as possible. You going to be okay?"

He nodded. "Don't worry about me."

I helped him to his feet, and although he was weak as hell, he at least could walk without help now. We were about to enter the Nowere territory and my nerves were on edge. How the hell was I going to keep this pack safe? We had werewolves and injuries, and had grown in size more than I'd anticipated.

I walked to the edge of the clearing and peered into the woods, tilting my head up to get a scent. There it was. A very faint strain of Nowere drifting on the breeze. They were out there, and no one felt the responsibility of keeping everyone alive like I did.

A hand settled on my back, and the smell of Reese replaced the lingering stench of Nowere.

"Hey." He had that submissive look in his eyes, the one I hated. It reminded me of how he'd reacted to me back when we first met. Had he already shut off the part of him that cared about me? Maybe he never had. Maybe the mate bond was all that was there.

It was going to take some time for me to cauterize my

raw wounds over the loss of my mate. I slid my eyes to him, then straight ahead. "We need to move."

"Look, Dare—"

I didn't want to do this now. "Are you ready?"

"Will you let me speak?"

I went silent, the plea in his tone like a twisting knife in my skin. He waited a beat before starting over. "Thank you. I don't know how else to say it. You risked so much, and still *are* risking a lot to save my family."

I turned my head and locked eyes with his. What was I looking for? A sign that this hurt him as much as it hurt me? I was going to miss him with every bone in my body, with every beat of my heart. I slipped a hand into his hair, and his eyes fluttered before popping back open. His body swayed into mine, and his hand settled on my waist.

The naked need shone in his blue eyes, and this was all too much for me. I had to finalize this, stab one last knife into the bloody body of our bond. He deserved to know the truth before he gave me hope. I steeled myself for this reaction. "We have reports that Astria, and particularly the Whitethroat pack, are being repopulated."

Reese's entire body froze, and his eyes went wide. He blinked at me a couple of times before taking a step away, his brows lowering. "What did you say?"

"Our scout saw what looked to be inhabitants of Astria again, in the old Whitethroat compound. She smelled werewolves."

Reese's fists clenched at his sides. "When?"

"Weeks ago."

"She saw them weeks ago or you found out weeks ago?"

I didn't hesitate. "I found out weeks ago."

Reese sucked in a breath and turned away, the muscles in his jaw clenching. If he thought some of his pack was still alive, he'd be drawn to them, and despite our mate bond, it'd be hard to resist that draw. "You didn't tell me when you found out."

"I did not," I said. "I'm telling you now. And I'm also telling you to take your family and return home."

"You withheld this pretty fucking important information from me, but now that I lied to you, this is your excuse to send me away, is that it?"

It *was* an excuse to send him away, but it had nothing to do with him lying, and everything to do with wanting him to live the life he'd been denied. But I wasn't going to tell him that. It was better for both of us if he wasn't conflicted about his choice. "Do you not want to go?"

"Of course I want to go," he growled. "Everything inside of me is pulling toward home right now, knowing I have family there. But I'm coming home with you first. I want to say bye to Bay and Mav."

"'Course."

Our eyes locked. "What about you?" he asked.

"What about me?"

"What are you going to do?"

"I'm going to do what I did before you came, Reese." *Now with a hole in my heart.*

His mouth dropped open, but I was done with this conversation. "Gather your wolves. We need to leave."

"Can't we talk about this?"

I gritted my teeth. "Gather. Your. Wolves."

His nostrils flared, and his eyes narrowed. "Fine." He turned to stomp off, but while I was done with words, I wasn't quite done with him. I gripped his bicep, and tugged him to me. He smashed against my chest with a grunt, and I didn't let him get a breath before taking his mouth.

He was stiff for about five seconds before melting against me, opening his mouth and kissing me the way only Reese kissed. The way I'd taught him. With everything he had.

I gripped his head, controlling the kiss, controlling him, wanting him to know how much I didn't want things to be this way.

When I broke the kiss, his eyes were half-closed, lips red, swollen, and glistening. He blinked up at me, taking a moment to come back to himself. I let him go, and he stumbled before righting himself. "I'll, uh, go gather my pack, then."

I nodded, swallowing down words that threatened to come out. "That sounds like a plan."

When he left me, I inhaled sharply and exhaled slowly. Power flowed through my veins, tingling down to the tips of my fingers and toes. Selfishly, I was going to miss that too. I'd only just begun to understand all the power that the True Mate bond had given me.

But I couldn't justify clinging to power while my mate was miserable. I loved him, I knew. Beyond the mate bond, beyond anything in this world. I loved him because he was Reese, because he was smart and brave and loyal. I loved him too much to see him die a little inside every day he was denied freedom, denied his birth pack.

G stopped at my side, staring ahead into the woods of Nowere land with me. I could tell he was nervous too. Traveling with a party this large, moving slow because of injuries, wasn't a position any of us wanted to be in. His throat bobbed as he swallowed.

"Gav," I said.

At his full name, he turned to me, one eyebrow raised in his serious face. For so many years, I'd taken G for granted. His loyalty and strength. His bravery. I placed a hand on his shoulder. "What are your feelings for Jude?"

He was quiet for a moment, his lips pressed into a thin line. Finally, he said so quietly I could barely hear him, "I'm his."

I'd never thought I'd see the day G would willingly declare himself as someone else's. But then, Jude was something special.

I sighed heavily. "After this, I'm sending Reese and his brother and sister home. To Astria."

G's eyes widened, and his body vibrated with tension beneath my hand.

I forced out the words. "You're free to go with them."

He didn't move, his muscles freezing. "Alpha—"

"They'll need protection. And this way you won't have to be separated from Jude."

He just stared at me, clearly at a loss for words.

"I told Reese about the scout reports from Astria. He knows. He wants to go home to his family. I'm within my rights to keep him with me, but I can't, G. I can't leave my pack and give him his home at the same time." I tilted my head. "What would you do in my position?"

I held my breath until he said, "Same as you, Alpha. I'd do the same as you."

I clapped him on the shoulder and dropped my hand. "Well, let's hope our instincts are right, then."

I turned to call to the pack, but G stopped me with a hand on my arm. "Did you discuss alternatives with Reese? Other options?"

"What's the point? He said he wants to go, that he feels the pull."

"What if your mate pull is stronger?" he asked.

Reese was standing with his brother and sister, drinking from a canteen. He handed it off to Jude, then wiped his mouth with the back of his hand. He laughed at something Selene said, and the vision of that joy was like a punch in the stomach. "It's not, G." The words barely hurt anymore. "It's not."

CHAPTER SEVENTEEN

Reese

MY BODY, MIND, AND HEART were three separate beings, all with different goals and ideas on what I should be doing. My heart wanted Dare. Full stop. It only wanted Dare, his arms around me, his mouth on mine, his whispered words in my ear. But I'd lied to him, and that was a deal breaker. I was done in his eyes, no matter the bond we shared. No matter what my heart wanted.

My body wanted to run home to Astria right now. The pull was unmistakable. Just knowing some of my pack could be alive had me in flight mode.

And my mind? It was a jumbled mess, trying to reconcile the heart and the body in a way that was logical. Except nothing was fucking logical in this. Fate had given me a True Mate in a fucked-up world during a fucked-up lifetime.

Because of the mix of Were and werewolf, we decided to travel in our human forms to make communication easier. It was slower-going, though, which had Dare on a razor-thin edge. His entire body was tense, his hands balled into fists as he led us through Nowere land.

He'd given us a game plan before we'd left the clearing.

In the event of a Nowere attack, Weres were to shift and surround the wolves as protection. If we had to move like that, we would, in a sort of pod. In theory that was great. But we all knew if we met with a large Nowere pack, it wouldn't fucking matter what kind of formation we had. It wouldn't be an organized fight. It'd be a chaotic massacre.

Selene held onto Hans, who only needed minimal help now. She was still wearing her dirty, blood-stained dress and her hair now hung in ragged, sweaty clumps. I couldn't wait until we got home. I was going to burn that fucking dress. She met my gaze and shot me a wobbly smile, which I returned.

Jude hadn't left G's side since he was rescued, gazing up adoringly at his giant. Even now, G's hand was planted on Jude's shoulder, a symbol of protection I appreciated.

The injured Were, Nash, brought up the rear. Watching him try to walk was painful, and his gaunt face was pinched in pain. The Silver Tip pack had some great healers, and I hoped he wasn't too far gone. I worried though, as he was as close to walking death as I'd ever seen. Other than Noweres, of course.

The terrain wasn't bad, a mostly wooded area. The underbrush was low and easy to walk through. Still, I worried we were making too much noise, and Dare must have had the same thought, because he would occasionally glare at someone who was hacking away at nearby branches too loudly.

The path began to look familiar, and I hoped we were close to the Silver Tip compound when Dare stopped suddenly. His head went up, his nostrils flared, and he raised his hands as a signal for us all to stop. I expected someone to grumble, but everyone in our group must have sensed the alarm in Dare's body language.

Slowly his head turned, his eyes cutting right to me. For a moment we locked eyes, and when he parted his lips, my brain pulsed. *Pulsed.* As if there a thought that was fighting its way out. My heart beat double-time, like an echo, and I gripped my chest. Dare looked away, and the sensation fled as fast as it had come. Had I imagined that?

I didn't have time to dwell, because the smell hit me next.

Nowere.

We all scented it, and Dare began to issue quiet orders. "Everyone shift. Weres, close ranks in a circle around the wolves. Wolves, surround the wounded." He pointed at G and Rua. "We're on the offensive. Everyone else, defense. Got it?"

"Dare—" I began.

"They're coming," Dare said. "I thought we had more time, but the pack must be moving."

"How many?" G cracked his neck.

Dare sniffed, and I strained to listen, catching the unmistakable sound of Nowere chattering. "Fuck," I muttered.

"Close," Dare said. "Another minute."

Selena and Hans were in an embrace, her lips moving as she spoke to him quietly. His focus was on her, nodding diligently. Jude was in G's arms, and G had to forcefully shove him off before he dropped a kiss on my brother's head and shifted into the massive Were that he was.

The chattering was closer now, along with the sounds of many feet crashing toward us. Dare stood five feet away, still human despite the entire pack shifting. He swallowed, his Adam's apple bobbing. "Reese."

"Stay alive," I blurted out. "You gotta stay alive."

He blinked, those green eyes flashing at me before they turned black. "You too," he said. His hand shot out, and he grabbed me, hauling me in for a kiss as he shifted. The hair on his chin sprouted against my face, and I wondered if this would be the last time I'd see him.

I stumbled back, and a fully shifted Dare roared so loudly the ground trembled beneath my feet. Did Noweres feel fear? Because that was fucking terrifying. I was still shaking as I shifted into my wolf form.

I retreated behind the ranks of Weres just as the first Nowere crashed into view. He was missing half his face, and one hand dangled from a disjointed wrist. His fur hung in mangy clumps, and he fucking *stunk*. He gnashed his teeth as four Noweres arrived at his back. Then he charged.

After that, *chaos.*

We wolves huddled around Hans and Nash, prepared to take on Noweres who crashed through the ranks of the Weres protecting us. G was a massive tornado, his large body cutting swaths of carnage through the onslaught of Noweres—ripping off heads, stabbing torsos. Dare fought more efficiently, cleanly breaking necks and felling Noweres with swipes of his claws.

Rua was a smaller whirlwind, ducking behind Noweres

to kill them with a slash across their necks, never letting them gather a large offensive.

The rest of the pack held formation, protecting us when Noweres got away from the main three killing machines and tried to make a run for us. I was well aware I wasn't as equipped as the Weres. I couldn't kill without getting too close, and even a scratch from a Nowere would bring me down. So I held back and growled and seethed, preparing to do anything I could to protect my family.

A shout went up behind me, and I whirled around to see Caro down. Three Noweres were on him, dragging him away, and by the amount of blood on Caro's body, I knew he was a goner. I didn't have time to mourn, because his absence left a gaping hole in our ranks. Three more Noweres advanced, ready to infiltrate. Two were taken out by the Weres on either side of the gap, but one Nowere was heading right for me. His leg had a gaping thigh wound, exposing muscle and bone. He was missing an arm, but still had a full jaw—better to eat me with.

I lowered my head to the ground on a snarl, searching his body for vulnerable spots where I could tear out a brain or spine or other vital part of his existence.

His massive, clawed hand came swiping down, intent on taking off my head, so I leaped. He screeched, chattering at me, as I opened up my jaws, ready to rip out his throat. But his other hand lashed out, catching me in the midsection. The crack of my ribs drove a piercing pain through my chest, and the force of the blow sent me flying into a nearby tree trunk.

I hit it on my other side, and another crack sent raging flames of pain across my chest. The edges of my sight began to darken, the pain consuming me. As I fell to the ground, the last thing I heard was Dare's roar before everything went dark.

Dare

MY HEART STOPPED WHEN I turned to see a Nowere swipe at Reese. His wolf body flew through the air until he hit a tree trunk with a pained squeal. An immediate crippling flare of pain slammed into my ribs.

The pain, the sight of my mate's crumpled body at the base of the tree, and the advancing Noweres sent me into a tailspin of destruction.

I roared, power surging through me like I'd never felt before. I raced toward my mate, taking out Noweres on either side of me. I didn't care about formation or rank anymore.

Mate. Mine. Hurt.

A Nowere was advancing toward his prone body, teeth bared, and I picked up the filthy, disgusting thing, bashing its head into the tree repeatedly until it was no more than a mass of bloody flesh. Then I slashed my claws across his neck and beheaded it.

I picked up Reese, cradling his wolf body in my arms. His eyes didn't open, and when I ran my hands over his sides, I could feel his cracked ribs beneath his beautiful gray fur. His white throat was stained with blood, and I screamed, my lungs burning as I filled the forest with my frustration.

When I turned around, my pack was watching me. There wasn't a Nowere in sight. Jude had shifted back to his human form and he clung to a bloody, heaving G, also in human form. "We dispatched the pack," G said, his voice hoarse.

I shifted back, still cradling Reese's body to me. Selene ran to us as I knelt and placed Reese on the ground amid some softer brush. Now that I could look at him closely, I determined he was breathing, although labored. The blood on his throat came from his nose and a cut on his mouth.

I ran my fingers down his spine, testing for any injuries to his back, and a front paw twitched. Selene wasn't making a sound, but tears ran down her cheeks, and she pressed her fists to her mouth as she blinked up at me, pleading for me to do something.

We were vulnerable here, and I didn't like it. With my mate injured, I didn't have a choice. I could carry him the rest of the way home, but the thought of hurting him worse during transport was unacceptable.

My pack stood around us, silent and restless. Rua hadn't taken her eyes off me, and it hit me that she was concerned about me too. If Reese died, so would I. My main priority was to keep him alive because he was *Reese*.

I shifted him slightly so his head was cradled in my lap. G handed me a wet cloth, and I carefully wiped away the blood on his fur, my stomach churning when his beautiful white throat remained stained pink.

His instinct had been to protect. He hadn't cared that the Noweres were really no match for a wolf his size. He'd do anything he could to protect those he loved. I wanted to see those pretty blue eyes, that cocky grin. I wanted to feel his arms around me, his lips on mine.

"Reese," I said softly. "Wake up, baby. Wake up." His tail thumped once. I stroked the fur on his head. "Let me see your eyes, little wolf."

His sides heaved, and a shudder ran through his body. His eyes opened, the blue cloudy, but they were open, and he was alive, blinking at me as a whine started low in his throat.

He shifted immediately to human form with a pained cry. He landed on his hands and knees, head low between his shoulders and livid bruises covering his sides.

His head swung to me, and through a cut lip and bruised cheek, he whispered hoarsely. "Hurts." Another tremble traveled down his spine.

I gathered him in my arms, pressing him to me as tight as I dared as he buried his face my neck, curling against me like my skin would make him feel better.

"I hit the tree and thought that was it." His voice was muffled. "I thought he broke my back and I was done." He blinked up at me with a popped blood vessel in his left eye, and managed a grin. "I guess I'm hard to kill."

My throat was closing up, and I was dangerously close to breaking down. "Good. I like you alive."

"I like me alive too." He twisted his body to look over his shoulder and immediately cried out, clutching his side.

"Okay, well, I'm alive but I'm seriously fucked up."

"Reese," I said.

"Yeah?"

"I felt it."

"What?"

I ran a hand down my side. "When you hit the tree. I felt it."

My words took a moment to process, and then his eyes widened. "What the fuck? The power draw and now this? Can you read my mind yet?"

I shook my head. "I thought earlier I could. I felt a pulse in my brain?"

Reese gripped my arms, his nails digging in. "Me too!"

"Fuck, I wish this wasn't happening now…"

My voice trailed off. There was no point dwelling on it right now. When we got back to the Silver Tip compound, maybe we could investigate it a little more. Before he left.

I rose to my feet, Reese pressed to my side. I was about to address my pack, when my nose caught a scent.

No. No no *no*. G smelled it too, and his eyes widened a half second before the chattering reached our ears.

Another pack, and this time, I wasn't confident at all we'd make it, not with our ranks depleted. Most of my Weres were hurt, and my mate severely injured.

For the first time in my reign as alpha, I didn't know what to do. Reese's nostrils were flaring, and he was muttering "oh fuck, oh fuck," as he smelled and heard the Nowere pack drawing closer. We couldn't run, we could barely fight, and how had I let this happen? My gaze met

Reese's, and this time there was no grin, there was only resignation.

"Go on," said a craggy voice. Next to us, Nash stumbled to his feet. He waved his hand at me. "Now. Go."

"What do you mean?" Reese asked.

"Nash—" I began.

He was walking away from me, his ribs sharp beneath his skin. "I'm heading out to meet the pack. It'll distract them long enough for you guys to get away."

"No," I said firmly. "Absolutely not—"

He turned to me with a snarl. "Don't. An alpha's job is to do what's best for his pack. What's best is for you to sacrifice one to save many. You know it. I know it. I'm half-gone anyway."

Reese's hand tightened on my arm as he sucked in a breath. The Nowere stench filled my nostrils, searing my lungs, and the chattering distracted me. Nash was right. Fuck, but he was right. To save my pack, I had to let him go. Allow him to sacrifice himself.

"I don't want to do this," I said.

He chuckled darkly. "I know, but as alpha of the Silver Tip pack, you will."

I nodded. "I will."

Nash's shoulders sagged in relief. He met my gaze. "C-can you tell Bay?"

I wasn't sure what he wanted me to tell him. So I said what I planned to tell my brother. "I'll him you're a hero."

Nash made a sound in his throat, like a sob, before smiling. "Perfect." He gave himself a shake, face hardening.

"Now, fucking go."

Right, if Nash was willing to do this, then I had to make sure his sacrifice was worth it. "Everyone shift," I ordered. "I'm carrying Reese, we gotta really put some distance between us and the Nowere pack, all right?"

When I was surrounded by Weres and wolves, I shifted, picked up my mate, and we all began to run.

I glanced over my shoulder, and the last I saw of Nash was his broad back, head high, as he crashed through the forest on his way to the pack of Noweres.

He was a hero, all right.

CHAPTER EIGHTEEN

Reese

EVERY JARRING MOVEMENT OF DARE'S heavy and swift footfalls was a bolt of agony through my body, but I gritted my teeth and rode it out. He panted at the burden of my extra weight as he ran at a relentless pace with the rest of the pack. I'd shifted back to my wolf form, and he wore me across his shoulders and neck like a scarf, holding onto my front and back paws as he ran. My injuries were too severe to heal quickly and would take time.

I think I passed out a couple of times from the pain, going limp only to flinch awake with a whole new level of suffering.

The only good news was that we saw zero signs of Noweres. After encountering two deadly packs back-to-back, fate was taking it easy on us the rest of the way. Still, the speed we were traveling was nearly impossible to sustain with the amount of injuries we bore.

Dare directed us to stop at the same clearing where we'd rested on the way. Everyone shifted and took the time to rest up, eating and drinking what provisions we had left.

My mate hadn't let me out of his sight; in fact, he hadn't

let me out of his arms. We sat against a tree on the soft ground. He ran his fingers through my hair, over my ribs and the bruises on my face and back. "You're healing well," he muttered.

The broken bones had begun to knit, which was *not* a comfortable feeling at all. "Yeah."

He held my head in his callused grip, studying my face before sliding one finger down my forehead. "You're in pain, though, I can see the tenseness."

I nodded. "It's okay, Dare."

He frowned, his nostrils flaring once, before shoving a canteen of water in my face. "We'll get you healed up. You'll be fine. No worse for wear."

"I know." I wanted to dwell on the care Dare had shown me after I'd been wounded, but I was sure it was only relief I hadn't died. As he'd said, if I died, he'd perish shortly after. The True Mate bond fucked him that way. He was sending me away; my welfare was only important because he needed me to stay alive.

He ripped off a piece of jerky with his teeth, chewing half and giving the other to me. He stared at the grass beneath us while swallowing. "When I saw you fall to the ground, my skin got hot, like I was burning from the inside out." He shook his head before lifting his eyes to me. "Never felt that before."

I moved closer. "Right before the pack hit us, did you..." I couldn't think of words to describe the sensation. "Did you feel like something was in your brain?"

He pulled out another piece of jerky silently, his brow

furrowed. He took a bite and swallowed before answering. "I did."

"What was that?"

He shook his head. "I'm not sure. I..." He waved a hand, a hard mask slipping over his face. "It doesn't matter now."

"What if I come back?" I blurted out. "What if I go to Astria and come back?"

He raised an eyebrow but wouldn't look at me directly. "Why would you want to come back?"

"What if no one is there? What if your scout is wrong?"

He took a long time drinking his water before he pulled off with a gasp. "Do you think the scout is wrong? What do you feel in your heart?"

My stomach rolled. "I don't think the scout is wrong."

His smile was grim. "Neither do I. And you'd leave your pack to return to me?"

I stayed silent at that. Would I? Yes, my wolf nature begged to return home, to be reunited with my pack, but what then? Dare would be back in Eury, wasting away without me. What if I returned home, only to feel the pull to be back with Dare?

He stood up, towering over me. "It's best if you leave with no intention of coming back. If I think there's hope..." He shrugged his massive shoulders. "It'll be much worse."

A sick feeling spread through my body like poison. "Of course."

He nodded, then walked away to see to his pack. My gut tightened as the distance spread between us. I didn't know what to rely on anymore, instinct or my heart. Were they telling me the same thing?

As soon as Dare left my side, Selene and Jude descended on me, touching and hugging and assuring themselves I was okay. I batted their hands away. "Quit crowding me."

Selene's careful touch now turned into a slap to my shoulder.

"Ouch!" I said rubbing the skin.

"I will touch you as much as I want, brother. I thought you died!" The fury in her eyes quickly melted away as the tears began to run. She dropped her face into her hands, and sobs shook her body. "Just when I'd gotten you back."

I gathered her into my arms. She'd been through so much, and I was eager to get her behind stone walls where she was safe. "I'm sorry. That was a dick move on my part."

Jude sat on his haunches next to us, nibbling his lip. I reached out and drew him into our hug. With a kiss pressed to Selene's temple, I said, "But I'm all right. In pain, but I'll heal."

Selene leaned back and picked at the ragged hem of her dress. "So what's the Silver Tip pack like?"

I poked a finger through a hole in the fabric. "They're good Weres." I hesitated, thinking of Gage. "Okay, well most of them are good."

"More good apples then bad?" she asked.

"Definitely," Jude answered. "Most of them are like G and Dare. They want their pack to survive peacefully."

She still didn't look convinced, her eyes wary. "What about how they treat heat?"

I threaded my fingers through hers. "The female gets to choose her mate during heat. Nobody is forced."

She blew out a breath and offered me a relieved smile. "That's great."

"Wait until you meet Bay," Jude said, his grin huge. "He's Dare's brother. He's funny, and everyone loves him."

Selene's grin grew larger. "I can't wait."

I didn't know how to broach the subject, but they needed to understand what was in store for us. "There's something you both need to know, something which will affect our future."

Selene's fingers tightened in mine as she leaned closer. Jude frowned. "What?"

"Dare told me a scout reported that Astria is being rebuilt. There could be Whitethroat pack members there."

My sister gasped, her hand going to her mouth, while Jude's jaw dropped. "Really?"

"Really." I decided to wait until after we were back at the Silver Tip pack to announce we'd be leaving. There'd be time once we rested and ate. "We'll talk about what we'll do when we get home, okay?"

"Home." Selene tested the word in her mouth, gaze holding a little bit of wonder. "Will we have that again, Reese? A home?"

I drew her closer, wrapping an arm around her shoulder, while I patted Jude on the back. "Yes, we will. I promise you both, we'll have a home again." *Somewhere.*

Selene sighed in my arms, Jude rest his head on my shoulder, and I closed my eyes.

We'd have that again, in this life.

Dare

I DIDN'T WANT TO LEAVE the clearing. It was peaceful there, the trees lining our sanctuary providing shade from afternoon sun. But we needed to get home. The pull of my pack was strong. I'd been away from them for far too long, and I was restless.

Reese sat with his siblings on the outskirts of the clearing. I watched as he opened his eyes and looked right at me, as if he knew I'd been watching him. I felt pulled toward him too, in my heart, in my body. My Were would rage when he left.

I thought once again about forbidding him to leave and making him stay with me. But would he be the same if he was denied his pack?

If he left, I couldn't think about the possibility he'd come back. That would only lead me to madness. Once I sent him away, I was going to have to do everything I could to forget about him, to erase him from my existence.

My chest tightened, pain sliced down my heart as it cracked, and I rubbed the skin over it. Reese's eyes tracked my movements before returning to my face. I nodded at him, and he began to rouse his brother and sister.

I turned back to my pack. "We'll shift again, maintain a fast pace, and be home by nightfall. Anyone think they can't handle that?"

There were no objections.

Everyone shifted, and I once again picked up Reese, knowing he wanted to protest but was unable to in wolf form. Which made me smile a bit.

Then we were off again, racing through the woods. We weren't stopping until we got home. The ache of missing Bay and Mav and my pack was now a cramping in my gut. I knew Reese was healing every minute he was in wolf form, but that still didn't stop my desire to get home and see him curled up in the middle of my bed, getting my blanket covered in gray fur.

I wanted his pink-stained throat white again.

And then I'd say goodbye.

By the time we reached the gates, the sun was half obscured by the horizon. My shoulders ached from Reese's weight, and something sharp had wedged itself between my footpads.

I shifted to human form, the entire pack following my lead—including Reese—and I hollered out to the scouts who manned the gates. "Your alpha is back, open up!"

I waited, eager to get inside and see my pack while Reese stood at my side, still holding his ribs tenderly. All around me was the ragged breathing of the group I'd pushed to the brink of exhaustion.

The gates remained closed, and I huffed out a breath and approached them to bang on the wood with my fist. "Hey! Wake up!"

No response.

I glanced around, hoping my shouts didn't draw Nowere

attention. I raised my fist to knock again as the gate finally began to open. I stepped back out of the way, and sighed in relief...which was cut short as soon as I caught sight of what was happening behind the walls.

Gage stood with his arms crossed over his chest, several wolves flanking him, blocking our entrance. My heart pounded, and a trickle of sweat dripped down my back. A low growl next to me signaled Rua was not pleased, and I could feel the waves of hatred coming off G. Vaughn cracked his knuckles.

Next to me, Reese began to shake.

Gage smiled, and I didn't return it. "So I see you made it back," he said. His gaze scanned the rescue group. "Looks like you had some trouble."

"I'm not in the mood for this, Gage. It's been a long day and we'd all like to get inside and rest."

"Ah." Gage held up a finger. "See, this is awkward." He waved his hand, and from behind him came a shuffling sound. Gage stepped to the side, and a mass of flesh and blood and rags was tossed to the ground at his feet.

"Gage—" I began, but my words died as the mass raised its head, and Bay blinked at me with two swollen eyes. He tried for something like a grin, though it was red and lopsided. "Hey, brother."

Gage swung his booted foot and caught my brother in the ribs. Bay didn't make a sound, but curled in on himself. The ratting of the silver chains binding him echoed off the stone walls.

I didn't move, my gaze on my brother, my Bay, the best

thing my parents every produced. A better Were than me. A type of calm descended over me as he went still. I'd known this day would come, but I hadn't thought Gage would stoop this low. I shut off everything—my exhaustion, my worry over Reese, my sadness about him leaving. Inside, my blood was pumping liquid fire into my veins, every muscle on alert. I only felt the steely determination that I would kill Gage. My focus narrowed to him and only him as I raised my eyes to lock with his.

He held out his hands at his sides, striding forward to stand in front of Bay's prone form. "You left, Alpha. And it wasn't hard to gather several Weres who've had enough of your passive rule."

I didn't say a word, as I was already envisioning slitting his throat.

"I promised them things you didn't," he said. "Things you won't do. We don't want to toil behind these walls anymore. We're Weres. We want to raid and take. We want different food, and riches, and wolves to fuck." His eyes drifted to Selene, then back to me. "We want the rule my dad and your father envisioned. Until you and your bitch mom fucked it up."

I ignored the jab as best as I could, knowing it was supposed to make me lash out irrationally. "Where's the rest of the pack?" I asked, my main concern for Mav.

"They know better. After they saw what happened to Bay when he tried to fight us… They knew better."

I got to the point. "Are you challenging me?"

Gage laughed, an evil sound rumbling from his chest.

"Yes, Dare. I am."

I pointed to my pack behind me. "They're vulnerable out here. Let them inside first."

He made a face. "Nah."

More incentive to get this over quickly. I sneered. "Spoken like a true alpha who really cares about his pack."

"Maybe you should have thought about that before picking all your most loyal Weres to accompany you on your little mission for one fucking wolf."

I clenched my fists. "I'm going to really enjoy seeing your body at my feet."

His eyes narrowed, and he curled his lips. "So you accept the challenge?"

"Accepted." I shifted immediately and leapt.

CHAPTER NINETEEN

Reese

My heart slammed up into my throat, nearly choking me, and my ribs screamed as every muscle in my body tensed.

Dare was...magnificent. Despite our journey and all we'd been through the last couple of days, he looked stronger than ever. Were my eyes playing tricks on me? He seemed larger and bulkier, his claws sharper.

I guessed if the True Mate bond power was kicking in now, it was as good a time as any.

I didn't have much time to dwell, because Gage and Dare were circling each other, snapping their jaws. Gage bobbed on the balls of his Were feet, kicking up dust.

I glanced behind me, sniffing the air for Nowere scent, but I smelled and heard nothing. Jude stood in front of G, his teeth bared, his eyes wild. I hadn't had much time to witness my brother's actions after his muto, but pride swelled at the sight of his anger. In another couple of months, he'd be even tougher. Behind him, G met my eyes, and I swallowed nervously. He gave me a short nod, then turned his attention back to the challenge.

Dare attacked first, swiping at Gage with one clawed

hand before turning and lashing out with a high kick. Gage dodged the claws, but not the foot, catching a nasty blow on the side of his face. He roared and advanced, swiping at Dare's vulnerable stomach so that Dare was forced to retreat to avoid being disemboweled.

"You have to beat him, you have to beat him," I muttered. I wished I could do something. Like send Dare power, or encouragement, or anything to help him defeat Gage and take back control of his pack and compound. But I didn't know how. Why didn't the True Mate bond come with a damn manual?

Bay was conscious now, laying on his side, watching the fight. His gaze slid to me, and I thought he'd smile, give me a sign that this would all be okay, but instead, he only gazed at me intently, his expression solemn, before dropping his head back to the dirt. My heart sank.

The front of the compound was a tornado of dirt now as the two alpha Weres scuffled over the ground. Gage's face was bleeding, and he was limping slightly, while Dare's shoulder was cut.

The Weres supporting Gage began to close ranks, making a circle around the fighters. I started forward, pissed off they were blocking more of my view, when G stopped me with a growled warning. "You enter that circle and you're fair game, remember?"

Shit, he was right. The last thing Dare needed was to have to save my ass as well as his own. "But I can't see everything."

G's eyes were on the fight. "I know. I don't like it either.

Normally we'd be on a platform, looking down, but this is…an unconventional challenge."

Dare was winning, though, that much I could see. For every blow that Dare connected, Gage missed when he tried to retaliate. While Dare still stood strong on two legs, his eyes clear, Gage was stumbling and glassy-eyed.

Something shiny flashed, and a pained cry came from one of the two Weres. I darted forward, as close as I dared, to see Dare stumble back, clutching his side, as Gage advanced. Dare's hand fell away to reveal a ragged, raw wound that bore the unmistakable mark of silver. The pungent stink of burning flesh filled the air.

"G, he cut Dare!" I called over my shoulder. "He cut him with silver!"

G's eyes flared. "You're a cheating motherfucker just like your uncle, Gage! The pack won't get behind a cheating alpha—"

Gage's response was powerful swipe of his claws, catching Dare in the face and rocking him clean off his feet. He fell to the earth with a thud.

The ground shook, and every cell in my body seemed to swell to the point of pain. Every instinct in me screamed to help my mate. The silver would have weakened an already exhausted Dare. Gage advanced on him, and I felt that same pulsing in my brain as I'd felt earlier. This time it was stronger, sharper, the pulsing slowly giving way to a constant ache that grew, pain intensifying, until my vision began to short out, and my legs gave way. I fell to the ground, holding my head. A scream rent the air and it took me several seconds to realize the sound was coming from me.

Just when I thought it was too much, that my skull was going to crack open to reveal only gray mush, the pain subsided, and in its place, was a voice.

Run.

My head shot up.

Dare stumbled to his feet and swayed, but managed to stay upright while Gage advanced on him.

Go home now. Run!

That was Dare's voice. In my head. His gaze slid to me. *Please, little wolf.*

Where was home? I wanted to say. Instead I shook my head. *No. I won't leave you.* I inhaled, gathering all the power I had in me, all the energy I would normally expend to shift, and shoved it at Dare through the new-found mental connection we shared.

His body jolted like he'd been struck by an imaginary fist, and he darted his eyes to me one last time, narrowing them. *Why did you—*

Gage caught him on the cheek with a punch, the sound of flesh hitting flesh drawing a gasp from Selene. Dare didn't even move his feet as he absorbed the blow. Then, with an upward cut across his body with his massive clawed paw, he caught Gage on the chin and knocked him off his feet. The other alpha went soaring, landing on his back in the dirt and sliding five feet.

There was a scuffle behind me, my name being called in what sounded like G's voice but I was too focused on the fight.

Dare headed toward Gage, and I knew this was the moment he'd finish him, despite the silver wound in his side. My power combined with his was unbeatable. I smiled as Gage rolled onto all fours with a groan. Then he turned his head and looked right at me.

He returned my smile with a bloody one.

And my stomach dropped.

A nearby Were grabbed me. And I realized my mistake too late. While I'd been focused on sending Dare my power, I'd entered the circle. I was now fair game.

Fuck.

The Were who grabbed me held a silver knife up to my throat, and in my now weakened form, I couldn't fight or shift. G had tried to warn me, I realized as he watched me with concern. I shook my head at him, ignoring the pained look in Jude's eyes.

Gage held out a hand, pointing to me, and Dare stopped, Were eyes widening in horror as he realized what was happening. Gage shifted so he stood in his human form, covered in blood and dirt. And that fucking smile was still on his face. Dare shifted too, not taking his eyes off me.

Gage crossed his arms over his chest. "I waited patiently for you to find a mate, Dare. Because I knew, once that mate came along, then I'd finally have your weakness." He laughed bitterly. "I especially love that your mate is a wolf, and has little wolf siblings he loves. Because what your mate loves, you love, and that makes you even weaker." Gage's bloody smile was carving out my heart. He waved a hand toward the Hive rising tall toward the moon in the distance.

"The pack doesn't care about these ancient rules. They care about the stronger alpha winning."

"What's fair about using silver to win, you bastard!" I yelled.

The Were knocked me in the back of the knees, and I fell to the dirt. Dare started but when the knife pressed closer against my flesh, he stopped, nostrils flaring. Finally, he turned to Gage. "What do you want?"

"Your surrender," Gage said simply.

"You think I'm going to leave my mate with you?"

"He can leave. He and his siblings. I'll let them walk out of here free and clear."

"Wait, what'll happen to Dare?" I asked.

"I'll kill him."

"That's not a fucking surrender, that's—" This time, the Were shoved me forward, then grabbed me by the hair and forced my head back while he growled stank-breath in my face.

Gage waited. "So what'll it be, Dare? Fight and kill your mate *and* yourself, or save your mate and lose your life?"

Fight. Fight. Fight. I repeated it like a mantra in my head.

You die, I die, remember?

Well, I'm not leaving here knowing he's going to kill you!

Dare shook his head, not speaking back, and with slow movements, lowered himself to his knees and bowed his head.

My proud alpha. My True Mate. The same Were who delivered me food in bed, who could name every pack member, and who risked his life to save my brother and sister. The love of my life who touched me with kindness and called me his little wolf. He was willing to do this for me. He was willing to sacrifice himself so I could be free.

The soft sound of water hitting the earth had me looking up into the night sky for rain. Until I realized they sound was coming from the tears dripping off my face. My mate, my proud alpha, was now bowed before a weaker leader.

Under Gage's rule, this proud pack would be cowed and abused just like the Bluefoot pack.

Mav. Cati. What would happen to G and Vaughn and Rua? No way could I let this happen. Dare's hands were figuratively tied, but mine weren't. I was the alpha's Mate, damn it. His True Mate. The pull in my body was over-whelming, making it impossible to remain passive. I wanted to fuck up some Weres and defend my mate, and there was no denying it.

Despite my depletion of energy, I called my shift, and immediately, a unique sensation flared like a struck match in my chest. Normally, my feet, hands, and head shifted first. But as the burning intensified in my core, my chest began to expand. And *expand*. The inferno spread to my limbs. The Were who held me dropped my arms with a hiss and, when I turned to look at him, he was whining and clutching his hands as they smoked. *Smoked.* Like my flesh had burned him.

When I held my hands out in front of me, they morphed into massive paws, double the size they normally were. I screamed as my skull stretched, and I fell to the ground on all fours. This shift was pure agony, and for several moments,

I swore I was going to die. Why did this hurt so bad?

When my vision cleared, I stood on four paws, and the ground was much farther down than it normally was. I swung my head to my brother and sister. Selene's hands were clapped over her mouth, and Jude's eyes were bugged out of his head.

"Reese." He gaped. "You're fucking huge."

I shook my fur, rippling my muscles, reveling in the power and strength in them that I'd never had before. The Were who'd been holding me snarled, his palms now red and blistered. I slashed my paw across his throat and didn't bother to watch as he bled out.

And all around me was chaos. While I had shifted, G had too. Rua and Vaughn were off to the side, protecting my brother, sister, Gale, and Bay, while G tussled in a pile with about three Weres pummeling him.

A yell went up, and I turned to see Gage with his fist in the air, his other arm locked around Dare's throat. My mate's entire side was a massive burn now, as if Gage had ripped the silver knife through him again. The sight of Dare's swollen human face and the smell of his burnt flesh sent me into berserker mode.

I leaped into the air, easily clearing the heads of the eight-foot Weres in front of me. A sick smile stretched across Gage's face as he gazed down at a struggling Dare. Dare saw me coming first, his eyes wide, mouth open as I descended onto the man who sought to kill my mate.

My front paws collided with Gage's chest, and he released Dare as he fell back, me on top of him. A strangled sound rumbled from Gage's throat, but it was too late for him, too late to stop the fury and killing instinct that was consuming me.

I dug my claws into his skin, blood pooling around the puncture marks. With a growl, I opened my jaws as wide as they could go, bit into his neck, and twisted, shearing his head clean off his body. It rolled away as blood poured from the open neck wound. Gage's body twitched beneath me as his life blood mixed with the dirt.

I whirled around with a growl. G had dispatched several Weres, and bodies littered the ground. But they were all watching me now, and, when the remaining Weres who had been loyal to Gage saw their leader was dead, they bowed their heads with a whine.

A low moan drew my attention. Dare was on his stomach, crawling his way toward me. "Reese," he gasped.

I immediately raced to him as he rolled onto his back and fisted my fur. "You're huge." He ran a hand down my flank, his eyes taking me in with reverence. "I can't believe you..." He glanced behind us at Gage's headless body. "I take that back. I can believe. I just never would have predicted it."

His side was a riot of burned flesh. Without thinking, I bent my head and began to lap at the wounds. The taste was horrible—metal and ash and sickness. But I kept going, because wherever my tongue touched, wherever my saliva soaked, the skin began to close and heal. Dare panted beneath me, one hand on my head, stroking my ears, as I sought to heal my mate.

Dare

I SIFTED MY FINGERS THROUGH Reese's dark fur, unable to believe the size of him. He was double the wolf he'd been just earlier today. That, along with the mental connection we now shared, made my head spin.

Also? He was healing me. With every lap of his wolf tongue, the burned flesh of my side slowly began to heal. The pain receded to a mild tenderness. He lifted his muzzle, blue wolf eyes admiring his handiwork, before swinging his head to me and nuzzling my hand with his snout.

"You're beautiful," I said.

He shifted to human quickly, and I actually kinda missed the warmth of his fur. Of course, nothing beat Reese's grin. "Hey," he said.

I smiled back. "Hey, yourself."

"How're you feeling?"

"Better now." His skin was slick with blood, and I fingered his previously injured ribs. "You hurt?"

He shook his head, and shifted closer to me, laying a hand on my thigh. His fingers curled in slightly, and he didn't take his eyes off me.

I slowly lifted my torso with my hands braced behind me. "What?"

"I don't even know. Everything. What Gage did, what happened to me, that choice he forced you to make. I'm not sure what to make of it."

I swallowed. "Me either."

"Did you really want me to run?"

"I wouldn't have said it if I didn't." It would have killed me to watch him leave, but knowing he had a home to return to helped. "I was going to die either way. My pack would have been vulnerable no matter what I did. So protecting you was the only legacy I had left."

He pushed himself forward, lips meeting mine. And as quickly as he kissed me, he pulled away and rose to his feet. "Let's check on everyone."

He was the perfect alpha mate, thinking of the pack. I clasped the hand he offered me and stood up.

I heard that, he raised an eyebrow at me.

Good.

All around us was carnage. Bodies in various forms of dismemberment lay on the bloody earth. G had the attempted-mutiny crew lined up against the wall, his arms crossed over his chest. There were only three of them left out of about a dozen. Vaughn was playing with Gage's head, making the jaw move and saying things like, "I'm Gage, I'm a cheater, and a wolf still took my head off."

"Vaughn!" I barked.

He started and dropped the head, quickly folding his hands behind his back. "What's up?"

That Were. Couldn't take him anywhere. "Close the gate."

"Yes, Alpha!" He trotted toward the gate.

I immediately went to Bay, who was attempting to break the silver collar around his neck. Just the sight of his beaten face was almost enough to send me into a rage on Gage's body, but I controlled myself. I knelt next to him and ripped the collar in half.

Bay collapsed into my arms. I squeezed him tightly, noting his one arm dangling at his side. It was probably broken. Those fucking bastards. "I'm sorry," I said into his matted hair. "I'm so sorry."

Bay chuckled against my chest. "You didn't know they'd do that, and I didn't either. We can talk later about the bad decisions we made. For now, though, let's just be happy it ended the way it did." He pulled back. "My heart stopped when you bowed your head, Dare. I thought we were all goners until your mate went Super Wolf."

Reese ducked his head, his cheeks coloring.

"Yeah, that was something else," I said. I patted my brother on the back. "So what happened?"

"Spineless shits. Broke into my room while I was sleeping. Beat me up, chained me, then made a pack announcement that Gage was the interim alpha until you arrived back home and he could challenge."

"Mav?"

"He's fine. He and Cati hid. That was one of the reasons they went all out on me. They wanted to know where Cati and Mav were."

I growled. "I need to get back to the pack. They inside the Hive?"

"Yeah, Gage set curfew and everything."

"You okay?"

"Sure, I just need to shift and heal up. Sleep for a week."

"Good idea. I don't want to see you for seven days."

Bay grinned, then shifted to his wolf. He shook out his fur and, with a look at me over his shoulder, slowly trotted away.

Beside me, Reese swayed on his feet, and I grabbed his arm to steady him. He shot me a smile that didn't look all that happy. His face was pale, and his eyes didn't seem to focus, right. "You need to rest."

"So do you," he said back.

"Yeah, sure, but I'm alpha, and I'll rest after I check on my pack."

He tilted his chin. "I'm the alpha's mate. I should check on the pack too."

"Reese," I said firmly. "You were severely injured, then you gifted me all your energy, then you shifted into a wolf twice your normal size and tore the head off my challenger. I think you can rest while I check on the pack, okay?"

He was quiet for a moment before mumbling, "Yeah, sure, whatever."

"Code to our room is 247283. Got it?"

He nodded.

"G," I called. "Get Selene and Hans a room, walk Reese up to my room, then you and Jude get some rest."

The big Were frowned and gestured to the Weres he was guarding. "But what about—?"

"I'll handle them," I said.

He hesitated for a moment before following my orders, gathering a stunned-looking Hans and Selene and leading them along with Jude and Reese into the Hive. I watched until they entered safely before turning to the traitors as well as the rest of my pack. "Vaughn, stay with me. The rest of you, head on inside and call a pack meeting. I know it's late, but I want everyone up."

Murmurs of assent greeted my directions, and then the only living beings that were left on the grounds were Vaughn and three other Weres who I once thought were loyal. I stood in front of them, pissed off I had to deal with them rather than heading inside to see my son. I crossed my arms over my chest and braced my feet apart. "Why?"

No one spoke for a long while, until finally a young Were, barely months from his muto, said, "He told us this wouldn't last. That he had proof the Noweres were getting stronger, smarter, and that they'd eventually take over our compound, so we needed to start conquering other packs."

"What kind of proof?"

The older Were beside him shrugged. "He never said."

"And you believed him?"

"We didn't have reason not to."

For once Vaughn was quiet, frowning as he digested the Weres' words before turning to me with a quizzical look.

"Sometimes it feels like we're just waiting," the third Were spoke up. "Gage said it's not in our nature to be passive, that—"

"You think I'm passive?" I cut him off with a deep voice that rumbled with suppressed anger. "I'm not passive about the Noweres. But I don't think the solution is to use resources to take over other packs. That's not how I operate and if that's what you want, then the gate is there. Leave." I stepped closer. "But know this, there are many ways I'm actively working to keep us safe and happy. Maybe I should have done a better job of communicating that to the pack, and I'll remedy that from here on out." I straightened my back. "So, do you want to leave or stay?"

"Stay," the youngest Were said quickly. "We shouldn't have believed Gage and...I'm sorry."

"Stay," the other two echoed meekly.

I flicked my fingers toward the Hive. "Go to your apartments. Stay there until I decide on your punishment. Because trust me, there will be one."

They rose with muttered thank-you's and walked with their heads bowed. When they were out of sight, I sighed. There was still so much to do, and all I wanted was to crawl into bed with Reese. Hold him tight, try to convince him to stay with me even though I knew he wouldn't.

Vaughn rubbed my shoulders. "You okay, Alpha?"

"Fucking exhausted," I said, rolling my shoulders into his touch. "Little to the left."

He laughed and smacked me. "Come on, let's get inside, then you can screw your mate."

I rolled my eyes at him as we trudged toward the Hive.

As soon as I walked through the doors, a small novus crashed into me, his skinny arms wrapping around my thigh. I bent and buried my face in my son's neck, breathing him in, so glad I'd secured a hideout for him in the event of a challenge, and thrilled he had a mother who made sure he was safe.

I glanced up to see Cati watching us with wet eyes. I stuck out an arm and she ran, hugging us.

"Thank you," I said into her hair. "You did good protecting him."

"I got him to the safe place like you taught us," she said. "And I had my knife, and I would have died protecting him."

I ran a hand down her cheek. "I know you would have."

Lowering Mav to the ground, I knelt in front of him. "You okay?"

He nodded, biting his lip. "I am now."

"I'm sorry that had to happen, that you had to hide away with your mom, but it was for your safety, you understand?"

"Did you kill Gage?"

I hesitated. "Reese did."

Cati made a small gasp, and Mav's eyes widened. "Is he okay?"

"He's fine, but he's resting."

"When he's awake, can I see him?"

My heart cracked. "'Course, buddy."

I rose to my feet and patted his back, then walked further into the Hive. The chatter of a large group of Weres grew louder, and when I reached the Forum, applause began.

I gazed around me and above me at my pack, all gathered on the floor and along the balconies, clapping and hollering. I waved, a swell of pride filling my chest. This was what Reese had done, given me back my pack which Gage had tried to steal. Never again would I be lax and allow a usurper to gain power.

I made a motion for them to quiet down, and when they were silent and listening intently, I began to speak.

CHAPTER TWENTY

Reese

DARE'S PRESENCE WAS DIFFERENT. AS I watched from my perch on the balcony on the top floor, hidden behind a column from his view, I sensed the change in him.

The pack did too, because after cheering his arrival, they were now silent. Rapt. Hanging on to Dare's every word.

I should have been resting like Dare ordered me too, but watching him command the attention of his entire pack was mesmerizing.

"I'm sorry for what you went through in my absence," Dare was saying. "But Gage lost the challenge, and he'll receive a proper burial. From now on, there will be no more tolerance for members of this pack who threaten my leadership. If you have concerns, then I welcome discussion. But outright hostility and aggression will be met with swiftly. That is an error I made, out of guilt for the death of Gage's father, and I'll always regret the terror you've been put through over the last couple of days."

He was larger, his voice deeper, and the power emanated from him in waves. There was no way anyone could miss the difference in him. I thought he'd been powerful before. I hadn't known how much *more* he could be.

He went on to describe the fight, and his voice grew louder when he talked about my shift. "My mate knew I had no choice, and shifted so he was able to defeat Gage. He kept me alive. He's resting now, but when you see him, please thank him for what he did."

Dare dropped his head, and I strained to read what he was thinking. I was met with silence. My mate wasn't allowing me to hear his thoughts, but his expression was somber when he lifted his head, and it wasn't hard to imagine what he was thinking about—me leaving.

My chest tightened, and my lungs cramped, as if oxygen had been sucked from the air. I'd heard enough of Dare's speech, seen that the pack was once again happy, so I ran up the stairs to our room, spun the lock to the correct numbers, and walked in.

Our room. Yep, I'd said that. In my head. It was, wasn't it? The room that Dare and I had made ours, where we'd officially mated, where we'd feasted on fresh food, where I'd read his son stories and slept under the skylight.

After securing the door behind me, I stripped off my clothes, giving myself a quick wash before crawling into bed. But I didn't sleep. As exhausted as I was physically, my mind was racing.

Home wasn't a concept that had made sense to me for a long time. Home had been Astria. But it'd been Astria the way it was before the Nowere attack—when the threat of them had seemed more like a fairytale than a reality. We'd lived and loved in bliss. Even if some of my pack had lived, even if they were rebuilding, there was no way it'd be the same. Not after the devastation we'd seen.

Not after the losses we suffered.

Home was Jude and Selene.

Home was…Dare.

I clutched the pillow beneath me, breathing in my mate's scent still left on the bedding. When Dare told me that some of my pack might still live, I'd sworn the pull of my wolf was telling me to go back to Astria.

But now that we'd returned to the Silver Tip pack, I didn't feel that pull any longer. There was no ache in my gut, in my heart. My wolf was content here. The only pull I felt was toward Dare.

My mate. My True Mate.

Home was…the Silver Tip pack.

I had to think about Selene and Jude, because my actions affected them. Would they want to stay here? Because I couldn't be separated from them again; the thought alone made me nauseous. We hadn't risked all we had and nearly lost Dare's life just to be separated again.

I squeezed my eyes shut and imagined what it would be like to leave Dare. To walk out the gates and go home to Astria without him. My mouth dried up, and my stomach clenched. My inner wolf whined, and everything inside of me screamed, *No!*

Dare had ordered me to leave, though. He hadn't given me a choice. So if I was going to stay, I'd have to convince him that this was the right decision. That this was what I wanted. Looking back, I realized his decision to send me away wasn't because I'd lied. His choice had been about my happiness and *his* sacrifice—he was willing to live in pain for the rest of my life if it meant me being happy.

I stayed awake for a long time, and, finally, I heard the door open. Dare's footsteps were heavy and irregular. The shower ran as he rinsed off, and then the bed dipped as he joined me.

I pretended to be asleep, shutting off my brain to the connection as best as I could by imagining a wall between Dare and I. And the fact that it felt unnatural was a red flag.

Dare's arm wrapped around my waist, and he tugged me back against him. He nuzzled his face into my hair, muttered something, then his breaths evened out almost immediately.

I matched my breaths with his, expanding my chest as his pressed against my back. I wiped my mind clean, and then, like my mate who held me close, I fell asleep too.

Dare

When I woke, the sun was only beginning to creep through the windows, casting the room in a hazy pinkish glow.

Reese breathed deeply, cradled against me. My arm was around his chest, elbow bent so that my forearm lay on the mattress. His hand lay beneath mine, our fingers laced together. I wasn't sure we'd ever held hands like this, as a form of intimacy rather than me leading him somewhere.

Had we linked in our sleep?

As I inhaled, Reese's scent was heavier, coated with permanence and contentment and home. I craved him and my dick hardened where it lay against his ass. It'd been a long time since I'd been inside of him and everything in me lamented at how wrong that was. I needed that reminder that he was mine, that we were stronger together.

I tugged him closer, and he stirred in my arms, bringing our linked hands right up to his mouth. With his eyes still closed, his mind still heavy with sleep, he pressed a kiss to my thumb.

"Reese," I rumbled into his neck, and he moved again, turning in my arms until he was blinking up at me with unfocused eyes.

"Dare." He smiled, raising our hands above his head as he stretched out his body with a yawn.

I slipped between his legs, pressing him down onto the bed, and taking his lips in a kiss. He moaned into my mouth as our tongues tangled, and his strong thighs squeezed my hips, his heels digging into my ass. I ground into him as our cocks slipped together with pre-come.

I grabbed his other hand, linking our fingers, and held both to the bed over his head. His eyes were still unfocused—not from sleep anymore, but from arousal. His lips were wet and swollen from my kisses, his cheeks flushed, and his neck red from where I'd sucked on the skin. He arched his back, squeezing my fingers. "Fuck me."

My mind was a jumbled frenzy, but I had enough awareness to realize that my Were wasn't anywhere to be found. This was me, Dare. Wanting the soul that was Reese.

I let go of his one hand so that I could guide my cock to his entrance. He was slick as hell, dripping on the bed below us. I slid in with ease, and he immediately clamped around me, throwing his head back, muscles straining. He groaned. "So good. Oh fuck, so good."

I began to thrust as I held both of his hands above his head. I wanted to watch his face, see every expression that came over his eyes. I needed to commit it all to memory so that after he left, I'd have something to look back on to remember the best thing that ever happened to me. He was a sight, his chest flushed, his mouth open, nostrils flaring.

"I love you, Reese." I drove into him so hard, I moved us half a foot on the bed. His eyes widened, and his mouth opened but no sound came out. "I love you because you're smart." *Thrust.* "And loyal." *Thrust.* "And because you make me a better alpha."

No sound came out other than a strangled gasp as I continued to pound into him. I leaned down, sucking on the mark I'd made earlier, wanting it there for weeks.

"Dare," he whispered, then his body shuddered beneath mine, and a hot splash of his come coated my stomach.

The smell sent me over the edge. My canines punched down through my gums, and I sliced into his flesh on his shoulder just as I released inside of him. He jerked beneath me as I came. And came. And came. My orgasm must have lasted a full minute before my hips stopped, and my teeth withdrew from his skin.

I fell to the side, unable to support myself any longer, my body depleted of all its energy. Usually Reese was the one who was dick-addled after sex, but I couldn't seem to keep my eyes open. I made the last-ditch effort to draw Reese into my arms and lick at the bite on his neck, but even then, I only got a few licks in before I felt like I was going under.

"Dare. Hey." Reese's voice held a tinge of alarm as he shook my shoulder. "You okay? What's wrong?"

"Tired," I mumbled. "Need to sleep."

"Okay." Concern still laced his tone. "Okay, you sleep. I'll be here when you wake up."

The last thing I heard as I passed out was Reese whispering. "Love you too."

CHAPTER TWENTY-ONE

Reese

I LAY AWAKE FOR A long time staring at the ceiling. Dare never fell asleep after sex. If anything, an orgasm energized him. His breaths were deep and even, which was the only reason I hadn't run to a healer yet.

That and...well, I needed to sort out some things in my head. Every time Dare fucked me, I'd always felt like his Were was there with us, like a third being. And, well, my wolf had been there too. I'd never felt like I was just with *Dare.*

Until now.

There'd been no Were. No wolf. That had been nothing but Dare craving me, and me craving Dare, and us...loving each other.

I dropped my forearm over my eyes. I loved him. When I thought about leaving him, not only did my wolf wail, but so did my heart. My soul. Whatever made me *me* in all my forms protested the idea of leaving him.

When I searched my heart and my instincts, nothing was pulling me to Astria.

Because I was already home.

I slipped out of bed, careful not to wake Dare. I cleaned up, then pulled on a pair of pants. Another glance at him ensured he was sleeping and would not be awake soon, so I slipped out, closing the door as softly as I could behind me.

I went straight to G's apartment, hoping I could catch my brother awake. I knocked, waiting as muffled voices conversed on the other side of the door before it swung open. G stood inside the doorway, nude, and when I glanced past him, Jude was sitting on the bed, an array of plates around him.

And the room smelled like sex.

I raised an eyebrow at G, who blushed, a deep crimson creeping up the dark skin of his neck. Jude opened his mouth, but I held up a hand. "I don't want to know. You happy?"

G walked to the side of the bed, and Jude brushed the back of the Were's thigh with his hand, then gazed up at him adoringly. "Of course."

"Great, then that's all I need to know. Look, we need to talk."

Jude wasn't even paying attention to what I was saying. "G is going with us."

I stopped on my way to the bed. "What?"

"Dare told him to go with us, to help protect us." Jude beamed. "I can't wait to meet our pack." His face quickly fell the longer I stared at him without reacting. He dropped his hand in his lap and patted the bed next to him. "I'm sorry. Let's talk. Are you okay? Dare?"

"Yeah, that's what I wanted to talk to you about. G,

would you mind getting Selene? I want to talk to her and Jude. Privately."

G didn't hesitate. He dressed quickly and was out the door with a promise he'd be back in five minutes. I sat on the bed next to Jude, taking a bite out of a leftover cookie. "Mmm these are good."

Jude grabbed a carrot and stretched out on his back as he munched on it. Jude would always be my little brother, and it was taking me some time to get used to the fact that he wasn't a novus anymore. He was a full adult wolf. His biceps bulged, and the muscles of his thighs shifted beneath the skin. His face was no longer puffy with baby fat. "So what's up?"

"I want to propose a change of plans, but it affects you and Selene. We make decisions together, okay?"

Jude's body tensed. "Does this involve me leaving G?"

I shook my head. "No, brother."

His eyes fell, and a flush stained his cheeks. "I feel lucky he's even speaking to me again after what I did."

"He was so worried about you."

Jude crunched his carrot, but didn't have a chance to respond because the door opened, and Selene walked inside. G kept his hand on the door. "I'll be right down the hall if you need me."

"Thanks, G," I said.

After he closed the door, Selene held her arms out at her sides with a smile and twirled. "So? What do you think?"

"Your hair!" Jude rushed to her side, fingering the now short locks. She also wore a new dress. A simple short one dyed a light blue.

"I always wanted to cut it. The length was so heavy. But Xan wouldn't let me," she said, with a jut of her chin. "But he can't tell me what to do now, can he?"

I stood up and held out my arms. She hugged me, and then a third set of arms wrapped around us, and Jude's scent filled my nose.

"We're safe," Selene whispered. "Right? No more fighting, or forced labor or mating? We're safe."

How could I move them? How could I make the dangerous journey to Astria knowing we were happy and healthy here? "Yes, which is why I want to stay."

Jude's arms tensed before he pulled back with wide eyes. "Stay? And not go to Astria? But what about our pack?"

I directed them to sit on the bed, and they huddled shoulder to shoulder while I paced. "So here's the bottom line. We make this decision together, so if you both want to go, we'll leave. As soon as we're ready. We'll go home to Astria and reunite with what's left of our pack, and that'll be it." I stopped with my hands on my hips, my heart racing. "Or we stay. Dare is an amazing alpha, and this pack is self-sufficient. We're welcome here, and as the siblings of the alpha's mate, you'll be treated well." I paused. "You have been treated well, right, Selene?"

"Oh yeah. Hans and I are in a nice room. They brought in a healer and food, and then let us sleep."

I breathed out in relief. "Great, I'm glad to hear it."

"I thought you said you felt the pull," Jude said. "To go home. Are you just ignoring it? Are there any long-term consequences to that?"

I kneeled at the foot of the bed. "I read it wrong," I said. "I was being pulled here. To the Silver Tip pack. With Dare. *This* is my home now. I won't deny that I want to know who still lives in Astria, but leaving here, leaving Dare, seems inconceivable to me."

"Tell me," Selene prompted. "Tell me about him. I don't know much."

"You will," I insisted. "You will get to know him. You've already seen what a great leader he is, but you'll also get to see he's a great dad and brother and friend. And an amazing mate. We're unlocking powers of the True Mate bond we didn't know existed. I shifted into a wolf double my size! And we can communicate silently."

"Whoa." Jude's mouth formed an *O*.

"The thought of leaving him hurts you," my sister said. "Is that what you're saying?"

I nodded. "Like my guts are being ripped out."

"Then why the hell would we still insist on leaving?" Jude asked.

"I don't know," I said. "Because maybe you still feel drawn home, maybe—"

"You're home to us, Reese," Selene said. "You've always been home. And if you're here, then it's home to us. If this is where you want to be, then we want to be here too."

"You're nuts," Jude huffed. "Thinking we'd still want to leave? What's wrong with you?"

I threw my hands in the air, laughter bubbling up my throat as the vise that had been squeezing my chest for weeks released.

I could breathe. I could relax. I could be content that I had a home, that my family was safe, and there was no more running. Collapsing onto the bed, I let the laughter out, curling onto my side until tears streamed down my face and my stomach cramped.

Something warmed pressed against my back, then Jude's arms wrapped around my waist. Selene cuddled into my chest, and my laughter sputtered out as contentment set in.

Once upon a time, back in Astria, our parents tried to get us to sleep in separate beds. We never listened, and each morning they'd find us tangled together. We hadn't been able to do this since leaving home.

When I'd blinked all the tears out of my eyes, Selene was watching me. She trailed her hand down my face. "This is what you want? To stay here?"

I nodded.

"Do you love Dare?"

I nodded again. Her mouth stretched into a wide smile, and Jude made a happy sigh against my neck.

"Good," she said softly. "Then we'll stay here."

"Stay," Jude echoed.

I closed my eyes and let the warmth of their bodies take me under.

Dare

WHEN I WOKE, I KNEW he was missing. I didn't smell him or

feel his warmth pressed against my side. He was gone.

I shot out of bed, taking a second to pull on a pair of pants before I raced out the door. I leaped down the entire staircase and landed on the fifth floor with a thud. I told myself he wouldn't have left, not without a goodbye.

Had his whispered "I love you" been a goodbye?

Fuck no. Couldn't be.

He wouldn't leave without Jude, so I took off down the hallway toward G's room. I was at top speed when my neck collided with something hard, taking me off my feet and slamming me onto my back on the floor.

My instinct was to shift, my senses on full alert against a threat. I went to rise, but was pinned to the floor by a bare foot. My gaze rose up the leg, massive torso, and thick neck to the face of an amused G.

"Fuck, Dare," he said. "Thundering down here like a goddamn Nowere. Chill out."

"Reese is gone," I growled.

G's face didn't change. "He's not gone, you asshole. He's in my room asleep with Selene and Jude."

I blinked at him. "Oh."

With a sigh, he removed his foot, and I rolled to all fours before standing, wiping off my hands, and avoiding G's eyes. "Are they okay?"

"Fine." He pointed to the door. "See for yourself." He sat down on a chair in the hallway, resuming carving a piece of wood and ignoring me and my massive freak out.

I opened the door quietly, took a step in, and paused. On G's massive bed was a pile of Whitethroat wolves. Reese was in the middle, Selene tucked against his chest while Jude wrapped them all in a bear hug from behind. When the hell had Jude grown? He looked as big as Reese now.

I closed the door behind me, and the soft click made Selene stir. She blinked open her big blue eyes, so like Reese's, and stared at me for a moment until she rolled away from Reese's grip and stood with a stretch.

Her hair was shorter, and she was finally in a dress that wasn't torn and covered in blood. In fact, this was the first time I'd seen her clean. Like Reese's features, her cheekbones were high and her lips full. Her presence and scent were all her own, beautiful and graceful with a backbone of steel.

"I'm sorry we met during stressful circumstances," I said.

She padded toward me on bare feet. "There's nothing to be sorry for. You reunited me with my brothers."

Reese muttered in his sleep and turned his head into the blanket beneath him. "I'm glad I was able to do that for you."

"Reese said he wants me to get to know you."

What was the point if they were leaving? "Oh? How so?"

"Well he doesn't know that I've already seen all I need to see to have an opinion on your character."

I couldn't help but smile. She was certainly Reese's sister. "Enlighten me on my faults, then."

She shook her head, stepping closer until she had to tilt her chin up to see me. "Your only fault is you probably let my brother get away with too much."

Now I laughed. "You might be right about that."

"His life with Xan was so hard. I haven't been here long,

but despite the challenge from that other Were, I can see your pack is happy. I can see he's happy."

That sobered me. "He'll never be fully happy here knowing his pack is still alive."

"Why?"

"Why? Because it's in his blood to be called home. He'll be miserable if he's kept away from them."

"Who says?"

Damn, she was tough. "Says fate."

She snorted. "Fate murdered our pack. It disrupted our lives as we knew them in Astria, a place that will never be the same. Fate killed our parents and sentenced us to a lifetime under Xan's rule. As far as I can see, the only good thing fate has done is brought you into our lives. And now we're making our own choice. Fuck fate, we're done with her."

"I don't understand."

"We're not leaving." Reese's voice threaded into our conversation. He was awake now, sitting on the edge of the bed, Jude still laying on his side beside him, but alert.

"You're what?"

"We're staying," Reese said firmly, rising to stand and running a hand through his bed head. "Fate chose you for me initially, but now I'm choosing you. I'm choosing this pack as my home. I'm choosing to stay here. The thought of leaving…" He shook his head. "Is like having my heart ripped out. I won't do it, Dare."

I knew the feeling. "Ten minutes ago, when I thought you'd left already, I did feel like my heart had been ripped out."

"I know what you were doing," he said. "You were will-ing to live with the Mate Pain if it meant making me happy, right?"

He was right. I understood why he'd kept Selene's exist-ence from me, and I trusted he wouldn't lie to me again. Sending him away was meant to make him happy but if it didn't... "Yes."

He nodded. "Right, that's what I thought. But leaving won't make me happy, Dare. Ever since we left Astria, I thought this pull in my gut was telling me to go home. I guess I suck at directions, because that pull was leading me here the whole time. This is my home. This is my pack. And you're my mate."

"Reese," I whispered.

He stepped closer. "You choose me too, right?"

I cupped his face, running my thumb along his bottom lip. "Of course I choose you."

"I come with a brother and a sister. And a wolf named Hans and another wolf named Gale who I'm pretty sure is fucking Rua right now."

I barked out a laugh. "I choose them too."

He wiped his brow dramatically. "Whew, that's a relief."

I dared to hope. "This is your final decision."

"I won't change my mind." He settled a hand on my waist. "I want to be here with you. I want to watch Mav grow and see my sister have pups—"

"Hey!"

"And try to ignore G and Jude while they eyefuck each other—"

"We do not!"

"And be your mate. In your bed. Until we're gray."

I said against his lips, "Fate can go fuck herself." Then I swallowed his laughter with a kiss.

CHAPTER TWENTY-TWO

Dare

I LEANED AGAINST THE OUTSIDE wall, chewing on a piece of grass as Reese, his brother and sister, Hans, and Gale played a game with Mav on the side lawn. Reese called it soccer, which wasn't something I'd ever heard of, but apparently they used to play it in Astria when he was a novus.

The only rule I'd gathered so far was that players couldn't use their hands, and Mav was a natural, while Hans purposefully tripped over his own feet to make my son laugh.

Bay stood beside me watching the game, so close he brushed my arm, a habit that had become common since the challenge with Gage over a week ago. I thought it had to do with my being his alpha, but Reese had rolled his eyes when I'd expressed that to him. *It's because he's your brother, dumbass*, he'd said.

I ruffled Bay's hair. "I have something to tell you."

"Something bad?"

"Just something."

Bay's smile faded a little. "What's up?"

I'd put off telling Bay about Nash until he was fully

healed and back to his old self. The last thing I wanted to do was pile more anxiety on him, and I'd instructed the whole rescue party to give me time to break it to him. Nash's story deserved to be told, and I planned to tell the whole pack later that night.

"When we rescued Jude from Xan's place, you know he was in this hole that was dug in the ground, right?"

"Yeah, you said there was a locked gate on top of it."

"Well, there were several holes. Hans was in one and in another one was a Were."

Bay frowned. "A Were? Really?"

"Look at me."

"I'm looking at you."

His gaze was wandering to the wolves playing soccer. "Bay."

He sliced his eyes to me. "What?"

"The Were was Nash."

Bay's body went tight, the only moving part was his eyes as they studied my face. Slowly, his fists clenched, then released. His lips parted to say on a whisper, "Nash?"

"Nash," I confirmed. "I didn't recognize him at first. He smelled like a Silver Tip, but it wasn't until he said my name—and yours—that I recognized his eyes."

"He said my name? Wait, so he's alive? What—?"

"Hold on, Bay," I said, laying a hand on his shoulder. He shrugged me off quickly, backing up a step, glaring at me with a wary look I'd never seen before. I held up a hand, palm out. "Please let me talk."

He nodded with a jerk.

"Nash was badly injured and starved. I wasn't even sure he'd make it all the way home, to be honest. But he managed to keep up with us. We ran into a pack of Noweres and fought them off, but Reese got injured when they dragged off Caro."

Bay swallowed, his Adam's apple bobbing.

"So we thought we were okay, taking stock of our injured while Reese struggled to breathe. And that's when we caught the scent of a second Nowere pack." I stepped closer to my brother. "You need to listen to this part closely, because it's important, okay?"

He nodded.

"We were going to stay and fight. Even though I was sure we'd be wiped out. There was no other choice. But Nash volunteered to meet the Nowere pack, to divert their attention. To get them off our scent. Bay, you can ask anyone who was there. I didn't want to say yes, but I had to think of what would be best for our pack, and that was saving as many as I could. Plus, Nash wouldn't take no for an answer."

"H-he sacrificed himself?"

"Yes," I said. "He did. The last I saw of him was his back as he headed in the direction of the Nowere pack. He saved us. He saved all of us."

Bay lifted his hand to his mouth and turned his back to me. His shoulders shook, and I let him have that time to process what Nash had done for the pack. Finally, his breath hitched, and then he turned around, wiping his eyes. "Do you know how he ended up at the Bluefoot pack?"

"No, I hoped to get answers later but…"

"Right." He stared at the top of the wall. "I've wondered for so long what happened to him. And now…I guess I know. I guess I have closure."

"I'm sorry, Bay. He asked how you were. And I said you were happy. And that seemed to give him peace."

"He asked about me," Bay said thoughtfully.

"He did."

He shook his head, making an odd sound somewhere between a chuckle and a sob. I finally tugged him to me, patting his back until he shoved me away with a grin. "Been meaning to ask you something."

"Sure."

He chewed the inside of his cheek. "I want to go to Astria."

That was the last thing I expected him to say. "What?"

"We have reports the Whitethroat are rebuilding, and even though Reese is choosing to stay here, we have ties to that pack. What if they need help or supplies? What if they have information about the Noweres that we don't since they survived an attack?"

"Bay—"

"I need this," he said quietly. "I need to get away for a little. Complete something successful."

"I told you what happened with Gage wasn't your fault—"

"It's not about that." He waffled his hand. "Okay, it's a little about that, but damn it, Dare, I'm restless. Something out there—" He pointed to the wall. "—is calling to something in here." He beat his chest with a fist. "So let me go. You can handpick my team. I'll go and report back. Help ease your mate's mind."

"I have you safe and healthy and now you want me to be okay with sending you off on a journey that could kill you?"

The muscles in his jaw clenched. "Don't make me disobey you."

"You would?"

He paused. "I would."

I thought about my answer. He didn't leave me much of a choice, but I knew he wanted my blessing, my cooperation. And I sure as hell wanted to handpick his team. "Okay, fine. But let me have a week with you before you leave, okay?"

He smiled. Not quite the Bay of old, but close. I'd take it. "Sure, brother."

I slung an arm around his shoulders as we began to walk toward the soccer game. Reese was running with Mav on his shoulders, weaving around everyone on the field while my son laughed hysterically.

Beside me, Bay laughed. "I need to learn this game so I can kick your ass."

I grinned. "Would love to see you try."

Reese

"ARE YOU WORRIED ABOUT BREAKING the truce?" I asked Dare.

We were lying in bed at night, drowsy after sex, but I

wasn't in the mood to sleep. My mind was on a zillion different things, one of them being my sister's heat. To the surprise of no one, she'd chosen Hans to get her through it, and, although I trusted the wolf, I was still hoping everything was all right, and that her first experience was positive for her and…

"Reese, you gotta stop."

I turned my head to see Dare's eyes glowing green in the moonlight. "Stop what?"

"Thinking. You're doing it so hard, I can hear everything, and it's giving me a headache."

I gaped at him. "Well excuse me that I have a sister in heat, and I can't stop thinking of Zin and Zen, and that Astria—"

He cut me off with a kiss, and I promptly shoved him away. "That was not nice."

"My kisses aren't nice?"

I scowled. "You know what I mean."

He sighed, his barrel chest expanding. "Little wolf, we're not doing anything about any of that right now. Tomorrow, we'll sit down with my guard and make a list of all you're worried about and how we plan to deal with it. But tonight? Let's relax."

He was right, of course he was right. The stars in the clear sky twinkled down at us through the skylight. While that ache in my gut was gone, I still wondered if there were members of my pack looking at the same stars right this minute down south in Astria. "Okay, a plan is good. I appreciate that."

"I'm concerned about the same things you're concerned about, but it's nothing urgent."

I gulped. "Right."

Dare didn't speak for a long moment, and when he did, his voice was low. "Bay is going to scout Astria."

I turned my head so fast, I pulled a muscle. "What?"

"He wants to leave. He said he's restless and wants to make a difference."

"So he's..."

"It's a little bit for you, and a little bit for him. But this will give you peace of mind. He plans to open up communication between the packs if he makes contact with a Whitethroat."

I wanted to go hug Bay. Right now. "That's...so nice, I don't know what to say."

"He's not leaving for a week." Dare folded his hands behind his head. "You can talk to him tomorrow." He yawned. "Can we sleep yet?"

"I'm not that tired."

He raised a dark eyebrow. "Oh yeah?" His lips tilted up, and he rolled over, gripping my ass and pulling me astride him. "I can make you tired."

I curled my nails into his chest as my cock quickly hardened. Another round would be a perfect way to—

A knock at the door interrupted us. I slipped off his lap, and Dare stood up with a growl, stalking toward the door. He flung it open to find Cati and Mav. Cati's smile was anything but apologetic. "Sorry, but I'm needed to help with a birth. Can you take Mav?"

I smothered a smile as Dare tried to cover his irritation. "Uh, sure."

Cati smirked, then ushered Mav inside. She waved to me. "Hey Reese."

"Hey there."

"You boys have a nice night." She winked before leaving.

Dare shut the door, and Mav made a beeline for the bed, taking a flying leap and landing in my arms. "Hi Reethe," he said.

"How you doing, buddy?" I gave him a playful shove and he growled and lunged at me again. I fell back onto the bed with a laugh as Mav pretended to bite my neck.

The bed dipped as Dare came back. He watched us wrestle until we both lay on the bed, panting.

"Okay, I think I'm tired now," I said with a grin.

Dare rolled his eyes, and muttered, "'Course."

Mav hugged his father around the neck, and the three of us settled down under the sheet, Mav in the middle.

He fell asleep quickly, and little snores escaped his lips.

Dare kissed his hair, then watched me over Mav's head. "Tomorrow," he said quietly. "We'll figure it all out tomorrow. For now, relax. You're home."

"Yeah." I grinned. "I'm home."

THE END

Sign up to be the first to know when the next book releases!

Go to www.meganerickson.org

to sign up for Megan's newsletter!

Glossary

Astria: Home of the Whitethroat pack and several other werewolf packs

Bluefoot Pack: Werewolves, run by Alpha Xan

Eury: Home of the Silver Tip Pack, the Blackfoot pack, and several other werewolf packs

Muto: A shifter's first change, usually occurs around age 18

Novus: A shifter who has not had their first change yet

Nowere: An undead Were. Stuck in Were form. Roams in packs. Kills werewolves and turns Weres.

Silver Tip Pack: Weres, run by Alpha Dare

Were: A type of shifter who has three forms—Human; four-legged wolf; upright wolf/human hybrid

Werewolf: A type of shifter who has two forms—human; four-legged wolf

Whitethroat pack: Reese, Jude, and Selene's home pack. Was decimated in a Nowere attack

About the Author

Megan Erickson worked as a journalist covering real-life dramas before she decided she liked writing her own endings better and switched to fiction. She's a multi-published author with Avon, Berkley, and Entangled. She lives in Pennsylvania with her husband, two kids and two cats.

Website: meganerickson.org
Twitter: twitter.com/MeganErickson_
Facebook: facebook.com/authormeganerickson

Other books by Megan Erickson

In Focus series
Trust the Focus
Focus on Me
Out of Frame
Overexposed

Bowler University series
Make it Count
Make it Right
Make it Last

Mechanics of Love series
Dirty Thoughts
Dirty Talk
Dirty Deeds

Gamers series
Changing His Game
Playing for Her Heart
Tied to Trouble

Cyberlove series (co-written with Santino Hassell)
Strong Signal
Fast Connection

Acknowledgements

This book was a book I wasn't sure I'd publish. Truth talk— I love reading shifter books. But I wasn't sure I'd ever write one. I didn't have an idea, but I went to bed one night thinking about Reese, and by the time I woke up, Dare was full formed in my head, as well as the first scene.

I wrote it down.

Then kept writing.

And here we are. A published book.

This is my first solo self-published book since my very first novel in 2013 (which I've now pulled to re-edit) so I was very, very nervous. I needed a lot of encouragement, and my friends had to listen to me whine, haha. I owe a huge thanks to Lia Riley, AJ Pine, and Natalie Blitt for putting up with me. You never let me down. Thank you to Santino Hassell for doing late night word sprints with me so I could finish this book. Also, thank you for reading the first chapter and encouraging me to keep going!

Thank you to Natalie Blitt, Eddie, Sara Beth, and Sasha Devlin for your excellent beta notes on this book. I know it wasn't easy. I have world building and shifter lore, and you all helped immensely.

Natasha Snow, as always, you nailed this cover. I adore working with you, and you are so talented.

Edie Danford, you are a wonderful copy editor. You

really made this book shine with your thoughtful edits. I can't thank you enough!

Thank you to my assistant Keyanna Butler for being the best damn assistant I could have. You are my friend, my confidante, my cheerleader, and lots of other things I don't have English words for. Thanks for putting up with me and for letting me freak out on you the day before I announced this book.

And last but not least, thank you to my readers, especially those in Meg's Mob. I don't know what I'd do without you all. You follow me as I hop from genre to genre. You are excited and right there with me along the way. I am so lucky to have you. I received a message on Twitter from a reader saying about this book, "It's not my genre, but I'm finding *you* are my genre." That's the best compliment ever. I hope I continue to do you all proud, and earn the faith you've placed in my books. Thank you.

Made in the USA
Middletown, DE
13 March 2018